D1453617

LINA:

A PORTRAIT OF A DAMASCENE GIRL

By Samar Attar

FRANKLIN PIERCE
COLLEGE LIBRARY
RINDGE, N.H. 03461

An Original by Three Continents Press

Copyright © 1994 by Samar Attar

A Three Continents Book

Published in the United States of America by
Lynne Rienner Publishers, Inc.
1800 30th Street, Boulder, Colorado 80301

Library of Congress Cataloging-in-Publication Data

Attar, Samar.
    [Lina, lawhat fatah Dimashqiyah, English]
    Lina, portrait of a Damascene girl / by Samar Attar.
        p.   cm.
    ISBN 0-89410-779-8: $28.00. –ISBN 0-89410-780-1 : $16.00
    1. Women–Syria–Fiction. 2. Syria–Social conditions–Fiction.
I. Title
PJ7814.T825L5613   1994
892'.736–dc20

94-25027
CIP

All rights reserved. The reproduction in whole or part, except for review, in any form or by electronic or other means, now known or hereafter invented, including photocopying, recording, xerogrophy, and in any information storage and retrieval system, is forbidden without the written permission of the publisher.

© by Samar Attar of Original Cover Design of Arabic Edition done by Al-Ja'Fari, used as portion of cover of this U.S. Edition; Entire Cover of U.S. Edition is Copyright and © by Three Continents Press, 1994

Alas! poor country;
Almost afraid to know itself. It cannot
Be call'd our mother, but our grave; where nothing,
But who knows nothing, is once seen to smile;
Where sighs and groans and shrieks that rent the air
Are made, not mark'd; where violent sorrow seems
A modern ecstasy; the dead man's knell
is there scarce ask'd for who; and good men's lives
Expire before the flowers in their caps,
Dying or ere they sicken.

(Shakespeare, *Macbeth*, IV, III, 164-173.)

To Professor D.P. Varma, mentor and friend, a belated apology for his house arrest and later expulsion from Syria in September 1961 by the military authorities.

Acknowledgments

I am grateful to the Rockefeller Foundation and the Center for Middle Eastern and North African Studies at the University of Michigan, Ann Arbor, for the residency fellowship 1990-91, which made the translation of this book possible, and to Professor Ernest McCarus, Director of the Center, and his staff for constant encouragement and help.

Contents

I	Childhood	1
II	Adolescence	52
III	Womanhood	179

I

CHILDHOOD

When the servant led Lina to the dining room, the white muslin curtains were drawn, and the big crystal chandelier was wrapped in a cover the color of *cafe au lait*. Lina turned her brown eyes in fright. Her brother, Khalid, occupied the head of the table, with her father's sister Samiya, her mother, her sister Bahiya and two other relatives down one side, and her two brothers-in-law and three sisters down the other.

—Lina, sit there. Aunt Samiya pointed to the single chair at the bottom of the table.

It was raining outside. The wood crackled in the stove. The feet of the servant, who was standing in a dim corner, looked like swollen balloons.

The smell of pies stuffed with meat, almonds, pistachio, and pinenuts filled the room. Plates of fried and grilled *kubba* lay at one end of the table and at the other end, on a bed of grape leaves rolled into the shape of small fingers and sauteed in tomato sauce, lay a plate of stuffed zucchinis. In the center of the table there was a dish of rice decorated with lamb slices, mushrooms, walnuts, and hazelnuts.

—God have mercy on the dead, said Lina's brother in a deep voice. Her aunt beat her chest with her hand, then pulled back the grey plait of her hair and covered it with a black mantilla hanging down her shoulder. Her mother uttered a soft cry. When Lina shut her eyes she could see nothing but hazy female shapes dressed in black, and men's unshaven beards.

A piece of grilled shoulder of lamb spilled onto her plate with the juice of mushrooms sauteed with yoghurt, parsley, and garlic scattered around the sides. As she raised her head, half protesting, the stern eyes of her sister Afaf were fixed on her. Lina felt suffocated; her face flushed.

No one said a word. The clatter of forks and knives increased,

1

then diminished, and the hungry mouths chewed hot pies. She saw her cousin Zahra take a big piece with her fat fingers and swallow it all at once.

Lina plunged her fork into the shoulder of lamb. She pinned her eyes onto the knife and cut off tender slices of meat. But when she noticed a speck of blood sneaking out and mixing with the yoghurt, it was as if a red winged cockroach was floating in her plate. Its eyes looked like those of her dead father. Lina gnashed her teeth and felt the cold piercing her ribs. No doubt her father was shivering now in his grave. How much she wanted to visit him tonight with her mother, to sit under the marquee watching the rain hitting the corroded tombstones. Perhaps, a blind boy would pass her to chant a verse from the *Quran*, or present her with a stem of myrtle which he stole from another grave. She heard the women's wailing mingle with the cries of the pastry vendors and saw boys quarrelling with one another while others urinated on the tombs.

—Why aren't you eating?

The question fell on her like a bomb. She couldn't recognize the speaker's voice. When she raised her head, the eyes of those present were vacant and glassy. Aunt Samiya was sucking lemon and garlic sauce from her fingers with a theatrical smile on her lips.

—God have mercy upon him, she said, he used to love grape leaves.

Lina saw her mother's face stiffen and the arteries of her neck grow tense. She wanted to run to her and hide her face in the black shawl.

—Well, if she insists on being stubborn, send her to a boarding school, suggested her brother-in-law Hisham, gnawing a round of grilled *kubba* with fat dripping from his chin.

—No doubt, you will not find her a suitor at an early age, added his wife Afaf mockingly.

The dining-room swirled around Lina. Her legs were twisted, her face felt inhuman. The lamb shoulder trembled on her plate, too. She saw the mushroom pieces walk in front of her, sticking their brown tongues out. Everyone was laughing at her, she thought. They jostled their heads together hysterically. But when she stared at their faces again she saw only Afaf's eyes, driving through her like the eyes of wild gazelles. Meanwhile, her cousin 'Aisha was licking the pomegranate sauce which gushed out of the hot grilled *kubba*.

Her brother wheeled around to face Ahmad, her brother-in-law, putting his glass of water onto the table.

—Why didn't your neighbor Ihsan come to the funeral?

—He had things to do, answered Ahmad restraining his laughter.

—What do you mean? Weren't we friends? Her brother took off his glasses, his hands trembling.

Leaning his pumpkin-like head a little forward, Ahmad twisted his moustache, then licked his lips, rather embarrassed, and said:

—Poor Ihsan. All he cares for is women's panties. He is always on the balcony casting amorous glances at people's washing.

Her two married sisters giggled, while her mother frowned, casting glances at Lina and at the servant standing by the fireplace. Aunt Samiya rolled her cigarette carelessly; her face was red.

—And how do you know he stares at people's washing? Her sister Rima turned on Ahmad and asked furiously, bending her chalky face and boyishly short brown hair towards him.

—Well! Her mother looked reproving. The black shawl dropped down her shoulders.

—Is Ihsan a peasant that you undertake to defend? asked her brother.

— No. But you're always psycho-analyzing others without even knowing them.

—The good soul! said her sister Su'ad, tightening her lips with scorn, as Afaf clapped her hands, summoning the maid:

—Bring on the sweets and fruit.

The maid rushed to the kitchen. Plates appeared and disappeared.

—The little socialist! mocked Lina's brother-in-law. He stuffed his mouth with a cream pastry.

—Take this piece. No, this one. This is bigger. For my sake, for the sake of the deceased.

Their words mingled. Lina saw their hands all search for a piece of pastry. She heard the women clamoring. Suddenly, her sister Bahiya, sitting next to her mother, burped and gazed stupidly at their faces.

The dining room enclosed her; the smell of freshly baked bread and melted white goat cheese, and orange and tangerine peels made her want to vomit. From the kitchen, the sound of bubbling coffee reached her, and she saw their faces slumping sluggishly. Her brother lit his pipe, leaning over toward Rima, shaking his head:

—Who taught you to be a socialist? Ha! Your professors at Damascus University?

—Why are you meddling in my affairs? said Rima dryly.

—Your affairs? Do you have special affairs?

She saw the heads of those present quiver with delight. Cousin Saniya suppressed her laughter, then plunged into a fit of coughing.

—Did you choke on something? whispered the women and she saw her sister Bahiya beat her cousin rhythmically on the back.

—You should answer your brother when he asks you something.

The voice of her brother was indignant, and she saw his angry face.

—No one here can force me to answer. I am free, said Rima, her brown eyes bulging.

— Free? Since when? You'll get a broken neck if you dare oppose your brother.

The coffee cup trembled in Aunt Samiya's hand.

—Your brother! Your brother! Rima struck the table with her fist. What do you mean my brother? If the truth be known, I am not a socialist, but a communist.

No one moved. Lina did not understand why everybody was angry. As she caught a glimpse of the servant standing in the shadow, she realized that she was not the only one who didn't know what was going on around her.

—For pity's sake, and for your dead father's sake, let us have no political discussion on this day, said her mother in agony.

—The little communist wants us to become poor, to give our lands away to the peasants, to make our women common property, to sit with that (her brother-in-law pointed to the servant standing like a statue in the corner) at the same table!

Aunt Samiya's head bent forward; her face was white as wax.

—Rima, do you know that the communists don't believe in God, and that churches in their countries are closed?

Rima burst into laughter.

—And why do you want us to believe in God, Aunt Samiya? she asked.

Lina saw her brother's hand rise into the air. But her aunt stretched her torso across the table and gripped his rigid arm.

—Don't hit her, she commanded.

—Do we have to listen to her stupid chatter in our house? asked Lina's brother.

—It is not her fault, her brother-in-law Hisham assured everyone. Haven't you heard how some leaders would like us to doubt the existence of heaven and hell?

—Nevertheless, they're very religious, cut in Rima ironically.

—Religious? What do you know about religion? asked her brother.

—Rima, Rima. Aunt Samiya shook her head and shut her eyes. Repeat with me that God may keep our beliefs, our land. God bless Muhammad, his blood relations and companions and grant them salvation.

—You won't eat any pastry stuffed with almond.

—Your father won't forgive you for what you've said tonight.

—You'll end up in hell.

—You'll marry our peasant's son.

—There won't be any difference between your hips and those of the servant.

Their voices became louder; their fingers threatened Rima's face. The room shook under Lina's feet. It seemed to her that

5

God was tumbling down onto the table from the ceiling. She pictured His cruel face spattered with blood, His legs covered in dust from the journey. He stretched His lean hand, picked up Rima and breathed into her face. A burning snake burst forth from His mouth.

Tightening her eyes, she dropped the orange onto her plate. Face to face with God, her feelings were quite mixed. She didn't know whether to love Him or dread Him. She dreamt of that cold night when her father made her sit on his lap and spoke to her in a low voice about the Night of Nights, on which the secret gates of the sky open wide. She saw the wind snap the trunks of trees, and heard the spikes of wheat broken in the fields. The animals left their holes; the people ran barefoot toward the mountains. Suddenly, a radiant halo appeared in the sky, slashing apart the dark sky around it. At that moment, her father told her that the gates had opened. She heard the people clamoring and saw their hands raised towards heaven in sublimation:

—Oh Lord, grant us the beauty of Joseph.

—...the wealth of Quaroon.

—...good health.

—...boys

When she rubbed her cheek against her father's shoulder it seemed to her that people were scurrying like the characters in the magic Box of the World Show. She heard the jingling of gold, the cries of boys and laughter of girls. The Ramadan cannon went off, and the smell of macaroni baked with cheese and parsley emanated from the kitchen. Lina heard delicate puff pastries being chewed. A plate of milk puddings sat in the middle of the table covered with syrup the color of glue, and shredded almonds.

—What did you say, Lina? asked her father.

—Nothing, she laughed nervously, biting her fingers.

—Why? He began to play with her hair.

—Will God answer my prayers?

—Of course, he said, quite confidently.

—And my nanny Fatima's, too?

—Certainly.

—What does He look like, this God, Daddy?

—Heaven forbid! he muttered.

—Does He like people, feed them when they're hungry, and cure them when they're sick?

—Yes, he told her, and she saw tears in his eyes.

Are there two Gods then in this world? One merciful and the other wicked? Is it possible that one feeds us with one hand, while the other burns us with another? Between the shuffle of feet in the kitchen and the cries of the muezzin at night God appeared to her in His split face: the clear looking half with features like her father's, and the other ugly half, a mixture of the faces of Aunt Samiya, her married sisters, and her brother-in-law Hisham.

—God bless Mohammad, his blood relations and companions and grant them salvation. God leave us our religion, our wealth, and health. God keep us from the Communists.

—Amen.

—Amen.

—Amen.

The troupe's voices called in unison. Then Lina saw Rima push back her chair, rising up in contempt. But her brother seized her and wrenched her forearm roughly.

—You're not going, he said.

—Khalid, her mother cried imploringly.

—Don't think you could change the world, girl!

—Oh God, keep us from evil, muttered Aunt Samiya, then breathed into the faces of those present.

—Let go of my hand, cried Rima.

—I won't let go until you say: 'Communists are filthy.'

—Say it. Say it. Say it. All the heads bent closer to Rima.

—I won't, I won't. Rima's voice became louder. And it seemed to Lina that every head in the neighborhood was craning through the windows and the passers-by had stopped in their tracks.

Suddenly she saw her brother's hand rise in the air, and slap Rima's delicate cheeks. Her sister fled the room and slammed the door behind her. Lina's mother bowed her head and broke into sobs.

—On the night of your father's death. . . Her words became disconnected, then turned into bitter lament.

Lina was led to her room by the servant. In the long dark corridor Afaf's fingers were groping for her father's silver candelabrum, then slipping it into her handbag.

* * *

Lina pulled up the woolen blanket. She tossed about, turning right and left. At times, she stretched out on her stomach, or her back. But the image of her father's bier crossing the narrow alleys and tall, dark skinned men following the dead with their heads bowed, appeared and disappeared in her dreams. On the balcony of her house specters of females were beating their breasts and wailing. Aunt Samiya was leading the chorus, the other women relatives gathered around her. Lina couldn't recognize their features. She only saw their grey mantillas billowing in the wind.

—Take us with you, brother.

—Who did you leave the orphans with?

—Your absence will be felt.

—Oh, absent one.

—Absent one

—Absent one.

The women repeated the chant. Lina found it difficult to swallow. She hid behind a black leather seat. When she looked with one eye, fraught with fear, she saw her mother lying on the floor with her sister Rima sprinkling rose-water onto her mother's face; the other strange women were standing around, holding long rosaries and chanting "In the name of God, the beneficent, the merciful."

A cold sweat began trickling down her back. Her neck stiffened. She saw herself alone in a dimly lit room with a white haired man who had peculiar features. As she ran to the closed door and tried to open it, she heard the man laugh in a loud voice. She turned to him, frightened, and asked:

—Who are you?

8

—I wash the dead. His voice echoed.

She watched her feet slip on the soap suds covering the floor. Then, she began to knock at the door. "Mama. Where are you?" But no one heard her. The old man was coming toward her, still laughing, and from his hands came the smell of soap.

Lina opened her eyes. Her heart was beating violently. There was not a sound in the room. The curtains shimmered in the gentle autumn breeze. She found herself murmuring: Oh God, oh God. Then the words stuck in her throat, and she didn't know what to say. She lay her head on the pillow, wet with perspiration, pulled up the covers piled on one side of the bed and hid under them. She had hardly dozed off when she began to hear strange voices. She saw herself wandering down an endless corridor in a castle. The smell of incense led her to a brass room with a fountain in the center. As she was about to enter, she noticed a group of big sturdy men with white flowing gowns and red fezes on their heads, dancing in a semi-circle. She hid behind a marble column and continued to watch the dancers, enchanted by their elegant movements.

Other men poured through the brass windows carrying drums and stringed musical instruments which resembled melons, or perhaps pumpkins. She didn't know what the adults would call them. The time passed slowly, while the men were dancing and repeating a single word: Allah, Allah, Allah. Suddenly, fear over-whelmed her. She saw the dancers' tassels get tangled bit by bit, their eyes close gradually. Then she heard their bodies tumble onto the floor, and the musicians vanished. When she left her hiding place, there was nothing around the fountain but rotting corpses.

She wanted to run away, but a woman with big breasts poured a bucket of blood into the corridor, then disappeared. The fountain dissolved like salt and a round table rose up in its place. The men's corpses flew in the air and landed on golden platters. She saw Aunt Samiya, her brother, her two married sisters with their husbands sitting on high wicker chairs, cutting the rotten meat with knives and forks. Just as she wanted to scream in their faces not to eat the meat of the dead, she heard her brother-in-law burp. "Oh God spare us our beliefs and our land," everybody said.

Staring at the table again, Lina realized that the corpse there was her father's. She saw his face decorated with mushrooms, walnuts, and parsley crying into dishes loaded with food.

She started swimming fearfully in the river of blood, but whenever she passed an obstacle, she encountered another. When she reached the castle's garden she flung herself onto the grass, utterly breathless. Suddenly, she noticed her mother dressed in black, around her were women sipping coffee out of little demitasses without saucers. She tried to eavesdrop on them, but they weren't using a language she could understand. She stretched out her hand and cried: "Mama, mama," but whenever she attempted to step forward, a thorny lilac rose sprouted in front of her. Her mother didn't notice her. Lina realized that her mouth was just opening and closing without issuing a sound. She started waving her hand to draw the women's attention, but she saw them move rhythmically, take off their clothes, then wrap their bodies in white shrouds.

She opened her eyes, alarmed, and jumped barefoot onto the floor. Her face was bathed in cold sweat. In a few seconds she found herself slipping into her mother's bed in the next room, burying her tired head into her mother's sagging bosom.

* * *

The sun sneaked warily over Lina's face. The smell of cut grass came from the open window. When she tried to get out of bed, her legs felt paralyzed. She could hear the chatter of women in the house. Through the partially-opened door she noticed her mother absorbed with Aunt Samiya in the next room, packing her clothes into a suitcase. Where was she going? she wondered. Would she be gone a long time or not? How much she wanted to cry! She didn't know why her mother had decided to send her away from home.

The smell of roasted coffee beans came from the kitchen. The green-grocers' boys were going up and down the stairs, joking with the servant and emptying their baskets in aluminum pots. Lina rose lazily and sat on the edge of the bed. The sun was warm. Her eyes fixed on the picture of her father hanging on the wall.

—Are you sick? Her sister Bahiya peeped through the door.

She didn't answer.

—Go back to bed. I'll get mum.

She heard her brother's voice in the bathroom, the shuffling of feet going and coming, the splashing of water in the basin, and she smelled the shaving lotion and the strong lemon-scented Eau de Cologne.

The warmth of the sun penetrated her ribs, and she remembered how her mother used to put her naked on the floor of the hot bathroom, sit behind her on a low stool, and wash her short hair, pouring tumblers of burning water over her thin shoulders. She couldn't see the opaque glass windows and heard nothing but the tongues of fire hissing in the stove and the olive seeds popping. Aunt Samiya used to believe that if olive seeds made a noise in the stove then any pregnant woman in the family would have a boy. Lina smiled contentedly, wishing her mother would carry her to the bath and rub her sticky back with a rough sponge.

Looking again through the door she saw her mother close the suitcase and Aunt Samiya rub her hands vigorously and then rush to the hall.

She plunged under the white sheets again and shut her eyes. Oh, if only her father would come back tonight. Her bag was ready. She heard her mother saying to Bahiya in the hall:

—Get her toothbrush, and don't forget her blue comb.

She thought she would escape with him through the back door and no one would see her. Perhaps he would buy her a bag of hot peanuts and tell her about his cold journey to the graveyard. She cried under the sheets till her eyes became swollen. No one had told her what her father was doing in the grave and who would prepare his meals, and whether he would visit her mother from time to time. All that had happened was the servant assured her he wouldn't be coming back.

—Did he want to go? Lina asked insistently.

—Of course not. God chose him to be by His side.

—Why didn't He choose someone else? Aunt Samiya or...

Fatima interrupted her:

—Because he's a good man.

—And Aunt Samiya is not?

—No. No. You are young and you don't understand what I mean.

—And heaven? Do you know where heaven is, Fatima? Will Daddy wait for us there?

The servant roared with laughter, and Lina resented her. She wanted to know what heaven was and why some people go there, while others go to hell. She remembered what the religion teacher said at school: "If you obey your parents, then you'll go to heaven." How much she wanted to raise her hand and ask him endless questions. But she was afraid of his white turban and his long beard. He didn't look at her face once. She never saw him laugh with other children. He always spoke in a resonant voice that pressed fear into their hearts, his eyes nailed to the bars on the window.

She thought of Samira, the girl with the mischievous eyes and curly hair, imitating the teacher in the school yard and the other children around her giggling. But one day, another teacher saw her and beat her hands with a cane. Samira then started doing her imitations twenty meters away from the school gates and on a sidewalk full of pedestrians.

She felt a cold shiver and curled up under the sheet like a damp kitten. No, she didn't want to go to school. She loathed her black school uniform, her starched collar and her Arabic language teacher who used to go between the seats examining the children's fingernails. One day this teacher said to a girl called Wafa':

—Conjugate the verb to vomit.

—What does vomit mean? asked Khadija.

—A boy is sick. His mother gives him an apple. He eats it, then vomits it up, because his stomach is upset. Do you understand?

The girl shook her head stupidly. Lina then saw Wafa's lips contort:

— I am vomiting. You are vomiting. We are.... She didn't know the dual.

Lina subdued a short laugh. The word was disgusting.

—Why are you laughing? the teacher asked her. Her thick glasses were trembling angrily on the tip of her nose. Lina didn't know what to say.

—Do you know the dual?

Lina put her head down. She wasn't thinking then of the conjugation of the word, and she heard Samira muttering behind her gleefully: "We are vomiting. She is vomiting..." and remembered how she saw a child vomiting in the toilet one day and how the cleaner Na'ima held the girl's head and bent her body forward. Then she heard the splashing of water and the shouts of boys outside imitating the girl: "I' I' I'."

The air in the old school kitchen was stuffy. Lina saw the children run with their boots caked with mud to buy roasted pistachio, cotton candy, or sugar coated apples from the janitor. Samira asked her:

—What does your father do?

—He's a lawyer, Lina replied.

—Your Honor, Ladies and Gentlemen, said Samira. She lifted up her starched collar and pranced around in front of the other children. They laughed. Pink strings of spun sugar candy flew all over their noses.

— Do the culprits escape the hangman's noose? ogled Samira, putting her hands into her pockets, questioning.

—I don't know, Lina said dryly. But the image of her father untying the rope from around the neck of a hanging man excited her imagination.

—Good-bye, Lina.

—Good-bye.

—Good-bye.

The children's words passed by, but Samira's mocking voice still rang in her ears. "Ladies and Gentlemen, Your Honor." She regretted divulging her father's profession. She asked herself about the profession of Samira's father. No. She didn't hate her, but she didn't like her either. Samira was always imitating other people, their voices, the way they moved. She often ended her sentences with abusive words.

Lina felt the blood gush through her temples. She wanted to drive away all the ghosts that chased her day and night, disturbing her mind and spoiling her health. But as soon as she opened her eyes she remembered Ahmad, the son of the village sheriff standing at the gate of her house carrying a bunch of red carnations on a stifling summer night. She heard her mother in the bedroom asking her father:

—What does he want?

—He has come as Afaf's suitor.

—A peasant son? Her mother said angrily.

—But he is educated, said her father contentedly.

—The son of a peasant is always a peasant.

She saw her mother throw a dress on the bed and heard her slam the door behind her. She realized then that a person's profession was a window to the world, and as soon as the person looked out he or she would either be accepted or rejected. She didn't wish to become a peasant. Her family, except her father, despised the peasantry. But her sister Rima had changed in recent years. Lina often heard the incessant quarrels between Rima and the rest of the members of the family at the dinner table. Expressions like feudalism, class struggle, exploitation, and capitalism were always on her sister's lips. But Lina didn't understand the meanings of these terms. Often she saw her family split into two camps: the camp headed by her brother who tried to attack Rima and expel her strange ideas from the family, and the other camp led by her parents who tried to change from the course of modern political events to any other subject. How much she felt like a stupid little fool during these heated discussions which often became violent. The adult world, with its cruelty and violence, its hypocrisy and double standards followed her wherever she went. How much she looked back at these ghosts from the past who spoiled her tranquillity with a mixed feeling of fear and curiosity.

She tossed about in bed; her forehead burning. She simply wanted to sleep.

—What do you want to be when you grow up? Wafa' asked her persistently one warm autumn day as they waited in the school yard for the bell to ring.

— I don't know yet.

Standing in one line with their black uniforms and starched collars, it seemed to Lina that the children were developing. She saw the young girls' breasts becoming rounded, their bottoms take the shape of apples, and the boys prance in their open shirts and unshaven beards. Some of them would work in commerce, or medicine, or law, and others in the state administration. She thought that the businessmen or the professionals would get houses, or perhaps cars, but the others would stay poor. She didn't know where to put the workers or the peasants. Do they go to school, too? And how do they choose their profession?

On the little table next to the bed were her reading book, an exercise note-book and a freshly sharpened pencil. Her mother must have put them there, but how then didn't she see her come into the room? She dragged her hand over the book without getting out from under the sheets which were clammy with sweat. There was a chapter on Al-Khansa'. Putting her fingers under the words and trying hard to understand the meaning, Lina found herself mumbling in a soft voice the elegy written by the pre-Islamic poetess to her slain brother:

> Is there a mote in your eye, or is it because the abode is
>   vacant since its people are gone?
> Bereft, it weeps abundant tears for Sakhr, over whom
>   lies a cover of new earth.
> Death must come and work its changes, for in the
>   turns of fate are change and alteration.

(Trans. James A. Bellamy)

Ah what a beautiful rhythm, she thought without understanding many of the words. She too wished to write an elegy for her father. She wondered how Al-Khansa' learned to write poetry and whether the devil had haunted her as the ancient Arabs used to believe.

She tossed back the sheets, almost throwing them onto the floor, then opened the first page of her notebook and wrote:

NAME: Lina Haseebi

GRADE: Seven

OCCUPATION: Poet

She heard her mother's footsteps approaching, then felt a cold hand on her burning forehead. No. She wasn't putting on a show. She was simply tired and didn't want to get out of bed. She felt her head getting bigger and bigger, and the vapor of the hot tea burned her face. She heard voices coming from the hallway talking about her and she smelled unpleasant medicines. Through her moist eyes she noticed her mother dissolve two aspirin tablets into a long glass of water, and she felt the salty taste dry out her tongue. She wanted to vomit.

Perhaps she would die that evening. They would wash her and wrap her in a white shroud. The women would wail from the balconies, while the men would carry her bier slowly to the mosque, and perhaps the muezzin would sing her name because she was a child. The shop-keepers would close their shops on both sides of the road and the housewives would cry holding their children as they looked down onto the street from their antiquated windows. At the weather-beaten cemetery they would bury her next to her father, and maybe her brother-in-law, Hisham, would feel bad because he was always cruel to her.

Lina trembled, the sweat dripping from her brow. She imagined her relatives sitting around the table. She saw her brother cutting roast turkey stuffed with mushrooms, rice, minced meat, and chestnuts, and heard Aunt Samiya crunching the wings of small fried birds as her sister Afaf slurped French onion soup mixed with melted cheese, laughing from time to time.

No. She will not let the sickness get a better hold on her, she assured her mother and pushed her face into the bowl of hot soup until her eyes reddened from the steam. The room was bathed in sunlight, and from the street came the grape vendor's voice calling, "The end of your days, oh grapes."

*   *   *

In the corridor leading to the outer door Lina stood on tiptoe listening to her cousin 'Aisha talking in a quiet voice to a short, thin-shouldered man. She saw her open a brown chest and show the man her dead father's suits.

—The grey coat will protect you from the December cold, she said.

—But it's too big, the man muttered.

'Aisha drew closer to him, pinned the sleeves to his hanging arms, then said:

—Ask Umm Muhammad to shorten them for you.

Lina saw the man's face frown a little. He shook his head without showing much enthusiasm.

'Aisha's voice grew louder. She rummaged through the clothing vigorously as if to stir up the stranger's glee.

—The black woolen pullover? Huh?

She tossed it aside and pulled out a navy blue suit that Lina's father used to wear on Fridays when he went out to see his relatives with his wife and children.

—What do you think? You'll look better than the *Efendis* in this.

The man took the trousers and put them up to his waist carelessly.

—Nothing fits me, he said.

Lina saw the trouser legs folded up around his ankles. She wanted to laugh but was afraid that her cousin would find her out.

—Your brother Saleh. Isn't he taller than you? All these clothes are brand-new.

The man bowed his head, then said in a gruff voice:

—But they belonged to the deceased.

'Aisha strode forward.

—Oh no. You don't believe in superstitions, she said patting his shoulder encouragingly.

For a few moments she rearranged the clothing.

—You will remember us in winter when you're wearing the grey coat, she said and pushed the chest in front of the stupid looking man.

—God have mercy on the dead, the man said coldly.

Lina saw her cousin close the door and sigh deeply.

*   *   *

The women gathered in the visitors' room. The door remained open. One woman entered, another came out. Lina glanced at her Aunt Samiya tossing her long yellow rosary beads, muttering incessantly. Her mother sat like a statue; her hair covered in a black mantilla reaching her waist, and her eyes stuck on a spot in the Persian carpet decorated with images of heavenly animals.

—Why are you standing here? The servant asked her as she passed by carrying a coffee tray.

Before she could answer, a woman guest pushed her from behind to the entrance. Lina saw the women look at her, their grey mantillas flowing down their backs and slipping off their heads.

—Black coffee. All right.

—This is sweet.

—I'd prefer black.

The whisperings grew louder. Lina found herself conveyed from one lap to another.

—How old is she?

—Did you stop sending her to school?

—Why don't you send her to 'Aisha's place?

—Her bag is ready.

Lina could not recognize the words or who spoke them. She felt her cheeks swell from the kissing. No. She didn't want to sit in the neighbor Farida's arms, and smell the sweat coming out from under her armpits. She didn't dare wipe her face. She was afraid. She heard her Aunt Samiya say in a low voice:

—She almost drove her mother crazy last night.

Farida edged closer inquisitively, her hand beating her chest.

The servant came in and carried her out of the room. On the clothes rack standing in the hallway, Lina saw her dark blue overcoat with the fox-fur lined collar. Her black leather bag was lying underneath.

—Where is she going? asked her sister Rima, who was getting out the key to the front door. She carried a pile of books.

—To her cousin 'Aisha's house, said the servant, putting the navy coat into Lina's arms.

—Why don't you send her to school? asked Rima.

—Because she's sick, the servant said in a soft voice.

Rima stood still for a moment. She put the books on the floor, then rushed toward Lina and hugged her:

—My little sister, my little sister, she muttered almost inaudibly.

Lina raised her eyes. She thought her sister was growing like a poplar tree, and she saw her long white fingers, like peeled asparagus, smooth the collar of the folded coat. From the visitors' room the women's ashen faces loomed, their persistent chatter buzzing in her ears. Then she heard her mother's slow footsteps and felt her dry lips press a kiss onto her forehead..

—Good-bye, Lina.

—Good-bye.

—Good-bye.

The door was opened, and from the street came the smell of autumn. Women's transparent veils billowed; their faces looked out of the windows, and the shopkeepers waved.

Then the neighbor Muhammad's carriage trotted on the asphalt road. The driver blew his horn: toot, toot, toot, and the children who were playing in the middle of the street ran away from the galloping horses.

* * *

The carriage driver Abu Mohammad smiled, then asked her, his black moustache twitching:

19

—Are you comfortable?

She nodded her head shyly and pulled her dress to cover her short legs which did not reach the carriage floor.

—No school today? asked the driver turning his head toward her again. His hands were loosening the rein of the two black horses.

—Mother called the principal today, and I was permitted to be absent for a couple of days, she said, feeling as if she had gained a new friend.

The driver shook his head, then laughed loudly.

The autumn sun fell over the street. Lina saw the housewives, some with light overcoats, others with tight sweaters and skirts that covered their knees, pushing babies' prams in front of them. At one of the corners of the street, she heard some boys climb the back board of the horse-drawn carriage. Lina leaned out, holding the top of the door to keep steady. The driver threw his whip backward and started hitting the back wheels shouting angrily:

—Get off quickly, sons of bitches!

The boys laughed. They began to flee in fear of the driver's whip.

Lina sat back. She was restless again on the torn leather seat. Abu Muhammad was sitting in front of her: his back bent, his hands pulling or loosening the rein of the horses. On both sides of the street rose old drab buildings. Khalil, the neighborhood idiot, happened to pass under a window as a woman wearing a night gown poured a bucket of water onto the sidewalk. He was soaked from top to toe. The street was taken by a storm of laughter. The woman who poured the water didn't make any attempt to hide. As the driver slowed down, the carriage shook with his laughter. Lina saw the woman holding the balcony rail and heard her shout at the idiot.

— When will you become a human being?

Some passers-by gathered around the idiot. No one helped him take off his clothes, or dry his hair. Putting their hands on their hips, they formed a circle around him and began to laugh. Khalil raised his head and muttered some words as he sobbed:

—Damn the father of your God.

Some people laughed, others said: "Forgive us, oh, Lord." The driver sped up, lashing his horses with his whip and muttering to himself: "I ask for your forgiveness, oh, Lord."

As the laughter died down, the carriage began climbing the mountain, and Lina felt like crying. The idiot's face with water dripping from it was stuck in her mind.

In an avenue lined with trees, the carriage slowed down, then stopped in front of a big white house. As the driver blew his horn: toot, toot, toot, Lina saw someone pull the velvet curtains off the big windows and faces look down the street, then she heard steps approaching. Within seconds, the carriage was surrounded by cousin 'Aisha's and the neighbor's children. Rasha carried Lina's bag, while Rana helped her get off, and young Omar shouted:

—Hi! Hi!

—We'll play together.

—Let's roast the nuts.

—No. We'll buy cotton candy.

—And when shall we go to the orchard of the peasant, Amina?

—Tomorrow or Friday.

The children's voices grew louder. Each child pulled her from her arm. When she turned her head to say good-bye to the driver she saw him busily preparing fodder for the hungry horses, and she noticed the servant Khadduj had left him some food on the seat.

—Mum will be late tonight, said Rasha cheerfully winking her eyes at her youngest sister who was sitting on the colorful carpet.

—Is your mum still in Lina's house? a thin girl, who was not more than 10 years old, asked curiously.

Rasha bit her lips and ignored the girl as if trying to erase Lina's house from existence.

— Are you hungry? the servant asked Lina.

—I am, Rana replied, jumping over the carpet, making some strange noises.

—And who is asking you? said the servant. She turned her back and disappeared in the kitchen, pulling Omar by the hand.

Lina sat on the sofa. She was afraid to speak. From the kitchen came the smell of cooked milk with rice. She had never liked milk, and she didn't wish to look at Rasha who was showing her scores of stamp collections. Pictures and names got mixed up in her mind. She couldn't remember the geographical locations of the various countries, and wished Rasha would speak a little bit slower. The geography teacher told the children one time, as she remembered, "The earth is round." Lina tried to recall the map of the world and to put each country in its right position.

—Is this the picture of the queen? asked the thin girl who was sitting to her right. But no one answered her.

—This bird is the nicest. The blond girl pointed her finger to a stamp on the opposite page.

—Did you see the Indonesian dancer? O, no, the plane... the apple...

—This is an Arabic lamp.

—Did you see the minaret?

The children's fingers landed on the stamps which were protected behind transparent papers; their words became indistinct.

Then, the blonde girl pointed her fingers to a man's face and said:

—Oh, this man looks like my father.

But Rasha jumped like a lioness, pulling the girl by her hand and taking her outside of the room. The children's faces drew closer. Lina saw their hands cover their mouths and knew they were warning each other not to remind her of her dead father. In her mind she tried to draw a picture of many men and women, all different in looks, clothing and temper, and she wished at that moment for the carriage driver to come back and take her home.

*   *   *

The sun was setting on the window pane of the dining room as the servant led the six children to the table and put in front of each one of them a bowl of rice pudding and a hot pie filled with melted feta cheese and parsley. No one began till Lina ate the first spoon of rice pudding, then the children's heads bent over the bowls. Lina saw Rana who was two years younger than herself purse her lips and loudly sip the syrup which almost froze over the pudding.

—What grade are you in? the thin girl asked Lina.

—Year seven.

—Are you good in school? asked Rana. The syrup dripped on her chin.

—I think so! But not in math.

—Really? said Rasha.

—The figures on the blackboard always make me dizzy, said Lina, forcing a short laugh. The mathematics teacher with her cruel face and big breasts came back to her mind. She had never liked the teacher. Lina leaned her elbows on the dining table and didn't feel like finishing the bowl of rice pudding. Her eyes caught the eyes of the servant, who sat contented sipping a cup of hot tea. Servants usually don't sit with adults, Lina thought. They stand at the corner of the room and wait for orders. Joy overwhelmed her because she was a child and because Khadduj could sit and sip tea with her calmly, without embarrassment.

From the street came the noise of a car pulling slowly up to the curb. The children ran to the window.

—Dad!

—Mum!

Rana threw her spoon on the floor and ran barefoot, and the others followed, except Lina. From the door she could see her cousin 'Aisha leaning on the arm of her husband Saleh, while Rana was clutching at their legs.

—What have you got for me, Dad?

In the midst of the noise, the thin girl and the girl with the golden hair disappeared, while Khadduj was clearing the remnants of the cheese pies and the bowls of rice pudding from the table.

*   *   *

Cousin 'Aisha closed the window of the bedroom, pulled the blue velvet curtains, then approached Lina's bed carefully.

—Consider me like your mother, she said, then bent down and kissed her on the forehead.

Trembling beneath the white sheets, Lina yawned. She pulled her legs to her chest. She thought her breath would warm up the bed, then she would stretch her legs gradually and her feet would become warm. She remembered her sister Rima running to bed on cold winter nights, carrying a hot water bottle and putting it under the sheets and then moving it from place to place while her mother stood in front of the door, laughing loudly. She had heard her relatives call Rima, "The old woman." Yawning again and enjoying the smell of the clean sheets, she thought of Khadduj who had spent hours washing and ironing them. As she felt herself getting warm enough to move her body to the other side, she heard Rasha, who was sleeping in the other bed, ask her in a soft voice:

—Are you asleep?

—No, said Lina raising her head a little from under the sheets.

—What are you thinking of? said Rasha.

—Nothing.

From the bathroom came the sound of cousin 'Aisha brushing her teeth and gargling.

—Don't you trust me? asked Rasha. She sat up and moved to the edge of the bed.

The room was almost dark. Rasha with her flowing white gown looked like a ghost.

—Do you think my father died? asked Lina hesitantly.

—But you are crazy. Of course he died. All of us will die. Her voice stopped.

Lina thought that Rasha understood things better than she did, because Rasha was older. She was encouraged again.

—Will he go to heaven? she asked. Her heart was beating violently.

—God will put his good deeds and bad deeds on a scale. If the good deeds outweigh the bad ones, then he will undoubtedly go to heaven, said Rasha in a confident voice.

Lina pictured God standing next to a huge scale like the neighborhood grocer, but His shop was open day and night. People were rushing in and out.

—But if his bad deeds outweigh the good ones? said Lina hesitantly, then felt ashamed.

—He will go to hell, replied Rasha, then added: Don't worry. The good deeds will outweigh the bad ones.

—What is heaven? Do you know Rasha?

From the hallway came the sound of Uncle Saleh's footsteps, then the light went off.

—Gardens, Rasha muttered, as if remembering what the religion teacher had told her in school.

—Fig trees? asked Lina.

—And apples.

—Plums, too?

—And grapes.

—Pears?

—And cherries.

She heard the rivers rush day and night and the bees buzz among the trees.

—The believers will trail their green silky clothes embroidered with gold, said Rasha, yawning in a loud voice, and diving under her sheets.

Lina listened very carefully. She thought her father would look ridiculous in a long green dress.

—And the river of milk and honey? she asked after a while. She couldn't remember who had told her about it. But Rasha muttered something incomprehensible, then fell sound asleep.

Lina felt the darkness swallowing her up. As she slept on her belly and hid her head under the pillow, God was pulling his worn-out sandal, just like Mahmoud the grocer, and standing busily in front of the metal scale. Around Him the people were pushing each other and chattering endlessly.

* * *

—Lina. Lina.

A cold breeze touched her face. She rubbed her eyes and yawned. The room was dark.

—Come on. Get up. It's a quarter to five.

She heard footsteps in the hallway and the toilet flushing. The room was full of light. As she tried to open her eyes, she saw Rasha wearing brown jeans and a yellow woolen sweater. She could hear young Omar sprinkling his sister Rana with water and laughing in the bathroom.

—Don't you want to go to Amina's farm? asked Rasha as she drew the velvet curtains and opened the window.

Cold air filled the room. It was still dark outside. Lina didn't hear a sound in the street. Flinging the sheets up with her feet she got out of bed, shivering. Rasha gave her a pair of dark blue jeans from her suitcase and a blue sweater with a high turtle-neck collar.

—Five minutes only, Rasha said and pushed Lina tenderly towards the hallway.

Cousin 'Aisha and her husband were still asleep. But the voice of Khadduj came from the kitchen, and Lina could smell the milk bubbling on the stove.

How much she missed those walks in the wheat fields while the sun was still almost hidden beyond the horizon. The cold air refreshed the sleepy eyes, and those circles the children formed around the heaps of threshed wheat singing: Tralala lala. Tralala lala. The colorful hats used to fly in the air, and the peasant women would stand in front of their huts carrying their babies. How much the smell of the wild flowers intoxicated her then.

She put on her clothes in a hurry. The children were already in the kitchen. Rasha, Rana, and Omar. Khadduj was busy pouring the hot milk in a big thermos, then she began folding the long pieces of bread covered with yogurt, olives, cheese, thyme, and oil in the shape of long cigars, and putting them in a straw basket.

The door was opened, and as the children stepped out into the thick morning mist, the cold wind blew against their faces.

—Wear your coat, Omar.

—Cover your ears, Lina.

—Tie your boots.

—No. No. Carry the basket carefully, Rasha.

—Do you have a handkerchief, Lina?

The children's cries grew louder and got mixed with Khadduj's orders. Then they walked loudly down the sidewalk, squashing yellow leaves under their boots. When Lina looked behind, Khadduj was standing like a specter at the door waving with her hand. Her hair was blowing in the wind.

* * *

They passed by the thin girl's house. But when they saw no light they didn't stop. The dawn was breaking slowly, and light was cast over the endless fields. Rasha and Lina carried the basket between them. Rasha held Omar's hand and Rana hung onto the end of the line. The children looked right and left. Rasha put her ear on the electricity post and listened. There was no car coming. The children lifted their feet and started to run towards Amina's farm.

The country path was dusty, and strange colorful flowers sprang on both sides. The muddy fields appeared beyond the fence as if they had been ploughed recently. From Amina's yard came the cries of cocks and the clucking of hens. Suddenly, the long line of children was broken. Omar started jumping around and shouting: Ki Ki Ri Ki. Lina watched as Rana filled her freckled cheeks with air, swelling them like balloons, while her lips rolled up and issued strange sounds: buq, buq. Lina felt confused. And the sound: buq, buq, went unchecked. Rasha threw a small stone on the broken fence and the birds which gathered around the berry bush flew away. Pushing her hair from her eyes, Rana giggled loudly. Omar measured the path with his feet in a zigzag way from right to left, stirring a cloud of dust behind him.

The door of the house was open. The children saw the smoke coming out of the chimney and they could smell the fresh bread. Rasha hurried to say hello to Amina's mother, while the rest of the children stood behind her, their faces red.

—Good morning.

—Good morning.

—Amina. Leave the hens and come with Mohammad, shouted the tall peasant woman, whose hands were withered.

Omar licked his lips and pointed to the round pieces of bread being baked on the wall of the open mud stove with the fire dancing around. Fascinated by the scene, Lina watched the peasant woman make the dough, slap it on a pillow, then throw it inside the stove.

As Amina and Mohammad came out, the children began to run.

—Who will carry the new basket?

The children grabbed at one another's hands. The smell of the fresh bread watered their mouths. Omar's fingers plunged into a piece of bread and made cracking sounds.

—Don't forget the tea, said Amina's mother as she bent over the stove, pricking the dough carefully with a long stick.

—Good-bye.

—Good-bye.

The voices became louder. Lina saw the peasant woman's white teeth and she thought of the pearl necklace on her mother's bosom, then visions got mixed in her mind. She thought of Aunt Samiya's false teeth. When Lina turned her tongue in her mouth she felt a gap between the last two teeth in her upper jaw.

* * *

The children walked to the apple orchard. Amina lay a colorful rug on the wet grass, Lina and Rana arranged the mugs, and Rasha distributed the sandwiches. Omar and Muhammad were jumping among the trees, gathering fallen apples with their hands.

When Amina whistled through her fingers, the children rushed to her and sat in a semi circle. Someone opened the thermos cover, and the vapor of hot milk touched Lina's face.

—I want tea, said Omar.

28

—No. Drink some milk, said Rasha shaking her head, as if to scold the boy.

—Would you like fresh mint with your yogurt? Amina asked her, and put a plate of mint in front of her.

The smell of thyme dipped with olive oil filled the air. Lina saw Mohammad's front teeth get smeared with yellow as he bit into a boiled egg. In the meantime, Rana was cooling the milk with her breath. Amina laughed, pushing her red locks away from her eyes and said:

—Who is going to tell us a story?

Omar clapped with both hands, and his milk mug fell down. The children jumped: Amina dried the rug with her handkerchief, Rasha beat the boy on his behind, Rana covered the thermos, and Mohammad jumped around the tree on one leg.

The sun drenched the apple orchard, and the birds began to leave their nests. From a distance Lina could see some peasants picking potatoes in the fields.

—Why don't we put on a play? she suggested shyly.

The children clapped their hands approvingly.

—Yes, yes, said Rasha.

—I'll play the role of the cruel father, said Omar, and pushing his small belly in front of him, he started walking like a peacock.

—And I'll be the princess, said Rana. She put her tongue out, mocking her brother.

—Will you take care of my garden? Omar asked the peasant boy.

—No, said Mohammad defiantly.

—Why? Don't you want to be like your father? laughed Amina and touched her brother's hair.

—Because I want to go to school, said Mohammad with a cruel tone.

—Just listen to who is speaking, said his sister mockingly. The Arabic teacher swore he would never learn a thing.

—Liar, Liar, shouted Mohammad.

—Didn't you flunk the exam? asked Amina.

Lina saw the boy's face become paler, his eyes seemed to sink deeper in their sockets.

—If only I had a private tutor like Omar, he said, gnashing his teeth, and didn't finish his sentence.

The children were silent. It seemed to Lina that heaven was falling on the earth, and apples were dropping before they were ripe.

—Why do we fight? asked Rasha.

No one said a word.

—O.K. Let's put on a play. What do you think? said Rasha again.

The anger was leaving Mohammad's face. His sister laughed and stretched her hand to him, but he didn't take it.

—Shall we play the game of the doctor and his patients? asked Omar, craning his head out from behind the tree. But Rasha followed him with a broken branch in her hand, threatening to discipline him.

—How about the guests' game, shouted Rana, and all the children laughed.

—Lina, what do you say? asked Amina.

She was hesitant at the beginning, then she said:

—The father dies, so his wife goes to search for him.

The children's faces became grim. Cries of protest were heard.

—No. Let her finish what she wants to say.

—Because her father. . .

—Shut up.

Her eyes were filled with tears. She had read in *One Thousand and One Nights* about the man with the thick beard who knew the way to the three miracles of the world. She felt Rasha's hand pat her shoulder.

—Don't listen to what Omar says, Rasha consoled her.

Lina raised her eyes with difficulty and looked at the children.

—On the way the woman finds an old man who tells her about her husband's place, said Lina.

—I'll play the role of God behind the tree, said Mohammad joyfully.

—Shut your trap, you imp, his sister interrupted him.

—We'll put a kerchief on your eyes, suggested Rana to Mohammad gleefully.

30

—And we'll make a pilgrimage around the tree, Omar jumped and clapped his hands.

—I'll play the role of the woman, said Rasha.

The children dusted the rug, then stood in a semi circle.

—Don't you want to be accompanied by your servant? asked Amina, hiding her smile with her fat hand.

—O.K.

Lina saw Rasha put the rug on her back, then walk in the circle like an idiot. Amina followed her. The children's eyes were fixed on the two characters. Rasha suddenly turned and shouted in a loud voice:

—Who ordered you to follow me?

—But Madam, Amina muttered some incomprehensible words.

Lina suppressed her laughter, thinking that the girl was a good actress, behaving as if she were born a servant.

—Now, didn't I have enough from my dead husband who used to cast amorous glances upon you? said Rasha, putting her hands on her waist and stretching her lips theatrically as the Egyptian actresses usually did.

—Upon me? said Amina in a frail voice, dropping her eyes down.

Rana laughed loudly, but Lina felt embarrassed. She had never liked those vulgar expressions used by the adults. Suddenly, Omar rushed to the middle and pushed Amina with his two hands.

—I'll play the role of the sheikh. Come on, ask me. His cheeks were swollen. He stood ready, as if to begin a fight.

—Now, sit down on the ground and pretend you are an old man, said Mohammad mockingly.

Omar grabbed a piece of bread and stuck it on his mouth, saying:

—This is my beard. Then he lay under a big apple tree and started snoring.

The children's eyes gleamed. Rasha fixed the rug again on her shoulders and pretended she was cold.

—Uncle. Uncle. She bent over the boy's face, then was taken aback, quite frightened when she noticed his long beard.

The children came closer to the tree. Lina's heart began to beat violently. She didn't know how Rasha would behave. Prince Bahman in the story of "The Two Jealous Sisters" had cut some of the old man's moustache in order to understand what he said.

—Do you know the way to the underworld? asked Rasha, shaking the boy's shoulder.

Omar's voice sounded funny from behind the bread. No one understood what he said.

—Let me cut some of your beard. Rasha squatted, and the rug spread like a peacock feather around her.

The children advanced, craning their heads curiously. When they saw Rasha bite the bread around the boy's mouth, they clapped and danced.

—I won't tell you, jumped Omar and threw the piece of bread on the ground.

The children gathered around him in a circle.

—Speak.

—Speak.

—Speak.

Their mouths yelled; their fingers threatened. The boy cried and tried to break the circle. Lina found herself stepping backward to let him slip by like a cat. Rasha threw the rug on the ground. She said to Omar:

—You've spoiled everything.

The children now were scattered, having lost their interest in the play. No doubt it was her fault, Lina thought, biting her lips. When she turned around, she saw Rana chasing the butterflies, the boys climbing the apple tree and throwing the fruits to the ground, and Rasha and Amina crossing the field, busy talking to each other.

She was sweating. The autumn sun was quite hot. Even the cows in the distant fields were lying down lazily. Lina was overcome by sleep, and the fallen leaves flew around her. She sat on the rug yawning from time to time. A grey squirrel jumped in front of her, then rushed towards the tree: its small eyes were full of fear. She wanted to scream, but the words got stuck in her throat. She imagined that the specter of Princess Perviz with her face yearning for knowledge rose behind her, and she saw a horse tied to a distant tree, stamping its hooves loudly.

—Perviz, take me with you, cried Lina in her dream.

—But you're young. The echo repeated the princess's words.

—You're young.

—You're young.

—You're young.

—How did you visit the underworld, Perviz?

—The Dervish helped me.

—Didn't he help someone else?

—No doubt. But the others didn't listen to his advice.

—Didn't the hidden faces behind the rocks scare you? Didn't the wailing of the ghosts deafen your ears?

—Never. I was determined not to see a thing, not to hear a thing.

—But the valley of the black stones, Perviz? And your dead brothers?

—Nothing will stop me from my goal.

—Will you ascend the hill?

—Yes.

—And you won't look behind?

—Never.

—And the voices that howl: Come back, come back.

—Not important.

—Perviz, Perviz. Are you seeking the speaking bird?.

—Yes.

—And the singing tree?

—Yes.

—And the golden water?

—Yes. Yes. Yes.

—And you won't forget your brothers?

—Never.

—In the valley of the black stones where the sunflowers grow.

—In the valley of the black stones.

—And you will speak with the dead?

—With the dead.

—And your brothers? Didn't they get old?

—Never.

—Never?

—Never.

—Perviz, Perviz. Wait for me. I'll come with you. Ah, where are you?

As she opened her tearful eyes, she found her hands pulling the rug nervously. And from the distant fields came the mooing of cows. She looked around, but her companions were not to be seen. She was afraid. She wanted to belong to the children's world. She didn't know why she felt alienated from those who were her age.

She began to run in the apple orchard, looking right and left. The cold sweat trickled down her face. There were trees everywhere: their tips were touching the horizon as she thought. Ghosts pursued her, stretching their long tongues along the edges of the road.

—Hey, idiot.

—Ha. . . Ha. . . Ha. . .

—Do you think you are like Perviz?

—A black stone. . . Your father a black stone. . .

—The underworld is a long journey.

—I'll break your legs.

—I'll pound your neck.

—I'll boil your stomachs.

—Ha. . . Ha. . . Ha. . .

The voices became louder, and the sun almost blinded her weary eyes. But through her wet eyelashes she began to see the specters of women wearing black and besieging her from every corner.

Her legs couldn't carry her any longer. She felt a sudden fatigue. How much she wished to be near the stove at that moment, watching her mother sip hot tea and her nanny, with her swollen feet, grill chestnuts on the fire. Her mother used to tell her stories sometimes from *One Thousand and One Nights*. How much she liked to listen now and again to the story of the poor fisherman who discovered by chance a brass vase in which a frightening genie had been imprisoned for thousands of years. The hidden vaults, deserted palaces, magic mirrors, princes with two halves: one human, one inanimate, all excited her young imagination. And when she went to bed, familiar faces often pursued her and crowded around her so she couldn't even breathe. How many a time Ajib bin al-Khasib, who brought blindness upon himself when he opened the golden forbidden door and gazed in the silver lamps dangling from the ceiling of the room, visited her. How many a time the specter of Sinbad, tied to the claw of the mythic roc, visited her in her sleep. And how many a time she heard Baba Abdulla in the middle of the night crying: "Whenever we own something we want more." But often, she used to ask about these wicked women in *One Thousand and One Nights*. They always betrayed their husbands, and preferred slaves. They were always jealous of those who were better off than themselves, and they did the impossible till others fell in their traps. How desperate she became when her mother repeated the story of King Shahrayar strangling a new wife every morning. She listened to the stories of Shahrazad out of breath, fearing that the king's cruel hand might stop the princess's mouth for good.

She thought of all these never-ending journeys in the *One Thousand and One Nights*: a merchant crossing the desert; another sailing on a ship; a prince hunting in the forest; a king walking at night in the city streets. Every story starts with a journey; short or long, but it is still a journey. It saddened her that the heroes were always men, and often belonged to the ruling classes or to the merchant class. She wanted to know why there was no woman Sinbad clinging to the claw of the roc, or finding herself alone in the diamond valley, or blinding the one-eyed giant with a pair of hot tongs. How much her mother laughed at her mixed up ideas and assured her that man was different from woman, and that he alone was capable of confronting difficulties. Lina withdrew and was saddened to think that her fate might be like that of the slave who was loved by Nur al-Din, or the wicked witch who transformed the lower half of her husband to a marble pillar, or the three girls of Baghdad who put make-up on, sang, and listened to the travellers' stories. She couldn't consider herself their peer. Sinbad and his love for the unknown, his determination to pursue his adventures, his boredom with the easy life; these things excited her imagination and haunted her day and night.

It didn't take long before the image of that sailor was blurred in her eyes, and in its place appeared the image of Perviz in the story of "The Two Jealous Sisters" ascending the mountain in man's clothing and refusing to look behind, or to take notice of the voices that insulted her. And, after her mother told her about Perviz, the whole world seemed different around her, as if something in its system had changed: the sun stopped circling the earth, the earth stopped circling the planets. But she felt that her mother didn't describe Perviz's journey in detail, the way she described Sinbad's. She was disappointed a bit, and she wished the princess could meet the old man who jumped at Sinbad's back and seized his neck for many days, or to be like the sailor able to get out of his island grave, or to confront the one-eyed giant; but at any rate, her own imagination supplied her with the stages of the journey, and she began to see Perviz in various poses with imaginary characters. How much she scribbled on her notebook before she went to bed, drawing the locations of islands, valleys, and mountains which the princess had crossed on her way before she obtained the speaking bird, the singing tree, and the golden water.

* * *

Lina looked around. The fields were silent like graveyards. There were no more peasants picking potatoes or lazy cows lying on the grass. Rasha and Amina would not leave her alone for long, she thought. It was time to go back to her cousin's house. She tried to whistle, imitating wicked Omar. She put her index finger between her lips, then blew, but nothing happened. She began to walk along the fence, looking back once in a while at the rug and the two baskets. It pained her that the two elder girls could have left her alone in the fields. She felt alienated from Rasha whenever the red haired peasant girl with the fat hands was present. Lina couldn't attract the attention of her relative, for Rasha was always fascinated by Amina's natural gestures, her wicked laughter and her worldly tales. Lina stopped interfering between the two friends, realizing she was an outsider, and that Rasha's kindness and care at this moment were only due to the circumstances which had led Lina to visit cousin 'Aisha's place.

She plucked a wild rose from the fence and breathed in its smell. The youngsters' world is not very different from that of the adults, she thought after a while. Children, too, take sides with or against each other without any apparent reason. It occurred to her that at the funeral dinner, her brother, her two in-laws, and their wives formed one block against the rest of the family, and everybody else was against her sister Rima. She didn't understand the secret of this hidden struggle. Her head turned upside down. Her ideas became confused and feverish. No. She liked Rasha. She liked Amina, the peasant girl. No one took sides against her. There was no reason. But when she looked around and saw the silent fields gaze at her like empty eyes, she felt like crying and began to walk on the edge of the fence till the long grass covered her waist. She could neither see the rug nor the baskets when she turned back now. Her short arms were buried in a sea of soft green blades. Feeling refreshed, she threw herself on the grass like a swimmer diving into the water. Suddenly, Rasha's laughter came ringing through the fields. She didn't want to jump from her hide-out till the sound came closer. She held her breath. Her heart was pounding violently. Rasha was running like a mare carrying a bunch of daisies, and close on her heels came Amina jumping on one leg: her red long hair flowing in the wind. The footsteps of the two girls came closer. Rasha said to the peasant girl:

—You're lying. And she laughed again.

—No, I swear by Almighty God, by my brother's head, said Amina.

Lina froze in her place. Her heart stopped beating. She didn't know why Amina would lie.

—Speak. What have you seen? asked Rasha curiously.

The two girls halted just two meters from her. She feared they would discover her hide-out.

—Haven't we come back to look for Lina? asked Amina, trying to irritate Rasha.

—Lina, Lina, Lina, cried Rasha angrily. We'll find her at the end.

—And what about Omar and Rana? asked Amina, giggling.

—Nothing to worry about. Aren't they with your brother? Don't they know these fields one by one?

—O.K. Let's sit here, said Amina.

Lina's heart was pounding violently again. She didn't know what to do. Rasha would be angry if she saw her coming out of the tall grass, or if she discovered her hide-out. Lina's feet became numb, but her ears stood up like those of a rabbit. She wanted to hear every word Amina said.

—I was almost asleep when I heard my mother's laughter ring in the opposite room. My brother was asleep. I went on tiptoe and put my ear against the closed door of our bedroom. But I heard nothing. All I could distinguish was my father's irregular panting. I opened the door carefully. My heartbeats quickened, then a cold wind touched my face. I remembered that the glass of one of the windows was broken. The laughter suddenly stopped, and I heard my mother cry: "Who's there?" I froze in place. When she realized that the sound was nothing but the rustle of leaves in the backyard, she turned in bed, then I heard a shower of kisses.

Lina felt the blood boil in her head as she heard Amina laugh devilishly. Rasha breathed loudly.

—Was their door open? asked Rasha.

—Half open. . .

—And did you go to the hallway? asked Rasha.

—I froze in my place for a long time. My head was outside the door, but the rest of my body was inside the room. I thought I was going to stay like that till the morning, and that I would not dare push the door, fearing it might issue the slightest sound. But the kisses continued, and my father's panting was getting quicker. I wanted to satisfy my curiosity, so I put out my right foot first, and I heard the door creak under the weight of my body, but I was lucky. Amina laughed loudly.

—Didn't Mohammad wake up? asked Rasha out of breath.

—No. Never.

—And your parents, didn't they hear the door creaking?

—No. When the mooing of the cows in the nearby stables grew louder I put out my left foot, and how I was afraid that the wind might slam the door behind me. I walked carefully, step after step. The lamp in their room was soft, and from the ajar door I saw my mother.

Rasha sighed deeply. Lina's limbs were paralyzed with excitement.

—She was wearing a pink short dress. Her hair was down on her shoulders. And I saw her ride my father's hairy chest. Her knees were bare under the light.

Lina sweated. Her heart was pounding again, the blood was flowing in her cheeks.

—His hands were touching her open legs. I heard her sigh and turn to both sides while her hair was scattered on her face.

Rasha's breath quickened till it became akin to snoring.

—When I gazed, said Amina as if to make her story realistic, I saw his hands looking for her breasts. And within a minute he tore the dress apart, and I saw him crush her under him. Then the lamp was turned off.

—Liar, liar, cried Rasha loudly.

—No, I swear by Almighty God.

—Then finish your story.

—I didn't see anything. The lamp went out.

—But he played with her breasts.

—I said that.

—Then what?

—I don't know. She was mewing like a cat in November.

—And he, didn't you see something?

—No. The door was half open.
—And Mohammad? Didn't he wake up?
—No.
—Why do you lie?
—I swear by Almighty God.
—And the doctor's game?
—What do you mean?
—Didn't you play with your brother?
—No. By God.
—Didn't you see your mother?
—No. By God.

Lina heard the footsteps of the peasant girl move away, and Rasha running behind her yelling like mad: Stop. Stop.

She sat down. Her legs were numb. She felt like she was riding on a flying chair in the amusement park. The trees looked funny, all upside down, and she felt as if the apples were falling till they flooded the fields. Her blue sweater was wet with sweat. When she calmed down and began again to remember the story of Amina, the peasant girl, the adult world which was blurred until now with darkness became clearer in her eyes. Her mother had told her about the stork leaving its eggs in beds, and how the eggs break, there emerging from them the soft heads of children with tearful eyes and withered cheeks. All these stories crumbled now. How much she wanted to ask the peasant girl many questions, for it seemed she knew everything. She thought of those evenings when her two married sisters used to whisper by the stove and laugh hysterically. How much she wanted to know why they were laughing then. The adult world was dark, vague, and she didn't understand anything about its rules or secrets.

The figures of both Rasha and Amina became small in the fields, then disappeared. Lina heard only the echo of their jingling laughter.

Oh, the warm autumn sun. She rubbed her eyes as if waking from a strange dream. As she stood up, she heard the grass break under her feet and saw a flock of birds hovering in the sky. The light was breaking on their fluttering wings. She pushed the entangled grass around her shoulders, then made her way to the country path. Her feet sank in a sea of fallen leaves.

—Lina, Lina!

She looked around. Who was shouting? The pale sun touched her face. Her eyes were blurred. Images from the distant past flooded her mind. Was she five then? She found herself counting on her fingers and heard the chattering of adults grilling meat in a field of daisies, while the youngsters gathered the scattered sticks and gossiped endlessly. She saw the pale-faced boy with the brown eyes follow her footsteps.

—Lina, don't go far, said her mother.

She saw the servant put a chunk of meat, tomatoes, green peppers, mushrooms, and onions on the skewers. Her in-law Hisham was fanning the fire with a thick piece of cardboard. She looked around. The boy was still gazing at her. She found herself moving further, bit by bit, from the crowd. And in the midst of the field he stopped her without saying a word and gave her a daisy. He was taller and older than she. When she tried to say something he put his hand on her mouth and smiled tenderly, and she saw his face glow with love. Was she wearing a white dress? White shoes? White stockings? She couldn't remember. But the smell of the daisies intoxicated her. She thought her feet rose and she began to fly on top of the daisies while the boy was holding her hand. His pale face was glimmering under the light.

—Lina! Lina!

Who was shouting? Her heart was pounding and the field of daisies disappeared along with her vision.

—Lina! Lina! The cries came to her like a procession of ghosts. And the fields with the empty eyes stretched endlessly. She began to run like crazy. The autumn leaves were flying around her.

*   *   *

The carriage driver, Abu Mohammad, could not stop in front of the iron gate of Lina's house. There was a crowd around the building, and some were pointing to the windows of the third floor.

41

Abu Muhammad put her suitcase on the sidewalk. His eyes were following the people curiously.

—What happened? She heard him ask one of the passers-by.

—I don't know exactly. But the army has apparently occupied the third floor.

—What? said the driver.

The man shook his head dumbly, then hurried and disappeared around the corner of the street. Her heart was beating strongly. She didn't quite understand what was going on around her.

—Don't be afraid, said Abu Mohammad, patting her on the shoulder. Then looking around as if thinking of something, he took out the fodder's bags and put them around the horses' necks while his eyes were following what was going on in the street.

—O.K., wait for me here, said Abu Mohammad. He ran lightly, his belly swinging over his legs.

Lina raised her head, but couldn't see a thing. The third floor windows were all open. She wondered what happened to her neighbors, the Sa'id family. She didn't realize they were going to move out, and regretted the fact she hadn't said good-bye to Nabila. She used to play with her on the roof sometimes, and tell endless stories.

Where was her mother? Her brother? And why was her house shrouded with terrible silence? The curtains were drawn, and she wished the driver would soon come back and that the crowd would disperse.

—Who occupied the house? she heard the butter merchant, Abu Mahmud, ask the ice-cream vendor just a few steps from her.

—A captain.

—A captain? whispered Abu Mahmud loudly. She saw him cover his right ear with his coat.

—They broke into the house.

—Who? asked the butter merchant and looked around. As he saw her trembling in front of the carriage, he turned his head away.

—The soldiers. The secret service. Who else, man?

—Ha! Ha! The butter merchant shook his head. And her brother? he said after a while, pointing to her.

—Her brother? Are you kidding? They came with machine guns.

—Machine guns?

Lina felt her legs paralyzed. Did they take her brother to jail? Did they kill him? No. She couldn't understand a thing.

A military car's horn sounded. The crowd opened and closed like a fan. She wondered where the carriage driver was. He seemed to have forgotten her standing at the sidewalk.

—A scene? Hey? shouted one tall soldier with strong muscles at the crowd. Haven't you ever seen anyone move to a new place?

When no one moved, the other soldier stepped forward, (after his comrade made a gesture,) lifted his bayonet in the air and threatened the crowd. People began to run. Lina saw the carpenter jump like a rabbit, his hunched back rising and falling among the crowd. Some women pulled down their black veils, gathered the edges of their long coats and hurried away, dragging along children with pale faces.

—Would you like some help, sir? Lina heard the butter merchant ask the tall soldier, craning his neck over the men's shoulders and winking at the ice-cream vendor.

Without saying a word, the soldier pointed to a blue metal box in the car as if ordering the butter merchant to carry it. Some men and boys who previously had stepped backward now gathered again. Lina tried in vain to see what was happening inside the circle. Suddenly, a woman appeared in front of the open window on the top floor. Everybody looked up. Lina could not recognize the woman's features because she covered her head with a colorful kerchief that had a black background. Lina knew that the stranger was a peasant, and she noticed the golden bracelets decorating her wrist.

—Saber. The plague be upon you, shouted the woman angrily.

Lina listened carefully. The woman's dialect was strange, not like what people speak in towns.

—Will you hurry up? Whatever happened to the rice, meat, and vegetables? The captain will break your neck.

At that moment the tall soldier stepped to the right. She saw him push his shorter comrade. His cheeks were flushed.

—Don't you see the crowd, Lady? Then this idiot. He pointed to his comrade with contempt.

—Hurry up both of you, shrieked the woman. She slammed the window violently.

Within seconds, the tall soldier became a wild beast.

—Now get lost, he shouted at the crowd, stretching his arms in a threatening way. His eyes burned red. First, the boys ran toward the other side of the street, then the men hurried away, their faces were grim. In the midst of the turmoil, the butter merchant carried the blue trunk on his back, the short soldier ran like a frightened rat, and the tall soldier kicked both men with the butt of his bayonet. Then Lina saw the carriage driver rush toward her from amongst the crowd saying in a loud voice: "There is no power save in God."

When the crowd dispersed, except for a small number of boys, the carriage driver carried her suitcase and motioned for her to follow him. Before they went through the entrance of the building, which had been transformed into a garbage dump by the crowd, Lina heard one of the horses piss outside. A foul smell issued from the asphalt.

* * *

—Mama. Mama. Lina put her mouth against the closed door and knocked, while the carriage driver stood behind her twisting his moustache.

There was silence for a moment, then a faint ticking noise was heard. Lina realized someone was behind the wooden door, looking through the glass eye. When the door was finally opened a strong smell of soap came from the wet corridor floor. She heard women whispering in the living room. Fatima kissed her and quickly took the suitcase from the driver, closing the door in his face before he could speak.

Walking on tiptoe, Lina felt no happiness in being back home.

And when she stopped by the living room, no one looked at her. Her mother was sitting on the sofa, her head down. All around her strange women whispered incessantly. Aunt Samiya stood behind the thick curtains. She watched what was going on in the street, while Sister Bahiya pointed with trembling fingers to the neighbors who filled their balconies as if watching a thriller.

—The peasants, said a blond woman contemptuously.

—They broke the European toilet, said Aunt Samiya and turned half way.

—Of course, because they are used to pissing in the fields, laughed another woman with wrinkled skin.

The women's heads nodded in agreement, but Lina's mother remained like a silent statue, the black veil coming down on her shoulders. Lina hesitated. Should she run to her mother? Should she hug her and tell her she missed her so much? She stepped forward, wishing some one would look at her. The women's mouths opened and closed incessantly; their heads came close then parted.

—They broke the doors' handles.

—Because they lived in the desert.

—They drowned the kitchen with water.

—Because they thought it was a pond for cows.

—They'll spread lice in the building.

—And a stinking smell.

—The rats will run.

—On the stairs.

—The soldiers will cast amorous glances.

—At the neighbors.

—At the girls.

—And the boys.

—And who will pay the rent?

—The rent?

—The rent.

A noise came from outside. The women ran to the windows. Their shoes sank into the Persian carpet; their hands clasped on their bosoms; their curious faces pressed against the hanging

45

muslin curtains. Lina stepped forward and gazed at her mother imploringly. Suddenly, the women shouted together: "The Captain. The Captain." Burying her trembling body in her mother's lap, Lina felt as if the soldiers' machine guns had riddled her head with bullets.

* * *

Lina's brother sat on the sofa, smoking nervously. The night had already descended on the city. The neighbors were closing the shutters of their wooden windows. She heard the clacking of wooden clogs coming from the ceiling. Her sister Bahiya was moving her eyes from corner to corner, but her eyes were fixed on the shaking chandelier. Rima was reclining on the other sofa reading a thick book. No one said a word. The old clock ticked slowly and the weary passers-by dragged their feet on the sidewalk. Fatima made coffee in the kitchen and hummed a melancholic peasant tune.

—They run with their clogs! Bahiya broke the silence, lifting one eyebrow drooping the other, and pointing to the ceiling.

—Barbarians, said her brother sharply.

—Did they have a chance to learn better? asked Rima mockingly, without raising her eyes from her book.

— And who asked your opinion? Her brother flipped the ash from his cigarette. He was shaking angrily.

Lina wished she could bury herself in a small room without doors or windows. How much these endless discussions tired her. Her family's evenings were all alike. They started with a fight, and they ended with a fight. She didn't understand what was said, but she knew that her sister Rima liked the peasants and defended them, and that her brother despised them without an apparent reason. Bahiya, on the other hand, sided with Khalid because he was a man, and because she believed sincerely that men understood the world, and that their ability to distinguish between good and evil could not be compared with the ability of women. From the corner of her eye, Lina watched her sister Rima's face. She didn't know whether she should love the peasants too. She remembered the neighbor's bosom dangling out of the window, her voice yelling, ordering the tall soldier to hurry up. No. She didn't like her. The woman was vulgar. Lina bit her lips and took the history book which was lying on her lap.

—Why don't you sit behind the desk? asked Bahiya scoldingly.

—Here?

—No. In your room. Don't you have a history test?

Lina nodded, then said:

—I am afraid.

—Afraid? asked her brother, putting his evening newspaper aside.

—Can I study here? she asked. Tears filled her eyes. She saw her brother put his forefinger on his lips, telling Bahiya to be silent.

—O.K. he said, taking a cup of coffee offered by the servant.

Lina put the history book on the desk in the corner of the room, lit the lamp, then sat on the chair. She had to review the reign of the Abbasids in Baghdad, especially at the time of Harun Al-Rashid and his son Al-Ma'mun. She remembered that her teacher insisted on the importance of the literary and scientific renaissance during the eighth and ninth centuries in the Islamic Empire. But when she flipped the pages of the book she couldn't concentrate on a single point. Her brother was sipping coffee loudly, while her sister Bahiya was repeating as she mended some stockings: "Do you hear the sound of water? Drip. . . Drip. . . Drip. . ."

Rima raised her head, stared at the ceiling, then went back to read as if the world around her was non-existent. No. She won't pay attention to them either, Lina thought. She remembered the history teacher. Cold sweat began to trickle down her forehead.

"History and myth are mixed together in telling the story of the golden age of Baghdad during the reign of Harun Al-Rashid. The city rose from nothing to a center of science and arts with no peer, not even Constantinople, the capital of the Byzantines." She read with a soft voice. The words became blurred in her eyes. The city

47

of Baghdad came to her like a veiled bride on the back of a caravan.

What will the teacher ask in the exam? The foreign policy of Harun Al-Rashid? She reflected for a while, then she thought of the relationship between Al-Rashid and Charlemagne and saw the Franks swarming the Arab court, then returning to Europe taking back with them hundreds of gifts like perfume, silk, and elephants. She remembered the delicate watch that Charlemagne and his companions thought was the witches' work. No. Perhaps, the teacher will quiz them about Al-Rashid's internal policy, his crushing of his rivals' rebellions, his support for science and the arts. Her weary eyes glanced at a short title: "The Baramkid's Massacre." Sadness overwhelmed her as she began to read about Al-Rashid's killing of his minister Ja'far.

—Didn't Ja'far Al-Barmaki invite physicians and scientists to Baghdad? She remembered asking her teacher one day.

—Yes.

—Didn't he build cities?

—Yes.

—Didn't he build factories?

—Yes.

—In short, didn't he make Baghdad the cradle of civilization?

—Yes. Yes.

—Then why did Al-Rashid kill him? Why did he attack the Barmaki's palace and the palaces of his relatives? Why did he confiscate his fortune?

She remembered her classmates thrusting their heads curiously; their eyes fixed on the history teacher's red face.

—Ja'far became very strong. Indeed, his authority surpassed that of Al-Rashid himself. Perhaps, this was the reason why the Caliph had killed him. The teacher was then silent for a while. But the students' eyes remained fixed upon her as if not satisfied by her answer.

—Furthermore, Ja'far fell in love with Al-Rashid's sister, added the teacher hesitantly.

The whispers increased in the classroom, and the girls in the

48

back seats laughed. The teacher banged on the desk angrily, and after she licked her dry lips she said:

—Well. The Abbasa had a child secretly.

The laughter resumed. .

—Al-Abbasa? Who is she?

—Al-Rashid's sister.

—Oh.

—I didn't understand what she said.

The teacher changed her posture. Her eyes were glowing in a strange way, Lina thought.

—This is what the historians assure us.

No. She wasn't going to review anything. She hadn't forgotten one single event. Not the dates, not the causes or the effects. As she closed her book, the massacre of the Baramkid glowed in her mind. She saw the common people loot their homes and throw their furniture from the windows and the roofs. And when she looked down at the flowing Tigris, she saw mutilated bodies floating on the face of the river; their eyes gouged out.

Lina felt Rima's hand on her shoulder. Raising her head, she saw her sister's face full of vigor.

—Are you still studying history? Rima leafed through the book with an air of mockery.

How much she wanted to cling to her sister's dress. She wished to know everything, to understand everything. But her sister was far away from her, always busy with her own thoughts.

—The sultans, eh? Their internal and external policies? said Rima flipping with her forefinger the pages of the book.

—Nothing about those who built the empire? she murmured as if she wasn't expecting an answer.

—You mean the Baramkid? asked Lina.

—The Baramkid? said her sister. They were loaded with gold.

Lina was dumbfounded. It hurt her that her sister didn't like the Baramkid.

—But Al-Rashid killed them one by one, confiscated their wealth. Is this justice? asked Lina passionately.

—Justice? What do you understand of justice?

Lina drooped her head and wished her sister would explain to her the meaning of justice. She always mocked her and considered her a young girl.

—History repeats itself, said her brother, squashing the evening paper, and throwing it on the sofa.

—Yes. Plunder is plunder since time immemorial, commented her sister Bahiya as she put the thread, needles, and scissors in the metal biscuit box which she had been using for some time for her sewing things.

Rima threw the history book on the desk, disgusted. She said:

—What do you know about Al-Rashid's baker? His cook? His guard? The builder of his house? The soldier who was killed for his sake?

—Ha! Why do you want her to know? said her brother defiantly.

But Rima ignored him. She shook Lina's shoulders and said:

—Al-Rashid and the Baramkid did not build the empire, but the simple and common people, those faces whom you do not recognize in history books.

She felt her sister was begging for her support. There seemed to be a struggle which appeared or disappeared between the adults in order to attract her to their camp and to buy her soul at any cost.

—We won't let you ruin Lina, her brother said and stood up.

Without saying a word Rima left the room.

—No. We won't let you do that, repeated her sister Bahiya like a parrot.

At that moment a strong knock was heard at the hall-door.

* * *

Saber stood in the hallway like a statue. He had his military uniform on. His face was full of anger. Lina saw her brother stare at him blankly.

—The captain sent me here, he said, and put his hand on the pistol which was dangling from his back pocket.

Her brother shook his head without smiling or frowning. Bahiya pushed her gently, thrusting her head carefully through the half opened door of the living room.

—Repair the door handles
—The water pipes
—The bathroom toilet
—Paint the walls
—The kitchen cupboards
—The window cracks.

The soldier said all this in one breath. Lina saw his chest go up and down. When he went to the door he turned slowly and said:

—My master wants you to know that he will pay the rent whenever he likes, and in the manner he likes.

He slammed the door. Lina saw her brother freeze in his spot, his face flinch. From the hallway came the voice of Bahiya sobbing. As Lina dragged her feet to the bathroom to brush her teeth, she saw Rima putting Nivea cream on her face and heard her humming a broken tune. How much she wished to know what her sister was thinking of at that moment. When she raised her head and stared at Rima's face again, it seemed to her that the sky was raining faces smeared with a sticky white substance.

* * *

II

ADOLESCENCE

As Lina walked alongside her mother one sunny day, bending her back a little, trying bashfully to hide her breasts which had become rounder during the last two years, she felt that every man who passed by was taking off her clothes with his sharp eyes. She remembered a night when she stood behind the slightly open door of the kitchen. Aunt Samiya was busy making coffee, and the light of the lamp was reflected on her white braid. She heard her say in a low voice:

—When did she have her period?

—Last week, laughed her mother as she was drying the Chinese plate next to the stove.

Aunt Samiya turned her head slowly, then said after a while:

—Be careful now. She is a woman.

Then, she heard them fall into laughter. When Lina withdrew quietly to her dark room, the light of the fire was quivering on the wall, and from the next rooms came the voices of her sisters loud one time, low another. Then the music became loud and blended with the tapping of the dancers' heels.

As she walked next to her mother, a vague feeling of fear grew in her and the strangeness of life suggested itself to her in the rumbling carts, the neighing of the horses, the rush of the porters' feet on the sidewalks, reawakened in her the unrest which had sent her to the window at sunset. Though she passed an array of shops adorned with the feast's candy dolls and moons made of colorful papers and she saw the children with their bright clothes pushing one another in front of the peanut merchant, thrusting their arms in the air, waving their heads right and left, her bitterness did not leave her for a second. Amid this bustling she fancied herself on the deck of a mythical ship, sailing to undiscovered harbors. But as she looked again at the stocked merchandise thrown in front of the old shops, she saw the porters with their torn shoes and baggy pants and her feeling of fear came back to her. Through the cigarette butts floating on the sewage, the whole world seemed to her like a rotten swamp.

—Hello. Hello, said Aunt Shamsa to her mother as she opened the door and motioned for them to enter. But when she noticed Lina, she rushed towards her with her hunched back and heavy steps and, standing on tiptoe, hugged her feebly to her bosom.

—Well. She has grown up, she said, putting her moist lips on Lina's cheeks.

—Our children are taller than we are, commented her mother laughing.

—Ah, the woman sighed as if she didn't hear what had been said to her, then she hurried in front of them, her head buried between her shoulders and a bunch of keys rattling in the pocket of her striped apron. As she crossed the interior yard, she stopped a second, put her right hand on her hip, then raised her head slowly to the upper floor and shouted in a thin voice: "Fattoum, Fattoum." From behind the espalier on which grapevines were trained and covering the balcony rail, the wrinkled face of her sister appeared. Lina heard her say in a nasal tone, "Yes, my dear." Then the fountain water drowned the funny voice.

Aunt Shamsa ascended the three stairs leading to the hall, bending her back, putting her hands on her knees, then she stood a little as if she wanted to catch her breath. She took out a big key and turned it in the lock three times, and when the door opened and the two women entered the room, a strong mouldy smell came to Lina's nose. She wished in her heart to sit in the garden, but as she noticed her mother beckon to her repeatedly with her hand to follow her, she stopped breathing and entered the hall whose ceiling was high and whose curtains were heavy velvet. Seconds passed and Fattoum came carrying a tray of coffee. She set it on the table, and while she was looking for the chocolate box in the cupboard in the middle of the room, Aunt Shamsa poured for them bitter Arabic coffee, and insisted with a weak voice that Lina try it without sugar, claiming that her sister's coffee was better than the bedouins' in the desert. But she stopped when she saw Lina's face shrinking after one sip. Fattoum then offered them chocolate and put scores of pieces in Lina's pocket in spite of the protest of Lina's mother that candy harms children's teeth. Between the clinking of coffee cups and the exchange of traditional greetings, Aunt Shamsa sighed and said:

—One feast comes, one feasts goes, and we grow old.

Lina saw her take her long rosary from the pocket of her apron and bow her head in assent. Then she heard her mother say:

—Ah. That's life.

—Of course, said Fattoum, pouring more coffee in Lina's mother's cup.

—You are a widow, and you know. Aunt Shamsa raised her head from between her shoulders, directing her speech to Lina's mother. Fattoum was in the graveyard today. She wiped the grave of her late husband. Left on it a branch of myrtle. Ah, one can't do anything.

Fattoum smoothed her grey dress over her knees and sighed:

—God preserve Sa'id for us. We don't want anything else.

Her mother brought her head closer to the woman with the pointed chin and the long nose and said with concern:

—When will we see Sa'id married?

Fattoum put the cup of coffee on the table, crossed her hands, then leaned her head against the velvet pillow and stared at the only sun ray coming through the heavy curtains, then she said in a low voice:

—God bless Sa'id. He is difficult. He washes and prays ten times a day.

—Na. . . Na. Aunt Shamsa interrupted in protest. But Fattoum didn't notice her; on the contrary she beckoned her to be silent and continued saying half jokingly,

—He takes the prayer rug with him to the office. And when I ask him 'Isn't there a nice girl who works with you?' he knits his eyebrows and says 'God save me from the cursed Satan.'

—People are different, said her mother, hiding her laughter.

—It is very true, my daughter. Aunt Shamsa took out her handkerchief and wiped her eyes, then began to praise God by flipping her rosary beads. Her head leaned lazily against the pillow.

There was silence. Lina got up and threw the chocolate papers into the ashtray on the table, then she came back quietly. She saw Fattoum look her in the eyes and heard her say after a long pause, directing the question to the mother:

—And your girls? Anything new?

Her mother shook her head no, then she laid her forefinger against her nose, frowned a little bit, bent her trunk forward, and said in a low voice:

—Last week while I was having a siesta in the living room, there was a light knock at the door. I said to myself, annoyed, 'Now who could come at this hour?' Then I heard the servant open the door and say cautiously: 'The lady is asleep.' 'Sorry,' said a voice which I couldn't discern. I got up in a hurry, smoothing my hair, and called upon the servant with a loud voice 'Who is there?' And before she could answer me, two strange ladies entered the visitors' room. I sort of guessed they were coming to see one of my daughters.

Fattoum laughed in a loud voice, while Aunt Shamsa let the beads fall from between her fingers and sat straight.

—I noticed something strange about the two ladies, said her mother, stressing some letters. They didn't introduce themselves to me. 'We don't like to lie,' said the fat lady folding her handkerchief cautiously and smiling wickedly. When things turn all right, then we could get to know each other. 'Isn't that right?' she asked the other woman whose legs were very thin. Then I heard them laugh, a short but clinking laughter. 'And what can I do for you?' I asked grinding my teeth. 'Well, we came to see Lina,' they said in one voice. Then I saw the fat woman nudge the other with her elbow, beckoning her to be silent, and I heard her say: 'My son is coming from Paris. Has a doctorate in law.' I stifled my laughter, knit my eyebrows in order to make the woman feel I was interested in what she was saying.' 'But Lina is young,' I said protesting. 'And who would find a husband after twenty?' said the woman with the thin legs. 'And a son returning from Paris with a prominent position and a great wealth?' she added, then she started to cough as if she choked. 'Of course, all these things are rare.' I told her, trying to hide my laughter. 'But Lina is young, plus she wants to finish her education.' 'Education?' The fat lady approached me shivering out of anger. 'And why should the girl have an education? Doesn't she know how to read and write? This is enough. Then if everything turns all right between us, your daughter does not have to work anyway. My son is rich and only the poor girls work.' 'You are right,' I told her. 'But the times have changed.' ' How did they change?' The other woman interrupted me 'if you don't marry your daughter before she is twenty, she'll become an old maid.' Then she put her light coat on her arm and left the room followed by the fat woman. And when I hurried to open the hall-door for them I felt that the man's mother was examining me with her small beady eyes and she was humming under her breath: 'Doctorate in Law. Doctorate in Law.'

—God forgive you, said Aunt Shamsa, scoldingly waving her forefinger in the air.

—Well, Lina is grown up. Didn't she have her. . . ? asked Fattoum as she rolled her cigarette cautiously.

—Of course, said her mother softly, but I swore not to choose a husband for anyone.

Lina bowed her head shyly, letting a remnant of the chocolate fall on her lap. Under the thin ray of the sun, she saw her mother's knees shine like pearls. When Fattoum got up and opened the window to get rid of the smoke in the room, Lina came close to her mother, leaned her ringleted head against her mother's shoulder and gazed at the light enchanted.

* * *

She couldn't sleep that night. Her mother's words were ringing incessantly in her ears. She found herself standing in front of the window, watching the evening invade the city: her head was leaning against the heavy curtains and in her nostrils was the odor of dusty velvet. She saw the idiot walk with difficulty towards the ruins, and she heard his footsteps clacking on the pavement. There was a garden one time. She used to watch every evening the neighbors' children play around the bitter orange trees. But one merchant from the city bought the garden and cut the trees, because he wanted to build modern offices to rent for high prices. Then, it was reported that he went bankrupt, or that the city council imposed high taxes upon him, and the garden fell to ruins, where stray dogs took refuge, or the idiot slept, or men urinated, or where the neighbors dumped their garbage. She recalled an evening when she stole away to the garden without telling her mother and stood behind the blossoming bitter orange tree, watching the children play with fire-crackers and throwing their cowboy hats in the air. The eyes of the pale boy traveled to her corner through the circling of the players that were exciting her heart and senses. In the garden the children who had stayed latest were gathering their spoils: crackers, leather pistol holsters, handfuls of bullets which had not been shot. The feast was over. She saw him coming towards her and in his hand was a small flute. And when he stopped close to her, her nostrils were filled with the odor of his clean shirt mixed with the fragrance of the blossoms of bitter oranges. The noise had already subsided, and only a few boys remained talking on the pavement.

He took her hand, then he let it drop. He came close to her, then he left her. She read in his grey eyes the tales of childhood. When she began to run on the lawn, lifting her long skirt a little, listening to the sound of frogs, she heard him laughing and knew he was following. Why didn't she let him kiss her? she asked herself bewildered. They were alone in the garden and the bitter oranges cast their dark shadow on the empty benches.

When she stood among the crowd in the well lighted square to buy ice-cream, he held her hand with his shaking hands. She knew that he was speaking to her, saying something, but she couldn't hear. She was looking for another face in the dark corridors of her mind, for an image which came to her by night through poems she read in her dreams, or the poems she read when she was awake. And without looking in his eyes, without saying a word, she took her hand away from his hands and ran away under the wing of the night.

How often she thought while she was standing behind her window watching the darkness invade the city that his face would come to her, not through the cover of an old book or a tune of a soft poem, but in the noisy world, on the sidewalk, in the cafe, in the garden, exactly as her soul saw him without shadows. She thought their meeting would take place at night, perhaps in one of the old lanes of Jerusalem and that he would take her hand silently. And she thought her shyness would melt away, and her masks would fall, and he would lead her half asleep to the foot of a steep mountain. And she thought she would hesitate to climb and he would pull her by the hand while the wind would be blowing her weak body. How far the white castle would appear on the summit then.

* * *

She always waited anxiously for the coming of summer. Although her mother very seldom allowed her to visit her peers, loneliness did not find its way to her heart in a society whose members were all adults. During the early hours of the morning, she used to accompany the maid Fatima to the nearby shops, helping her carry the hot bread, or checking on their account with the butcher, who was known in the neighborhood for cheating, or choosing the ripe peaches from the open boxes at the grocer. She often wondered why the grocer did not pay attention to her when she returned a rotten peach back to the box, but he would smile uneasily even before his other customers stretched their hands to touch the fruits and he would murmur:

—Everything is ripe. Everything is a bliss from God.

She noticed that most of the buyers would fill their baskets, then say to the strongly built grocer in low voices:

—On credit.

Sometimes, the grocer whose skin was well-tanned would protest and say:

—This is the last time.

Then Lina would see him running to his old office, putting his white glasses on his nose, leafing through a big book smeared with spots of oil. And when someone would call him: "How much is a kilo of sugar?" the grocer would raise his wrinkled face, answer slowly, then scribble something in his notebook as he murmured unintelligible words to himself.

As soon as Lina had crossed out bread, meat, vegetables, and fruits from her mother's long list, she would return home with Fatima through a narrow lane, passing by a number of peasants who put their cheese and cream pots on the sidewalks and tied their donkeys to the trees which lined the street. Fatima would hurry to escape the stinking smell of the fodder and Lina would follow obediently, though she did not share the servant's disgust.

Sometimes in the afternoon, when Fatima had finished washing the dishes and cleaning the kitchen, she and Lina would go to one of the public gardens. At other times, they would head to the mountain and walk for hours under the shadow of the trees to avoid the blazing sun, or they would choose the narrow lanes leading to the river in search of a cool breeze. They would hardly speak to one another. Fatima would always trudge, putting her left hand over her hip in a silent complaint about her rheumatism. They would often stop by the soft ice-cream parlour and watch the man put the cones under his electric machine, letting the vanilla cream fall generously like the braids of a child. Once Lina dared to offer to teach Fatima how to read and write, but the servant laughed loudly and said:

—What? At my age?

Lina didn't insist after that. It seemed as if Fatima were content with her life.

Lina and her family used to spend weekends at a summer resort. Abu Muhammad would come to the door at an early hour and speak with the servant while helping her carry the meat and fruits basket to the carriage. The brown horses would shake their bells merrily, rub their noses under the light of the green lamp. Bahiya often brought with her the table cloth which she had begun embroidering more than a year ago. She would sit in the middle of the carriage, stretching the linen cloth around her, leaving only a narrow place for her mother. On the small opposite seat, Lina and the servant would cram themselves, their heads almost touching the driver's back. As the carriage would start moving, Bahiya would try to pass the thread through the needle's eye and murmur: "Of course, Rima wouldn't like to come with us," then she would lick the end of the thread, bringing it closer to the needle's eye, narrowing her own small eyes. When no one would answer her and she would see that her mother was looking through the open window, while the servant was putting her hand over her mouth to hide the black hair which was growing over her lips and on her chin, bending her head and absorbed in deep thoughts, Bahiya would throw the table cloth on the leather seat in a dramatic way and would say to the two women in disgust: "Why didn't I stay at home?" Lina would hide her smile in one of the illustrated magazines which she used to carry with her on Fridays. Silence would prevail. When the carriage would cross the hanging cafes over the river and the noise of the city would die out, the driver would start singing.

In the garden of Aunt Samiya in the Zabadani valley, the family would spend most of the day. Lina used to love to collect sticks from the neighboring fields and help the servant start the fire, and then grill the skewers of meat. Her married sisters would drop in suddenly, accompanied by their husbands or cousin 'Aisha with her children. Then the garden would become full of noise: Bahiya preparing the table under the apple tree, her mother putting the meat, the tomato, and the onion in the skewer, the servant blowing the fire with a piece of cardboard and the smoke blinding her eyes, Su'ad mixing the tabboula salad and Aunt Samiya putting the onion skin, the parsley sticks and the lemon peels in the garbage bag. Near the hawthorn fence and far from the smoke, her sister 'Afaf would stand in her pink silk dress, a great necklace of pearls adorning her neck, and speak with the warden of the opposite house.

In the evening, Lina would withdraw to her father's library while the rest of the family sat on the balcony in search of a cool breeze in the midst of the hot July. When she had discovered the library for the first time, the face of Ali Baba entering naively the cave of the seventy thieves had come back to her in the darkness and suddenly, lo and behold, there were Persian carpets, Indian silk, and bags of gold and silver.

At first she had pored over the travel books. She saw herself move with Ibn Jubair at the end of the 12th century from Granada to Alexandria, from Al-Madina to Baghdad, and she heard the noise of the merchants, crusaders, and Moslems in the crowded markets of 'Akka and she walked in cities ruined by conquerors and she tarried at the gates of marbled floor bathrooms. But the image of the pious traveler standing one sunny day in the harbor of Tyre, watching a crusader's wedding with amazement, stuck in her mind and haunted her even in her sleep. Through the rustle of the golden silk and the footsteps of the bridesmaids on the wharf, the sound of wind pipes mixed with the cries of seagulls and the laughter of men rang in her ears.

The hot summer wind often awoke her while she was thinking that she was asleep in the yard of a mosque, or being on the board of a ship, or kneeling in front of the king of Sicily. How much she cried in her dream while walking in the gardens of Messina's palaces, waving to the anchored boats in the marina, gazing at the burning volcanos of the island.

In her mind her figure would rise like a thin, white-templed pirate standing on a deserted wharf, and in a proud gesture she would hunt the mythical bird *al-Rukh*, indifferent to the curse that would befall her.

* * *

The snow was falling slowly on the roofs of the houses one cold day of January. When the school gates were flung open in the Salihiya district about 12 noon, the deserted streets drowned in the children's noise. Steps hurried to the chestnut vendors who stood under tattered cloths, shivering while they grilled the brown nuts in primitive stoves, and sold them to the flowing students.

Lina carried her heavy bag and walked quickly home. She was hungry. The sight of the boys running towards the apple vendor, whose fruits were coated with sugar, whetted her appetite. From the corner of her eyes, she could see them snatching the sticky sticks and sucking the red dye, giggling.

The girls in the upper classes passed by her, swinging their hips right and left, and in their hands there were colorful umbrellas. She recognized Nihad with her short black hair and nicely shaped legs. Lina did not rub her eyes this time for she got used to seeing the girls without their school uniforms, and even without their winter jackets. As soon as the school gate would open, Nihad and her peers would run out, and a couple of feet from the school, they would pull off the uniform which hid their swelling breasts, folding them cautiously and putting them in a bag each one of them would carry in turn. Nihad would take out the mirror and the comb. All the girls' faces would come closer. All kinds of make-up hidden in pockets would appear. The eyes would be enlarged; the cheeks and lips would be reddened quickly, perfume would be patted behind the ears and on the wrists. All that used to take only minutes, as if these teenagers had worked as actresses in one of the city's theaters. The younger girls would watch this play with curiosity. But after some weeks, and when the burden of studies increased, the scene of the older girls became ordinary. Even Samira, who was known for her mischievous acts, stopped following them and mocking them.

Lina heard the short heels tapping on the sidewalk and saw the boys line in the corners of the streets, smoking and repeating once in a while words they had learned by heart from cheap love books. As she passed by the bookstore of the neighborhood, she saw through the storefront the bald owner standing the same way as ever behind a glass box and, around him, scores of children snatching colorful books and drawing supplies.

When she started crossing the street to her home, her yellow raincoat was drenched with water, her right shoulder reaching almost to her waist from the heavy bag. She wished that Fatima had prepared a glass of ice mixed with orange juice and sugar for her.

She remembered how the children of the neighborhood used to get up early when it snowed and run to the roofs, carrying with them pots and spoons. They would start working cautiously.

—Don't take snow from the bottom. It is dirty there.

—I know that.

—Take the cream on the top only.

—Cream? Is this milk?

—I love snow with lemon.

—With orange better.

—With *Ajaljiq* syrup.

—What?

—Don't you know the red fruit of the *Ajaljiq*? It looks like an olive.

—She speaks Turkish.

The footsteps would hurry on the stairs, the breathing would grow stronger, doors would fling open, mothers would run while taking the pots amidst the cries of children:

—Ice. Ice.

*   *   *

The smell of grilled liver was coming out of the kitchen when Fatima opened the door for her and helped her take off the wet raincoat. From the living room came familiar voices. She recognized some of them. But she was surprised that someone would visit them at this time, especially during the working hours.

—Your brother will leave us this afternoon, Fatima told her, pointing to his leather suitcase in the corner of the hallway.

—Will he? asked Lina surprised.

—Yes. To the front line, whispered Fatima and smoothed her white embroidered kerchief in front of the mirror of the antique *jardiniere*.

—Is it the military service? asked Lina putting her boots on a plastic sheet.

Fatima nodded, then hurried to the kitchen.

The wood was crackling in the stove when Lina thrust her head inside the door of the living room. Everyone turned at once towards her, then back to their original positions, except for her mother, who pointed to her to come in. On her tiptoe she entered, as if afraid of interrupting the party. She nodded, greeting the visitors. Her married sisters smiled, but her in-laws were busy talking.

—How was school today? asked her mother in a low voice, patting her on the shoulder.

—Like usual, said Lina without enthusiasm.

—Are you hungry?

Lina closed her eyes and hid her head in the folds of her mother's black dress. She was cold. She thought of a grey goat playing under the udder of its mother in the wheat field and, as she raised her head, she saw Bahiya busy weaving a woolen sweater while her fur slippers glowed in the firelight.

—Perhaps we will never witness the democratic life, said her brother rubbing his hands nervously.

—Don't you think it is better to remain under the authority of the military? asked her brother-in-law Hisham coldly.

—Are you joking? said her brother, and she saw fear in his eyes.

—No, said Hisham and moved in his rocking chair, stretching his legs on the Persian carpet.

—If we had elections in Syria today no one would win except the Communists and the socialists. Is that what you want?.

—Of course not. Khalid doesn't mean that. . . , interfered her in-law Ahmad. Lina saw his brown eyes glow. But his wife Su'ad thrust her head and said:

—We will prevent the Communists from participating in the elections.

The men did not pay attention to her.

—Who is responsible for our deteriorating condition? asked her sister 'Afaf, as if she were a leader addressing his defeated army. THE CIVILIANS. She stressed her last words.

Lina saw her brother-in-law Hisham raise his hand lazily, then let it fall down, as if ordering the woman to be silent.

—Why do we cause ourselves a headache, talking about nonsense? Hisham opened the upper button of his shirt and loosened his colorful tie. The political parties are banned. Elections are banned, and being next to the fire is better than in the frying pan. We have to exploit the situation to our own advantages.

—How can we do that when the army invades our houses? asked Lina's brother.

—You are right, said Ahmad.

—Wait a minute, said Hisham, almost whispering. He brought his head close to the two men. There is one party, the army's party. What did they call it? Then he scratched his cheek as if trying to remember.

—The Arab Liberation Movement, said Ahmad.

—Ah, of course, the liberation movement. My partner became a member today. He just applied. They smiled at him; he smiled at them and so we can hopefully solve all the problems of the company.

Lina saw Hisham sit like a cock. He was satisfied with himself.

—The imposter, said her brother in contempt.

—Imposter, or not, smiled Hisham cunningly.

No one said a word. Lina saw her sister Bahiya put her knitting-needle on the sofa, get up slowly, then stuff a big piece of wood into the stove.

* * *

The winter months passed slowly and gloomily. The family talked about nothing but the new arrests and the wide purge campaign in the country. Aunt Samiya used to come every Tuesday with a lot of news, sit down cross-legged on the sofa close to the stove, cover her legs with her wide dress, then put several pillows behind her back. As soon as Fatima would bring the coffee Aunt Samiya would take the tobacco box out of her pocket and start rolling the cigarettes, long and thin, then she would smoke one after the other till the air in the room became quite stifling. Lina often saw her mother open the window for a few minutes, then shut it, fearing that she might offend the old woman.

During these routine visits, her brother's letters were read several times. "The weather is rainy." "In the evening we play cards and smoke." "Perhaps I will come in for a short visit." The letter said nothing important. Yet her mother would put her glasses on her nose once in a while and repeat her brother's similar sentences as if she were a pupil in the second grade, trying to memorize verses from the Quran.

She imagined her brother waking up at five o'clock in the morning, putting on his military uniform quickly, having his breakfast with other reserve officers, then hurrying to the practice fields while the wind blew in his face. She was disappointed because he never wrote in detail about his daily life. She wished to know something about his training, his friends, the fields that stretched close to his camp. "The weather is rainy," her mother would repeat in a loud voice. "Rainy," Aunt Samiya would sigh and blow smoke in Lina's face while the gutters under the roof would moan.

When there was a knock at the door, Bahiya would jump from behind the sewing machine, putting her forefinger on her mouth and give warning:

—Change the topic. Then she would run to the hallway.

The fear of something unknown overwhelmed Lina. How much she felt that Aunt Samiya sincerely believed that the walls had ears. She noticed that the members of her family whispered and never talked in natural voices. Fear accompanied her wherever she went. How many times she would convince Fatima to tell her a trivial story on the edge of her bed. She was afraid to be alone in the dark. How often she woke up in the middle of the night hearing distant cries and remained frozen in her place till she heard the muezzin call for morning prayers, then the sweat would trickle down her ankles. She would repeat like a lost shell on the beach: "Oh God, oh God." As soon as she heard the footsteps of men going to the mosque, her heart would calm down, and she would relax, and then sleep would hover again around her tired eyes.

* * *

—Take Lina with you. It is late, said her mother to Rima one rainy evening.

—But she will be bored, said her sister, annoyed, getting ready to leave.

Her mother frowned, turned her back, then left the room. Rima tarried a bit, then looked in Lina's eyes, examining them. The rain was beating the wooden shutters and the fast cars were splashing water on the sidewalks. Lina heard her sister crackle her fingers, then say while looking out of the window:

—Put on your boots and coat. Come quickly.

She knew her sister didn't want her to come along. She thought there was some secret in the matter, but did not say a thing. She felt so badly that she wanted to gain Rima's confidence. When she ran to the hallway and put on her boots quickly, she heard her mother say:

—Well. Don't stay long in Asma's house.

—No, said Rima. We have to solve some mathematical problems.

—Will Asma be alone? asked her mother, as if she were doubting every word uttered by Rima.

—Probably, answered her sister indifferently.

As they descended the stairs, her mother thrust her face through the door. Lina heard her say:

—Rima.

Her sister looked up and said:

—What do you want now?

Her mother's eyes glowed. She looked afraid.

—You know what I want. Don't speak politics.

Her mother's voice came in a quivering whisper.

There was no one on the stairs, but Lina saw her mother hurry and close the door behind her swiftly.

Lina had not gone with her sister to any place before. The eight years separating them were like a barrier, difficult to destroy. She tried hard to be close to her sister. She offered to do all sorts of things for her, like buying a magazine, or taking her shoes for repair, or bringing a message to a friend who lives near by. But Rima used to force herself to laugh shortly, indicating that the courtesy between the two was over, at least for that particular day. When

Lina would open her mouth to protest, she would find the door closed in her face. She would stand there for a while, as if the whole world had stopped.

*   *   *

It was raining when Lina took the bus with her sister towards Qasyun mountain. People's faces looked gloomy as they looked out of windows blurred with vapor. Some men stood at the end of the bus carrying baskets full of fruits and vegetables. Lina's eyes were fixed on a sign hung over the driver's head: "Smoking is forbidden." But as she turned around, she saw cigarette smoke coming from every corner. Some women wrapped in black coughed under their thick veils.

The conductor passed by them. Her sister's hand stretched quickly.

—Two students please, said Rima putting two franks in the hand of the tall man.

Lina tried in vain to attract the attention of her sister. She felt that Rima was uneasy about something and seemed to be immersed in deep thought: her eyes fixed on the rain washing down the bus window. Lina regretted having accompanied her sister. Then she began to watch the passengers rush either forward or backward whenever the bus came to a stop. The conductor's voice roared once in a while, reminding people to keep order. She suppressed her smile when she saw the crammed bodies change their postures, rush backward to let new passengers in. Whenever the door opened or closed, a cold wind blew from outside, and the water dripping from closed umbrellas created a small stream in the bus.

When they reached the last stop, her sister nudged her. Lina smoothed the collar of her coat, put her wet hat on again, then got up. As soon as the wind blew against her face, she bent towards her sister and said almost emphatically:

—Trust me. I won't say anything.

She heard the clacking of her sister's heels on the sidewalk and felt her cold hand squeeze her fingers.

—O.K., said Rima after a pause.

Lina's ears stretched under the woolen hat. She thought her sister might be meeting a mysterious man. The image of the girls from the upper classes in her school shaking their hips in the street and the boys whistling came back to her.

—We will be going to Asma's apartment.

Her sister's words fell upon her like a lightning. She was disappointed when Rima's image and the other girls didn't coincide in her mind anymore.

—To solve mathematical problems? asked Lina naively.

—No. She heard her sister laugh loudly. There will be others.

—Others?

—From the university and perhaps from some high-schools.

Steps were heard on the sidewalk. Rima was silent. She squeezed her little sister's hand warningly.

At the bottom of the hill Rima looked right and left. The pale lamps of the street were shaking violently.

—You won't say a word, will you? Rima's voice came to her whispering, quivering.

—No. I won't say a word.

They began ascending the hill quickly, then they entered a dark building. When Rima was sure that no one was around, she knocked at the door of the first floor with the tips of her fingers. Lina's heart was pounding strongly. She was afraid, but happy. For the first time in her life, she felt she was not a child anymore.

* * *

Under the candles' light and in a room with drawn curtains, more than twenty men and women in their twenties were sitting around an old table on which leaflets printed in blue ink were scattered. Asma shook Lina's hand and asked Rima in the dialect of the coastal people:

—Your young sister?

Rima nodded her head.

—Why didn't we see her before? Hey? She patted Lina's shoul-

69

der kindly. Trust the young more than the grown up, she said, then threw their coats on the bed in the opposite room.

The people who gathered there were whispering about the leaflet when Asma introduced them with a friendly voice:

—My colleague Rima in the faculty of science and her little sister.

Heads nodded greeting them; chairs were brought closer to each other. No one seemed surprised by Lina's presence.

—Ok. Let us start the meeting, said Asma in a low voice. She knocked at the table with her fingers.

All heads turned towards a thin woman with big brown eyes and short curly hair. Lina saw her take a paper out of her small bag, unfold it carefully, then lick her dry lips.

—Yesterday, the secret police invaded the house of Professor Abd Al-Karim Al-Saleh at about 5 o'clock in the morning and led him to an unknown place after they threatened to torture his wife and children if they made any contact with the leftist groups in the country. They looked into his papers and books, and they gathered a great number of political leaflets which were against the present regime.

There was silence for a while. Lina felt her feet freezing.

—Did they find our names in the files of Dr. Saleh? asked one blond man wearing white glasses.

—I don't know exactly.

—But. . .the man interrupted. His hand was shaking.

—I believe the professor had destroyed the file last week when the raiding campaigns in the city were stepped up.

The man was obviously disturbed. Lina heard his cane chair squeaking under him endlessly.

—We won't meet again until we find out about the whole matter. But in the meantime, we will exchange letters and missions via persons who are not suspect and in the corridors of the university, said Asma, then pointed to the thin woman to finish what she had to say.

—The arrest of Dr. Saleh should not break us up. As long as we forget our political differences about socialism and the ways to implement it, and we form a leftist student front to stand in the face of military dictatorship and to stem the imperialistic rightist tide, our main duty remains to continue an endless struggle.

Lina saw the audience's faces glow again. No longer did she feel tired from the candles' lights which hurt her weary eyes. She was happy to learn new words. Leftist, rightist, imperialist, military dictatorship, socialism. She remembered how her sister Rima always mentioned the Soviet Union in her political arguments with the members of the family. She tried to remember the map. How ignorant she was. The gloom invaded her. No, she couldn't understand. The Tzars, the feudalists. She thought of Siberia. Who told her that the peasants and the workers were exiled to Siberia?

—What should we do in these circumstances? asked a man with a long neck, wearing a blue shirt.

All heads came close to Asma.

—What should we do? All asked in one breath.

—Our main task is to open the eyes of the people.

—But we are a minority, protested a fat girl with long black hair.

—The number doesn't matter, said Rima sharply.

—This is true, said Asma.

—How can we open the eyes of the people? asked another woman skeptically.

—By distributing leaflets and issuing secret newspapers, said the thin woman.

—You mean at the university? asked a man with a short moustache.

—In the high-schools as well, in the villages and the factories, said the thin woman.

Lina saw the fat girl look around, then heard her ask:

—Do we have members?

—No doubt, said Asma, then turned towards Lina calmly and asked:

—What is your name? What grade are you in?

Lina felt the blood flow in her cheeks. She saw all eyes fixed on her.

—My name is Lina, she said. I am in the ninth grade.

—Is your school secondary or high as well?

—Both.

—Great, said Asma.

—Wouldn't you like to work with us? We are against military dictatorship.

Lina bathed in sweat. No. She wouldn't miss a chance. She heard strange voices within her. Her brother too is against military dictatorship, but he despises Rima and her friends. Her brother-in-law Hisham, what did he say on that cold noon? She felt angry because the secret police were arresting people in their homes. She didn't know what to answer. She put her head down.

—We have educational meetings. Why don't you send Lina there? asked Asma, almost in a whisper.

—I'll try. You know the family, said her sister disturbed.

—Isn't it funny to open someone else's eyes and forget those who are close to us? commented the thin woman mockingly.

Lina felt insulted. Perhaps, the thin woman was right after all. Her sister always considered her a child.

—What is the name of her school? asked Asma.

—The First High-school for Girls, answered Rima.

—Great. Asma's face beamed. We have excellent members there. We will let one of them contact you soon. But be careful Lina, don't say anything to anyone, even your closest friend, warned Asma.

—I won't say anything. Lina put her head down, trying to get rid of her embarrassment.

Everybody laughed. The fat girl poured coffee in the cups. The leaflets were distributed, then disappeared into the pockets, or the briefcases or the books and the magazines. Suddenly footsteps were heard outside and the mewing of a cat behind a door. Asma blew the candles. The room became dark and everyone froze in his seats. Lina heard someone breathing. Seconds passed. The steps were distant now, but the cat was still mewing.

—Ok. Let us part, whispered Asma, and lit one candle. Two and two, and don't all of you wait for the bus at the same time.

Lina and her sister walked on tiptoe, and when they were putting on their coats, the thin woman whispered in Rima's ears:

—The instructions will reach you within the next week.

The rain had already stopped when they took the bus down to the city. The small houses which hung on the foot of the bald mountain appeared from a distance like pale stars. Lina felt her sister's hand press her fingers lovingly. When she looked in her eyes, she thought the wall of years separating them had fallen down forever.

In the corner of the street and next to their home, she saw the old Abu Amin cover his cart laden with oranges and mandarins with a grey plastic sheet full of holes, getting ready to sleep on the sidewalk.

*   *   *

When Lina left the bathroom and hurried to her bedroom to get ready to go to school one sunny day in March, she heard Fatima wash the floor of the living room balcony and saw her sister Bahiya open the windows of the house, then dust the pictures which were hung on the walls. Her mother called her:

—It is seven thirty. You will be late for school.

Lina hurried. The buttons of her uniform were still loose. Her belt was dragging on the floor. She sipped her coffee while standing.

—Won't you eat something?

—No. Perhaps during the break.

—O.K. I'll make you a cheese sandwich.

The smell of spring came from the wet street. Lina heard the vegetable vendors pull their carts on the asphalt and cry loudly:

—Ladies Fingers, O Green Okra.

—Your First Day, O Green Beans.

—Green Almonds. Soft Almonds.

When she carried her heavy school bag and ran down the stairs, the neighbor was bargaining with the tomato vendor from the hallway window while the housewives' heads were thrust out from the nearby apartments.

She passed by Abu Amin with the rosy complexion. His bed had already disappeared, and there was nothing but his carriage full of oranges and mandarins. He was busy sprinkling fruits with water so they remained fresh and shiny. His only son stood in front of another carriage squeezing red oranges for the passers-by.

As she crossed the crowded Salihiya street, the image of the man with the rosy complexion followed her. No one on the street knew whether Abu Amin's wife was alive or dead. She heard often the servants whisper about the relationships of the old man with veiled women who came to visit him at night on the sidewalk. Although some of the people in the neighborhood used to complain to the police and accused the man of drinking alcohol in public and having illegal relationships with both sexes, pissing and even shitting at the entrance of houses, Abu Amin remained forever on the sidewalk, summer and winter, day and night. The police could not find any decisive evidence to back up the accusations which the women of the neighborhood might have invented, and came to believe after a while. Thus, with the passing of time, the lies became facts. No one doubted them anymore.

Lina thought that Abu Amin became a basic thing in her life exactly like the rising of the sun, or the sunset. In fact, he reminded her of the changing of seasons. In the winter and beginning of spring he sold oranges and mandarins. Then the cart would be filled with almonds and green plums. When the summer came, heaps of apricots and peaches would pile up on a worn-out plastic sheet spread on the sidewalk, and Abu Amin would stand holding his scale, then he would put stones of different sizes in one scale and the fruits in another, and no one would argue with him about the weight. The passers-by always saw his son clean the sidewalk, or wash the carriage or shine some of the dirty pots. Often they would ask the old man: "Why doesn't Amin go to school? "The old man would laugh loudly, his blue eyes would glow, then he would say: "And who would buy him books? Selling is a trade, and the trade is better than reading books." The housewives used to whisper behind his back:

—What does he do with the piled pieces of gold under his pillow?

—Oh, from selling oranges? Honestly. Gold?

—From the balcony one night, I saw him counting the gold pieces.

The housewives would beat their bosoms and knit their eyebrows and sigh while carrying their baskets and standing in front of the gates of their homes.

Lina never really asked the old man about his favorite season, but she was dead sure that he would be counting the days and hours until the arrival of summer. His son Amin used to wash the sidewalk, then put the mattress down and cover it with a dirty colorful rug. When the darkness fell, he would light the lamp and prepare the tea, while his father lay in front of the piles of green watermelons, breathing with difficulty, and the sweat trickled down his forehead. Some men often visited him and sat with him on the edge of the bed, drinking hot tea. No one knew them. The rumors spread in the street. Some people said that Abu Amin belonged to the secret police, and that he was spying on the neighbors. Others stressed the fact that no one was allowed to sleep on the sidewalk winter or summer, no matter how poor that person was, and that the authorities always have pursued the beggars and prevented them from tarrying in the city streets.

When Samira passed by and hit Lina on her hips with the school bag, Lina looked around astounded, as if the whole world was transformed into one face, that of the vendor of the four seasons.

—Hurry up, said Samira, pulling her hand. Don't we have a test today?

—Ah, of course, said Lina lazily, but it is a composition test.

—Composition? laughed Samira. You are not afraid, I suppose. But I am. She slapped her cheek with the upper side of her hand and laughed loudly.

Behind them came Wafa' and other girls from the upper classes. The streets became crowded with people. The flower vendors stood at the street corners.

—Do you like the new Arabic teacher? Samira asked her.

—I don't know yet.

—You don't know? asked Samira. Do you need a long time to know?

—Perhaps, answered Lina and thought again of the vendor of the four seasons. What if the teacher asked them today: "Write about some personality." She wanted to laugh. Perhaps Samira would write about Harun Al-Rashid, or about some hero from history, or about her father. What did her father do? She couldn't remember, perhaps she never knew to start with. Anyway, Samira could not write about a poor vendor who slept on the sidewalk winter and summer.

—You are strange, Samira told her as they entered the gate of the school. The bell had just rung, and they ran and filed inside.

* * *

—Cheating is forbidden, said the teacher with the long brown hair.

The young girls laughed and took out their ink pens from tin boxes and had their rulers and scrap papers ready. Samira bent over her blotting paper, let the ink drop slowly from her pen, then dipped its point in the disappearing black spots.

—Don't you have another pen? asked the teacher.

Samira's face reddened. She bent her head.

—Do you need a pen? asked Lina and gave her a ball-point.

—Ok., said the teacher. You have 50 minutes. Then she turned her head and wrote on the blackboard in a clear handwriting: "Who is your ideal person in life and why?" Then she walked towards her desk, took a fat book out of the drawer and sat on a cane chair opposite the students and started reading. Lina saw Wafa' open her mouth stupidly and stare at the blackboard, while others yawned and scratched their heads, looking quite perplexed.

The noise in the street reached the class. Lina could not concentrate on anything. The personalities of the past and the future came to her endlessly. She saw Wafiqa in the opposite desk hide her head between her arms and write with enthusiasm. She heard her pen squeak on the old wood. Undoubtedly, the prophet Muhammad was her idol, said Lina to herself. The religion teacher praised her all the time, because she was veiled, and because she prayed and fasted. Lina thought that Wafiqa's paper would be full of Quranic verses and Muhammad's sayings. She closed her eyes, reviewed endless personalities in her mind. No. She would not choose heroes from history books, for most of them, if not all, preferred violence as a solution to everything. She remembered the massacre of Al-Rashid, in spite of the fact her teacher had justified everything. She dismissed the prophets because everything they've done could not be explained on a human level. She didn't want to write about her dead father, because she would not be objective, and she was afraid to babble. Everyone in class would laugh at her. She felt like crying. Thirty minutes had already passed, and the test paper was still white except for the name and the class.

—Oh Green Almonds. Soft Almonds. The sound of an old vendor passing by the window came to her. The students laughed. The teacher raised her head, listened to the cry, then continued reading.

Suddenly the figure of Abu Amin visited her. How mad! What will the teacher tell her? Won't her friends laugh at her? The watermelon vendor is your idol? In a minute the words of her sister Rima rang in her ears: "What do you know about the Rashid's baker, or cook, or guard, or the builder of his house, or the soldier who was killed for his sake?" The faces of all these men whom she never shook hands with, or read about in history, or literature books got mixed in her mind; they all looked like the watermelon vendor.

The bell would ring in about 20 minutes. Lina bent her head on the white paper and started writing like mad.

* * *

—Are you the sister of Rima Haseebi? A dark girl with brown eyes stopped her one day in the yard of the school.

—Yes. How do you know my sister? asked Lina surprised.

The girl smiled and pushed her hair away from her forehead.

—I've met her several times at Asma's house.

—Ah, uttered Lina a low sigh and stared at the attractive girl.

—What grade are you in? asked Lina after a while.

—Grade 11.

—Do you go regularly to Asma's apartment? asked Lina curiously. She was envious of the girl standing in front of her.

—No. But I go to a number of teachers' places. The girl bent and whispered in an almost unheard voice.

—What? said Lina surprised.

—Sh. The girl put her finger on her mouth. We have secret groups. Do you wish to join us today? She looked around, lest someone should hear her.

The noise of the girls in the yard was deafening. Lina saw the short woman supervisor run behind some young children carrying a stick.

—What shall I say to my mother? murmured Lina and the blood flowed in her cheeks.

—It is only an hour. Not more than an hour, said the girl quickly. She was still looking around her.

But Lina didn't reply.

—O.K. Will I see you then at the end of the next lesson? the girl insisted.

At that moment the bell rang. Lina nodded her head, then disappeared among the girls and stood in single file, waiting for the advent of the supervisor, not really conscious of what she had done. Is it possible that the new Arabic teacher is a party member? Which socialist party does she belong to? And how does she dare have these secret sessions in her apartment? The questions got mixed up in her mind, but she was determined to understand what was going on around her. She thought of the dark girl; she wasn't much older than Lina, and yet she was more mature.

* * *

78

There was a deep silence in the classroom when the history teacher with her white rosy face appeared. All eyes were fixed on her transparent blue shirt and her tight skirt which covered her knees. As she turned her back and wrote on the blackboard: "The Mamluks Period in the Middle Ages" whispers spread in the classroom, the laughter grew louder, and hands exchanged a drawing of a naked woman under which was written: "The divine history teacher."

—What do you have in your hands? said the teacher and turned suddenly. Her green eyes were glowing with anger.

The picture disappeared, and the teacher passed between the desks staring at the wicked faces.

—What did you see? She asked Lina after a while.

—Nothing, said Lina and bent her head.

—Nothing? Well. The teacher walked backward facing the class, then she took out the grades' notebook from her bag and said to Wafa':

—How did the Mamluks regime start in Egypt?

Wafa' stood on one leg and stammered.

—Didn't you prepare the chapter? asked the teacher angrily. The red pencil was shaking between her fingers.

—No. I was sick.

—Really? said the teacher mockingly, then she looked elsewhere at the girls. All right, who knows then?

Wafiqa lifted her head from between her narrow shoulders and smiled broadly. Lina noticed her yellow teeth.

—The Mamluks' regime started with the rule of Shajarat al-Durr who was most likely a slave of Turkish origin over Egypt after the death of her husband in the middle of the 13th century, said Wafiqa in a serious tone. The girls in the back benches laughed.

—Good, said the teacher, then wrote something in her small notebook.

—What do we mean by Mamluks? asked the teacher again and stared at the pale faces. Wafiqa put her finger in the air, moved her head right and left, but the teacher ignored her.

—Samira, do you know the answer?

—Yes, said the girl, without enthusiasm.

—Then answer. Why don't you raise your hand? scolded the teacher.

—The Mamluks were a ruling dynasty of slaves. They belonged to all sorts of nationalities, and they constituted the core of the army during the period of their masters, the Ayyubids. Samira was silent for a moment, then she confronted the teacher with courage:

—Why do we have to memorize these facts without attempting to analyze or criticize them?

No one said a word. The other girls were afraid. Suddenly, Lina felt a strong bond growing between her and Samira. When the teacher realized what had been said to her, she put her notebook quietly on the desk, then said scornfully:

—What do you wish to analyze?

Samira felt that the road was blocked, and the language which she was using could not be understood by the teacher, or the teacher did not wish to understand. Lina saw a grey cloud hanging on the girl's face. Was she bitter against the other girls? No one came forward to support her, although they always gossiped during the break about the authoritarian ways that some teachers adopted in the school.

—I mean we memorize historical facts, but. . . Samira's voice floundered.

—But what? interrupted the teacher.

Lina thought that Samira was right. She decided to express her opinion:

—When we studied that Shajarat al-Durr had ruled for 80 days as a sultana over Egypt, (the heads of her classmates turned towards her, and the new discussion seemed to amuse the teacher) and we said that the Caliph in Baghdad sent a letter to the princess of Egypt in which he wrote: 'If you don't have a man to rule you, let us know so we can send you one' we never discussed the content of the letter, nor did we comment on it.

The teacher laughed, and the class felt at ease. The tense arms and the shrunk muscles relaxed.

—Then you want an objective evaluation of the historical facts? said the teacher.

Lina nodded her head. She saw Samira's eyes glowing with thanks.

—But one does that at the university. You are young, said the teacher indifferently.

—Young? repeated Samira. He who grows up in our environment is not a child once he stops suckling his mother's breasts.

The teacher's face reddened. She took a piece of chalk between her fingers, then broke it nervously.

—Don't change the subject. We are not here to study politics, said the teacher.

—What is the difference between history and politics? protested Samira.

—This is enough! The teacher hit the desk with her fist. My duty as a teacher is to tell you what happened in the past.

There was silence in the classroom. Was the history teacher afraid? Lina asked herself. Did she believe as Aunt Samiya did that the walls had ears? What is the relationship between the Mamluks or their masters, or what happened in the past with what is happening in the present? When she moved her eyes, perplexed, she saw Samira put her head between her thin arms and stare at her old desk. Suddenly, Lina thought of these secret political meetings which were held in some of the teachers' houses. Samira had not learned these expressions in school. She regretted the fact that she had disliked her in the past. She remembered that she saw her often with that dark girl. Blood rose in her veins. She started looking at her watch once in a while, wishing the time would pass quickly. She would tell her mother that she had to go to the library, or that she accompanied another girl home to borrow a book. But her feet were frozen. What if her mother found out about the lie? What would her brothers-in-law do with her if they found out that she was attending a secret political meeting?

The history teacher's mouth was opening and closing. But Lina didn't hear a thing. It did not worry her in the least. She would find all the information in the history book; she would read quietly in the warm living room, and perhaps she would buy a special book, or she would ask her sister Rima about her opinion of the Moslem Sultana.

The events floated in her mind like corpses. It annoyed her that she couldn't relate the causes to the effects, or see history as an unfragmented entity in its past or present. One single event would shake suddenly in the depth of her memory, rise slowly, wear the white shroud, then crawl bit by bit till it appeared like a horrible big screen before her eyes. She never knew why that particular event came to life, while others remained asleep forever in the winding corridor of her mind.

The bell rang, but the teacher's mouth was still opening and closing. Lina heard the girls shout in the yard and run, and when Wafa' opened the window, a spring wind blew from the street. Lina felt as if Shajrat al-Durr was standing in front of her in her most luxurious attire, pointing with her long nailed fingers to men wrapped with black masks. She heard the Sultan of Egypt enter the bathroom, and she saw the vapor rise from every corner, then a scream pierced the air and vanished between the walls.

*　*　*

The girl with the dark complexion and the brown eyes was waiting for her outside the gate of the school. Lina moved with difficulty among the crowd of students. She heard the supervisor behind her say in a shrill voice: "Why are you pushing each other?" The janitor came with his long stick and big body, trying to force the girls to discipline, but they knew he would not hurt any of them, so no one noticed his presence. The students were flowing out of the classrooms like waves. No one could see anything but bodies and school bags placed either between the legs or raised in the air. The vendors of almonds, candy, Aleppo's pistachio, all were singing with monotonous voices on the edges of sidewalks. Young men wearing tight pants and white shirts with high starched collars were scattered in the street as if they belonged in Hollywood.

—Have you seen Samira? The girl asked her.

—You mean in class? asked Lina surprised.

—No, now.

—Is she going with us?

—Yes, said the girl. Her eyes were searching among the crowd.

Suddenly, everything became clear to her. Samira wasn't young. She didn't want to memorize historical facts. There was someone opening her mind secretly where the school had failed. Lina was overjoyed. She wanted to walk with her new friends, to learn from them how the young chick breaks the egg, then flies. Minutes passed, then Samira came running; her bag loaded with books and swinging vigorously.

The girls took the bus to the mountain. There was not a single empty seat. The conductor was moving with difficulty among the human bodies in order to give each passenger a ticket. The fat woman sitting in front of Lina turned her head nervously every time Lina's fingers touched her black veil unintentionally. Some teenagers took advantage of the crowded situation in the long bus and came close to the school girls. Lina saw their hands play cautiously with the rounded hips. She was afraid that voices of protest would grow loud, the bus would stop and the boys would be kicked out. She didn't have much time. She thought that she would not attend the whole meeting. It was likely that her mother would send someone to the school to ask about her.

The road seemed endless, and the bus was almost empty when the girl with the dark complexion squeezed her hand and said:

—O.K. Get your bag. We'll get out in a couple of minutes.

—What is your name? asked Lina.

—Ah, of course. Forgive me. Amal Madi.

—Are you Syrian? inquired Lina, hearing a strange accent.

—No. I am Palestinian.

The bus stopped. The three girls got out, and when the door was shut they were alone in the street.

—You'll find the meeting useful, said Samira and smiled.

Swarms of ideas invaded her mind. She felt like asking many questions, but she was afraid. What if the police raided the apartment and arrested the members of this secret organization? Who is this teacher that risks her job and could go to prison under a military rule that understands nothing but power?

—Are you afraid? Amal asked her as they entered the new building which was a dusty grey color.

Lina stared at the girl, couldn't say a word, and felt her lips quiver.

*　*　*

As Samira rang the bell of the third floor, the door opened and in the hallway stood a medium size woman with long brown hair. Lina remembered that she had seen her one time in the staff room in the school.

—Come in, said the woman; her smile making her round face shine.

Lina heard the water bubble in a pot and the clinking of tea glasses coming out of the kitchen. A score of school bags was piled in a corner of the hallway. As the girls entered the living room, they were met by friendly faces and warm hands.

—Lina is attending our meeting for the first time, said Amal.

The young bodies came closer to each other, and a space for the newcomers was made on the low Arabic sofa. Footsteps were hurrying from the kitchen to the room. Some girls came carrying trays of tea; their voices grew louder.

—How many spoons of sugar did you put?

—Two?

—I love my tea sweet.

—No sugar please.

—O, my God, it is too dark.

—How do you want it? Like water?

The air was filled with laughter. Lina recognized some faces: the girl with the red hair who was going to college next year, and that one with the striped blue and white dress in grade eleven. They looked old to her. No one was her age. Even Samira. As she sipped a little tea, the woman with the brown hair appeared in the middle of the room and welcomed the girls.

—Who is she? whispered Lina.

—The sociology teacher of the upper classes, said Amal quickly.

Lina thought that the teacher was married, or maybe she was living with her mother and sisters, because it was not likely for a young woman to live in an apartment by herself. But when she looked at the teacher's finger, there was no ring. She realized that the teacher was from out of town, and she listened attentively to her coastal accent.

—Comrade Raja' al-Jablawi will sum up for us the *Communist Manifesto* written by Karl Marx and Frederich Engels in the middle of the 19th century. The manifesto calls the workers of the world to unite and to revolt against their wretched conditions in the capitalist countries. When the comrade finishes reading the summary we will start the discussion, said the teacher in her clear coastal accent. Then she put a chair in the middle of the room and pointed for the girl to sit down.

All heads turned at the same time; eyes were fixed on Raja', the girl of medium height, with short blonde hair and white glasses. Lina didn't recognize her face. She thought the girl, perhaps, was not more than 18 years old.

—Comrades, she said, then coughed a little. Pimples were scattered on her white forehead. Her clothes didn't indicate she was rich by any means, or even a town dweller.

—All of you know Marx, but we have a new comrade here.

Sweat covered Lina's forehead. Everybody looked at her and smiled in a friendly way.

—Marx is a German philosopher. He lived in the 19th century and one cannot ignore his influence on our political, or social thinking. His famous book *The Capital* is translated into Arabic, and perhaps we could analyze some of its chapters in the next meetings, said the girl very seriously, then took a folded paper out of her pocket and started reading.

Marx. Where had she heard this name? Lina tried to remember, but in vain. The April sun was still shining outside, and Lina saw on the edge of the window a pot laden with narcissus. The girls were taking notes quickly. She heard Samira press the pen as usual onto the paper and saw Amal who was sitting next to her complete a picture of a man with a very thick beard.

—What does Marx say in his *Communist Manifesto*? What is his fundamental theory? asked the girl theatrically.

The pens were raised a little in the air, then descended on the papers.

—Marx proposes that there are two opposing classes throughout history. He calls the exploiting class in his times the capitalists, or the bourgeoisie: it is the class which owns the means of production. The other exploited class he calls the proletariat, or working class; its members are forced to sell their labor power in return for trivial wages. The German philosopher assures us that the struggle between the two classes will not be solved but through force and unless the working classes unite to nationalize all means of production and abolish the private property.

Lina looked at her watch anxiously. She couldn't concentrate anymore on what the girl was saying. She saw the sociology teacher move about in her chair, while other girls were busy drawing funny figures on the papers, their eyes were almost closed. Lina wasn't aware when the girl finished her summary. She was surprised to see the hands raised in the air, and to hear the whispers grow louder after the silence had prevailed for a long time.

—To what extent can we apply what Marx says about capitalist societies to our own society? asked a girl with a serious look. Her light hair hung across her face.

—Can you answer the question? The teacher asked the girl who had summed up the Manifesto.

—Yes, answered the girl with confidence. But before she proceeded, another girl gave her a cold glass of water. She drank a little bit, then said quietly:

—We can't consider our society a capitalistic one, because we didn't go through the Industrial Revolution like the West. Our agrarian society still has a lot of characteristics of the feudal one. But the relationship between the landlord and the peasant in our country does not differ greatly from that of the worker and the factory owner in the industrialized countries.

—You mean exploitation? asked the girl with the serious looks again.

—Of course. Both the peasant and the worker don't own the means of production; both have to sell their labour power in return for a limited wage from which they live.

—Didn't you find the book difficult? Samira asked the girl admiringly.

—Of course. I read it many times, then Miss. . . (she looked in the direction of the sociology teacher) helped me.

Lina wanted to say something too, but the time was making her nervous. She thought her mother would be standing in front of the closed school. Without quite realizing it, Lina found herself leaving the room, muttering apologies. She carried her bag and rushed down the stairs.

*   *   *

The street was bathed in brilliant sunshine. The neighbors crowded the balconies and the roofs. Some had decorated the windows with red, white, and black flags. The broadcaster's voice grew louder, transmitting the news of the Independence Parade. The planes flew over the sky of Damascus; leaflets were distributed in the city streets. The sidewalks were crowded with people. Some were waiting anxiously for the flower carriages, or the scouts, or the drummers, or the fleet of company caravans decorated with cotton, candy bags, and colorful bulbs. Fathers bought roasted pistachios and ice-cream cones for their children. Women stood next to their husbands, wearing their new holiday clothes and exposing heavily made-up faces to the warm sun of April.

—After the allies entered Syria and the troops of the traitor Vichi were defeated by the English and French and the Arab armies, General De Gaul proclaimed that the French mandate over Syria would continue until a new French government is formed.

The voice of the broadcaster came out from all the loudspeakers in the corners of the street. The passers-by did not, however, seem to hear any of it. The independence day was an occasion for many people to leave their wretched homes, enjoy the warm sun and watch the soldiers crossing the streets of the city carrying their new arms or riding the tanks which destroyed the asphalt, or the planes swooping from the sky in varied beautiful formations.

Lina relaxed on her rocking chair lazily and listened once in a while to the chattering people, or to the announcer's shouting.

—But you don't remember anything, said Samira, who was sitting opposite her sipping hot coffee. No, you haven't seen the tanks rolling in the narrow lanes, nor the bombs falling on the houses, the shops and the roofs. My mother was asleep when a bullet entered the window. My sister and I were not hurt, but my mother. . . The words got stuck in her throat, and her eyes seemed like glass.

Lina didn't know what to say. Then the broadcaster's voice flooded the street.

—Freedom is not given but taken, and the French troops, which stood in the face of the Nazis and promised to grant us freedom, bargained and tricked us. "Will we have concessions in this country? Will our economic, cultural, and strategic interests continue after our withdrawal?" In May, the year 1945, and for the third time in 20 years, the French planes bombed the oldest city in the world, not only to frighten its inhabitants, but to stop them from resisting the occupation.

— I can't understand, said Lina hesitantly.

—What? said Samira, as if she weren't listening.

—How can the French fight against the Nazis in their own country in order not to become slaves, yet deny the other nations the same right when they are the aggressors? asked Lina.

Samira nodded her head, then flipped her empty coffee cup on the saucer; the dregs spread on it. Both girls looked down.

—Do you read the future? asked Lina, surprised that her friend would believe in such an old practice.

— I don't believe in superstition, laughed Samira.

At that moment, the girl scouts started passing from under the balcony with their short white clothes and little colorful flags.

One, two. Stop. Salute. A fat man who looked like a trainer was shouting. The people applauded. Lina laughed loudly, while Samira was still looking at the coffee cup, its edges stained by the dregs.

—Why do you lie? asked Lina. You read the future. Don't you?

—The future? Samira stared in her eyes mockingly. No one knows the future, she said. But the sociology teacher told us one day in one of the political meetings: 'You make the future by what you do today, and in the way you like if you want.'

The noise in the street drowned Samira's low voice. Lina found herself obliged to come close to her friend and listen to every word.

Meanwhile, a musical group of 15 year-old boys passed under the balcony. Then the flower carriages started rolling, lightly carrying young girls in brides' clothes who waved to people. The broadcaster said through the loudspeaker:

—Independence. Yes, Ladies and Gentlemen. What does it mean?

Lina heard her sister laugh hysterically in front of the balcony door. Then she saw her approaching cautiously.

—Are you enjoying the celebration? asked Rima. Her voice was mocking.

—But it is the independence day, said Lina.

—What is the difference between today and any other day? Rima pulled a cane chair and sat on it.

—The difference is that today we spend lots of money that we badly need otherwise, said Samira in a confident voice, and she raised her head.

—This is true, but I meant other differences, said Rima.

Lina knit her eyebrows and stopped looking at the street. The independence day didn't please her sister. Sadness overwhelmed her. She remembered the day when her governess had carried her and stood on the balcony in the first floor. She hadn't yet learned to speak. A British soldier passed by, and Lina's big brown eyes had stopped him. He stretched both his hands. His rosy face was beaming with joy. Without saying a word, the governess understood what he wanted. She bent forward and pushed Lina towards him. As he embraced the child to his bosom and his breath touched her thin neck, she had begun to cry.

—You don't want the French and English soldiers to remain here, said Lina. Doubt was burning her soul.

—Don't be stupid, said her sister. Her eyes glowed.

—But independence day doesn't mean anything to you, said Lina defiantly.

—What do we mean by the word 'independence'? asked Rima, restraining her anger. Independence means in the language: freedom from control by other persons. Isn't it?

Lina nodded her head. Samira seemed interested in the discussion.

—But, said Rima, like a teacher, what control? the foreign troops, symbol of exploitation and oppression? Fine. Then we are free.

Lina laughed nervously. Her sister's language was confusing and contradictory.

—No, we are not free, said Samira.

—See? said Rima. Her eyes were fixed on Lina's bewildered face. Then, she looked at Samira and said casually:

—Do you know why we are not free?

—Of course, replied Samira. You are right. The peasant who fought against the occupying forces was and still is a slave in his land. Independence didn't change his economic or social status.

Rima smiled broadly.

—But isn't there a difference between the foreign occupier and the feudal or the capitalist in a given country? asked Lina. She had many doubts.

—No, said Rima. Both sides have similar interests. We will not achieve total independence until we rid ourselves completely of exploitation and slavery in all their forms: the exploitation of the feudal lord of the peasant, the capitalist of the worker, the military of the civilian, man of woman.

—But won't that take generations? asked Lina, still convinced that independence was a great step.

—No, cried Samira. Do you want the truth? We are lazy, lazy. And she stressed the letters of her last word.

At that moment, frightened voices came from the street. People started running toward the carriage of Abu Amin which was full of oranges. The onlookers on balconies pointed their fingers towards the man with the white silvery hair, and no one was looking at the soldiers anymore beating the earth strongly and cheering their leaders.

In a matter of minutes, people old and young started running everywhere, as if fleeing from the mouth of a mythical crocodile. A cry came from the loudspeaker: The Tanks. Lina saw the peasant women with their long embroidered clothes put the children on their backs and run for safety. "My son, my son." Lina heard Abu Amin sob loudly. She saw his blue eyes protruding. Then the voice of the broadcaster grew louder till it overpowered the noise of the fleeing crowd:

—Ladies and Gentlemen. Please be silent. There is nothing dangerous. Just a tank that went out of control. I repeat. There is nothing dangerous.

People's voices grew louder: "The murderers, the murderers."

As Lina, Rima, and Samira hurried inside, their faces pale as death, the broadcaster was saying in an euphoric voice:

—Ladies and Gentlemen. His Excellency the Colonel is now approaching the main platform.

The national anthem was playing from the loudspeakers, mixing with the sirens of ambulances.

* * *

(The darkness descends on the city. Abu Amin, the orange vendor, appears in the square. As he starts his monologue some passers-by steal away from the side streets carrying pale lamps.)

The lights of the houses overlooking the square were put out. People went to their beds wishing that the night would stay longer, so they would not have to face a day laden with worries. Once in a while a few shots would be heard, but no one was curious enough to look from the balcony to find the source. Abu Amin appeared with his blue torn out shirt and baggy trousers.

He lit his candle and put it on the edge of the street. He circled the orange crate several times. His blue eyes glowed with a savage look. A warm wind blew, penetrated his open shirt, and scattered the white hair on his forehead. He muttered certain incomprehensible words. He began to push the carriage madly; his bare feet rose in the air. The square turned in his head; the three story apartments tilted, and the roofs where the wash hung on the lines touched his broad shoulders. The black chimneys laughed at him. Then the trees crept towards him, threatening. The oranges rolled from the carriage. The wind was quiet.

He took out his knife and stood in the middle of the square, looking around. Then he started jumping in the air as if he were stabbing real enemies. His panting broke the silence. "One, two, three." He didn't say the numbers, but he was pointing with his fingers to the supposed corpses which were scattered on the edge of the square. As he finished counting, he took out a dirty handkerchief whose color had faded, wiped his forehead, then his throat, and then he blew his nose loudly. For a moment, he was fixed like a statue in his place, then he began to sob. The echo repeated his sobbing, but no one was curious enough to look from the balcony.

He put on his torn shoes, then took them off. He lit a match, examined the sore on the toes of his right foot, then the left one. He put on his shoes again and began to limp in his walk. He stretched the cloth dangling from between his baggy trousers, used it as a basket and began to gather the oranges slowly, piling them in the middle of the square.

He built a pyramid, then two, then three. The sweat washed his back; his blue shirt stuck to his body. As he looked at the heap of oranges, they seemed to glow in the darkness like the eyes of cats. He uttered a cry which froze the birds in their nests and awoke the evil spirits from the tombs of the city.

The candle was out. The square was enveloped in darkness. But the minaret in the east put on its green lights, and a short man appeared on the top. "Come to prayers," the man called in a dejected voice. Hurried steps were heard in the street and the pant-

ing of the orange vendor grew louder, till it dominated everything. The square seemed to hang between heaven and earth.
The houses tilted again and the laundry on the roofs hung like
the sails of traveling ships. The crazy man stood as if addressing
hidden enemies.

—On whom should I pour my anger? The knife gleamed in his
hand. The windows with iron bars stepped towards him as if they
were armies protecting themselves with shields. He jumped in the
air.

—Where are you? Come from behind your black masks. What?
Are you laughing? The orange vendor. The folk hero. Take it in
your chest! You and you and you. No. You don't know how bitter I
am! Your ugly faces. Your hands smeared with blood. Your nails
stuffed with human flesh. Your black suits. As if you are judges! As
if you are from a strange world. Speak. Answer! Why are you
laughing? I am a simple orange vendor. What did I do to you?
Why did you choose me?

—Did you see his long conical cap? said one man on his way to
the morning prayer.

—No. His long tail, said another.

—The devil is in the square. Hurry. An old man threw a stone,
then he wrapped himself with a woolen cloak and hurried towards the mosque.

—What does he say? Did you hear? asked the butter vendor.

—A language unlike ours, answered the grave digger.

The figures with the pale lamps hurried; all whispering in
scared voices:

—O God. O God.

—Who is there? Abu Amin threw the knife from his hand.
"This is an orange. That is an orange". The pyramid started to fall
like sandy hills. "How much he used to like oranges. His short
blond hair; his rosy cheeks. What did I do to you? Why did you
choose me out of all people?"

* * *

93

At The Mosque

(The worshippers sat on the carpet which covered the floor of the mosque; others stood in front of the water taps in the external yard and washed themselves. It was still dark in the city.)

—Our souls are dirty
Our bodies are dirty
Keep the devil away
From you and me, the sheik sang.

—What are you saying, man? one whispered in the ear of his neighbor.

—Did you hear?

—What?

—Bullet shots.

—Shall we go?

The water bubbled in the fountain in the outside yard, and the sound of wooden clogs was heard.

—Guide us, oh Lord, to the straight path, sighed the sheik. He rubbed his weary eyes.

—The path of those whom Thou hast favoured
Not of those who have earned Your anger
Nor those who have gone astray
Amen.

The echo repeated the men's voices.

—My sheik, the grave digger called. Are you content?

—God teaches us to be content, replied the sheik.

—Are you hungry?

—God feeds our hunger.

—And who lifts injustice that befalls you and me?

—Is there anyone but God, my son? Let us pray. Heavens' gates are open.

—Really? said the garbage collector joyfully.

—Do you doubt, man? asked the sheik.

—God forbid, said the garbage collector. God forbid.

—Oh Lord teach us to submit to your will

Oh Lord keep the devil away from us
and from our thoughts.
Lord make us in the company of your pious slaves.
Amen, the sheik sighed.
—Oh Lord preserve our rulers
we the weak
and teach us contentment
we the crippled
and make heaven our abode
on judgment day, said the sheik.

The garbage collector closed his eyes and dreamt that God had visited him in his wretched room and put a fresh loaf of bread, a big piece of goat cheese, and a bundle of black olives sprinkled with oil and lemon on his bed. When he wanted to shake hands with Him or to touch Him or to kiss Him, He disappeared like a specter.

Darkness still enveloped the whole city when the garbage collector carried his long broom, pulled his small cart, and began to whistle joyfully, for God had visited him.

*   *   *

—If only the weather cools down, said Lina to herself as she was crossing the outside yard of the university one hot day in summer. She felt stifled by her yellow shirt with the high military collar. Her leather bag was sticking to her moistened palm. The hot wind blew from the dry asphalt and penetrated the folds of her colorful skirt.

The university buildings, which were remnants of a French military post, seemed old and crumbling. From behind the dirty windows, dark skinned men thrust their heads, sipping cold lemonade and smoking lazily. Their hair was shining with cheap hair oil, their moustaches thick but short. This was to be graduation day, and the colonel himself was to open the ceremony (although no one knew for sure because the colonel's movements were secret) but those employees did not seem to be in a hurry. Some of them were watching the workers who were setting up the platform in the square, or the janitors who were putting the chairs on top of each other; others preferred to amuse themselves by watching the nests of doves on the bricks of the nearby buildings, or the group of students under the thin trees which were decorated with flags and colorful lights.

Lina looked at her watch, then she thought she had some extra time before she was supposed to meet Samira and Amal. She crossed the Law School, went to the interior yard and looked for a bench in the shadow of a big tree.

This was not the first time she had come to the university. She had accompanied Rima in the past couple of months either to listen to a lecture or to borrow some books from the library, or to participate in a discussion held by some secret political organization, or to join a short trip arranged by one of the departments to the villages, or the nearby cities. But this day was unlike other days. Lina had planned, with her two friends, to attend her sister's graduation ceremony and to meet her family later on in the gardens of the university and return home with them.

Some female students passed by her, strutting in their wide white dresses. The thin heels of their shoes tapped on the asphalt. One day, she thought, she too would graduate from the university. Her eyes were fixed on a girl with long brown hair reading under a jasmine bush. How many years will she need to read all the books in the library? Lina was suddenly distressed. She was afraid that she would grow old quickly, and her ability to read would diminish. "It is not important that one reads all the printed books," Rima told her one day " but to digest the most important ones." But who decides what is important and what is trivial? Who sets the literary standards? Who establishes the political, economic and philosophical concepts? What is the relationship between the difficulty of a certain work and its intellectual significance? She wanted to laugh in a loud voice. She remembered all these long weeks which she spent reading *The Wage Labour* and *The Capital* by Karl Marx. How difficult she found them. How many times she went to Rima, her fingers quivering under certain lines. No, the language wasn't easy, nor was the topic familiar to her. But her sister always told her "Go on trying, then ask someone in the discussion group about the vague points."

Those discussion groups. How much she liked them. She felt so close to the other people. But she was always afraid. She couldn't say confidently: "I am a Communist." She wanted to know everything about Communism, about its philosophy, its leaders. She began to listen to the accusations of those who supported different philosophies only to understand her own position. She knew she was young and that her intellectual maturity would not be completed overnight, and in the end she might find the solutions she had always sought, but she also might not.

From a distance she saw the path of the wild roses. She hurried, almost oblivious to everything around her. She passed by the thin gardener while he was watering short shrubs and singing in a desolate voice. The rosy flowers were sparkling under the sun; their leaves were green and shiny. As she knelt near a rusty sign on which it was written: "Walking on grass is forbidden", a beautiful fragrance came to her nostrils. She remained fixed in her place and felt as if the world were turning round and round at a crazy speed. She was overwhelmed by a yearning for Granada's gardens which she had read about in the poetry of the Andalusian poets. She imagined that the Generalife orchards with their endless brooks, flowing cascades, ever blooming roses, straight cypress trees and the fragrant myrtle paths, all stood in front of her, then she heard al Mu'tamid, the Caliph of Granada cry in his Moroccan prison. But as she touched the leaves of the roses affectionately, she started to shake in alarm, as she saw daggers dripping with blood, pointing toward her.

Lina dragged her feet and walked to a bench. "You are a prisoner," the Arabic language teacher told her one day. "A prisoner?" Lina had opened her mouth stupidly. "Yes. A prisoner of history," the teacher had assured her. "But aren't we all prisoners of history?" asked Lina surprised. "No," said the teacher firmly.

When she sat on the bench she felt the claws of history pulling her to the womb of the earth, and she couldn't cry. The Generalife gardens were melting in her eyes as the sunset would melt on the shoulder of the hill.

The sun was setting and the hot desert wind was calm. Through the moist earth some humid breezes came upon her and the tender petals of roses moved. When Lina looked behind her, the gardener in the dark blue shirt had disappeared and strange faces were appearing from every corner. The noise of people grew louder. The university yards were bathed in light.

* * *

—Where were you? Amal and Samira asked her in front of the door to the Arts Building.

—In the inner garden, said Lina apologetically. She walked with her two friends to the celebration place.

—We ought to be careful, Amal bent her head and whispered.

—What is the matter? Lina felt alarmed.

—There are pamphlets being distributed secretly. Probably something will take place tonight. Then she paused. Her face was void of any expression.

—But mother. . . Lina couldn't complete her sentence

—We will find her. We will sit next to her, said Samira assuredly.

Lina was worried. What if the army attacked and bullets were shot? She knew her mother would not leave till she found her daughters. Bahiya would not find the university gate, she will be fixed in her place like a doll and might even cry like a baby.

—Don't worry, said Amal and pulled her by the hand.

—And the rest? No one else will come? asked Samira.

—No, said Lina bitterly.

Aunt Samiya will sit behind the radio. Perhaps she will repeat the names stupidly: "'Ali 'Ammar, Faculty of Science: grade good; Su'ad Ghanim, Medical School: distinction." She will applaud alone in the room, then smoke. Perhaps, before Rima's turn comes, she will sleep on the heaped pillows on the sofa and snore loudly.

The students' parents were arriving at the university. Each family was trying to find seats close to the platform. Men in dark suits and white shirts with starched collars pushed their way, followed by wives wearing shiny clothes and golden jewelry. Although the university had opened its doors to all classes, and joining it was subject to an average point scheme, most of its students belonged to the bourgeoisie, while the feudalists preferred to send their boys to western universities. Sometimes the male villagers managed to come to the city; they worked and studied at the same time, but as they obtained university degrees they would turn their backs on their parents and refuse to return to their villages, not only because of the cultural and social gap that existed between the city and the country, but, above all, because of the bourgeois education which taught them to be arrogant vis-a-vis their background and to strive to change their social class.

It was hard to find a son of a laborer in the university. The workers were less lucky than the peasants. They lived in crowded, mud houses with tin roofs on the outskirts of town. They no longer lived off the land. They were neither villagers nor city dwellers. They were totally dependent on trivial wages which they received weekly from the factory owner. Their children (and there were plenty because God feeds the hungry bellies, and because children are the pleasure of earthly world as the Quran says) found themselves forced to work at an early age to help their fathers earn a living for the family.

Lina and her friends amused themselves by watching the passers-by. Samira, as usual, imitated men who walked like czars, or veiled women who moved on their tiptoe, fearing someone might hear their footsteps, or young boys who walked behind their mothers, their eyes glowing with anger to make sure no one would look at the black veiled figures.

The students tried their best to lead the people to the empty seats in an orderly fashion, but some men started cursing; the women's shouts grew louder, and no one liked his seat. Often, people stole the seats of others who had gone away for a few minutes to buy newspapers or to speak with friends. These scenes constituted dramatic material for Samira. She saw and heard everything. Minutes had hardly passed before she repeated all the events, acting with funny mime gestures.

Finally, Lina's mother appeared at the university gate in a black dress which covered her knees; her long veil hanging on her shoulders. Bahiya walked next to her, limping a bit, as if suffering from a sore on her foot.

—Mum, said Lina and rushed anxiously towards her mother. She saw the fascinating smile appear on her mother's face.

—Are you going to sit with us? mocked Bahiya.

The three girls laughed and made way for the two tired women.

—But we won't see anything here, protested Bahiya.

—Why did you come late? asked Samira.

—You're right. But the heat was unbearable a couple of hours ago, said the mother calmly.

They sat on the back benches. As the master of ceremonies opened the graduation evening, heads in front of them swayed right and left, and some people shouted angrily: "The loudspeakers." The man was confused a bit, then someone gave him another loudspeaker. He coughed lightly, then said:

—Hello. Hello.

—O.K., said voices in the audience.

— Ladies and Gentlemen, said the man, fixing his white spectacles with black rims on his nose. At that time men with grey hair and stern faces began to ascend the platform and take their places in an orderly manner. The people applauded, then the graduating classes began to appear: first the girls with their wide white dresses and coiffed hair, then the young men with their dark suits and colorful ties. Lina moved her head right and left, then she stood a little bit so perhaps she could see her sister among the crowd, but a woman behind her protested with a loud voice, and Lina lost interest in seeing anything.

—Ladies and Gentlemen, shouted again the master of ceremonies. We won't start till his Excellency the Colonel arrives.

—The Colonel? The whispers increased; the people sat in their seats as if expecting trouble.

Lina heard her mother sigh. She exchanged meaningful looks with Samira.

—Are you happy? Amal asked Lina's mother, attempting to make the atmosphere more pleasant.

Her mother's weary looks disappeared. Her face beamed with a joyous smile. Then she said, as if talking to herself:

—Happy? I only attended fifth grade. My father used to be proud of me and always said: "My scholar child." Indeed, I was a scholar in a society of ignorant women. I read and wrote, and that was the greatest thing a woman could aspire to in my time.

—How lucky you are, said Amal. My mother is illiterate.

—And mine too, Samira assured them.

—But times have changed, said Bahiya biting her lips.

—Undoubtedly, said Amal, nodding her head in agreement.

When Lina looked at her mother she could not recognize her. She saw the brown eyes glow under thick eyebrows, then she heard her murmur as if the world around her weren't there:

—He used to come with his carriage every morning. The girls of the house used to meet him in the living room. He talked to us about literature, history, and other sciences. No one except our social class used to educate his daughters. And yet, we were always told that our world was different from that of men, that we were born to get married and to beget children.

Her voice began to tremble a bit. "Happy, you say?" She stared at the people's heads sitting in front of her as she recovered her senses.

—And Rima, what will she do with her degree? She will get married too, and have children, said Bahiya, quite convinced.

But the mother didn't hear anything. She was in a different world. She looked healthy again.

—He used to tell me: "Oh, most beautiful girl." I was his student for only five years. My father, then, told me he found me a husband. I could not object.

Bahiya started moving nervously on the chair.

—Let us go, she said, and gave Lina a nudge.

—Five years, repeated Lina's mother as if she were in a trance.

—Ladies and Gentlemen. His Excellency the Colonel, exclaimed the broadcaster.

Suddenly, the yard of the university became like a fortress. Soldiers began to run with their machine guns. Some stood behind the windows on top floors; others stood ready to shoot on the stairs of the student union at the extreme right, or the library at the extreme left. The spectators looked around, then the applause grew louder.

—Ladies and Gentlemen. The broadcaster's voice was trembling with excitement.

Lina saw the short, bald university president rush to greet the colonel and his party, while the army musicians started playing national songs. The men with white silvery hair stood up on the platform and bent their heads in respect for the officials.

Darkness had already enveloped the city. When the broadcaster introduced the university president to the crowd, silence prevailed, and nothing was heard except the clank of some rifles in the soldiers' hands.

—Your Excellency, the Colonel. Ladies and Gentlemen. We cel-

ebrate today the graduation of a new group of the future youth,
said the president in a resonant voice, stressing the last two words.
Then he stretched his hand to the glass which was standing on the
lectern and gulped down some water.

Bahiya yawned and began to shift about on her seat. Amal and
Samira were following the movement of the soldiers on the windows and roofs. Lina didn't know what her mother was thinking
of. She saw her stare at the stars sometimes and smile quietly, or
gaze vacantly at the multitude of heads.

The time passed slowly. The wooden chairs squealed. People
began to sway right and left. Bahiya said: "Does anyone see
Rima?" No one answered. In the lights which were focused on the
stage, Lina could see the colonel's medals shining like wild eyes.
The students hurried, holding their degrees tightly to their
chests, shaking hands with the grey-haired men. Photographers
crowded around the edges of the stage, and the cries of the spectators grew louder. A woman sitting in front of Lina shouted when
her son got his law degree with distinction, then she became hysterical and began to cry loudly.

—I wish I stayed at home, murmured Bahiya, her small black
eyes screening the people. No one heard what she said.

Suddenly, a tall, narrow shouldered fellow dashed to the stage,
went instantly to the loudspeaker and yelled with a loud voice:
"Down with the military dictatorship." Heads froze in one position, then whispers around the stage grew louder. Other students
ran. When the spectators woke from their initial shock and realized that the battle between the students and the soldiers would
undoubtedly start, they began to jam the university entrance. Fear
paralyzed their tongues.

—Please silence, said the broadcaster, as the tall student was led
away from the stage.

—We will not let the agents and the saboteurs ruin this great
occasion. The voice of the university president rose shrilly.

—Where is Rima? The mother stood up, her face white like a shroud.

—Don't worry. We will find her, said Amal.

—Let us go, said Bahiya and held her mother by the hand.

—Go? said Lina's mother in a sharp tone.

People were still jamming the outside door, and the soldiers pushed them back. The broadcaster was repeating: "Please, go back to your seats." His voice was drowned in the sound of chairs toppling to the floor. Lina saw the colonel whisper with his comrades, while the grey haired men on stage looked like preserved animals. Only seconds passed when a new group of students started by. The faces, however, were grim this time; their heads were down. The broadcaster's enthusiasm decreased; his voice became quieter as if he didn't wish to address toppled chairs and an almost empty square.

The old city truck was sprinkling water on the edges of the sidewalks. The butter merchant was having fun killing the dancing flies on the window panes of his shop, while pots of black and green olives, white cheese, and yogurt were standing outside on dirty stone benches without covers. Bags of rice, lentil, sugar, and flour lay against the crumbling walls.

The ice-cream vendor yawned behind his white cart, standing under the shadow of a lean tree. But as he saw the city truck approaching, he hid in the entrance of one of the houses so as not to get wet.

The street was empty. The burning sun was fading the colors of the wash hanging on roofs and heating up the heap of watermelons covered with thick canvas, lying on the sidewalk near the butter merchant's shop. The buildings painted with brown, yellow and green looked grayish because of the winter rain and the summer sun. The paint had peeled off the balconies leaving ugly holes. The stone buildings, however, were not any better. Hardly one year, or two at the most, had passed since they were built, but the white stones had already become dark. Smoke from the chimneys had covered them with soot that no rain or snow could ever wash away.

Lina opened the window of the living room. The odor of burnt asphalt came upon her and the flies began to fly into the room.

How quiet her home was, she thought as she stared at the ice-cream vendor leaning against his white cart. No car passed by; no motorcycle. Undoubtedly, the people were asleep, especially after a heavy meal. From the kitchen came the smell of freshly ground coffee. Then Lina heard the water boil in the kettle and the steps of her sister in the hallway.

Early that morning, her family had left the city heat behind to spend the day at Bludan, a summer resort. She and Rima remained alone at home. When her mother asked her whether she would like to go with them, Lina had said she was tired. Didn't she think that the mountain breeze will make her feel better? asked her mother surprised. No, she said. No? she will regret it, Bahiya commented as she closed the door behind her.

Lina drew the transparent curtain, leaving it for the hot wind to play with once in a while. Then she put "The Four Seasons" by Vivaldi on the record player, and there came the sound of the violin: warm sometimes, harsh another. She thought the hot summer breath was mingling with the hissing of the fireplace in winter, and that the cider presses in autumn were nothing but the echoes of the shepherds' songs and the lambs' bleating on spring nights.

Lina was reading *The Mother* by Maxim Gorky when Rima entered the room carrying a tray of coffee, her rosy dress open at the neck, showing suntanned shoulders. Lina thought that her sister was undoubtedly happy. She had graduated from the university a few days ago, and within months she would start working and become independent. Lina envied her in her heart and wished the years would pass quickly so she could stand on the wooden stage with a long white dress and, with trembling hands, receive her degree from the president of the university. The thought of it overwhelmed her with joy and she felt she could fly. Suddenly, a ray of the sunlight was refracted in her eyes and the sky became a stunning lake of purple lights.

—Haven't you finished Gorky's book yet? asked her sister as she poured coffee. Hot vapor was rising in front of her face.

—I almost finished it, said Lina. How wonderful this Pelagueya Vlasova.

—Do you find her wonderful? asked her sister in a testing voice.

—I wish the mothers in this country were like her, said Lina regretfully.

—Do you think this could happen overnight? asked her sister mockingly.

—No, of course not. But we also are not like the son of Mrs. Vlasova. Are we?

—You are right, said her sister curtly. Her face was gloomy.

Lina watched the coffee cup shake in her sister's hand. No, there was nothing that separated them. They seemed to be aiming for the same goal.

—Do you know why we're not like Mrs. Vlasova's son? asked her sister as she raised the cup of coffee to drain it.

—Because he is a worker, while we belong to the bourgeoisie.

—This is true, said her sister, but you have forgotten that above all we are women.

What worried her sister at the threshold of freedom? And Mrs. Vlasova, wasn't she a woman? Wasn't she older than they were? Lina was disturbed to hear her sister's defeated tone. No one said, when Mrs. Vlasova joined the socialists, that she was a mere woman. No one laughed at her when she began learning how to read and write at a late age. She wanted to mention to her sister many names. Natasha, the fragile woman who always read out loud during the meetings. Sashenka, the strong willed woman who loved Pavel Vlasov. No, she didn't understand her sister's insistence on their gender being a hindrance. She remembered that, in all the political discussions she attended, a human being was always referred to either as poor or rich, owned or owner, but never as a man or a woman.

Lina stopped the record player and stared at her sister questioningly. At that moment, a noise came from the upper floor, and when Lina rushed to the balcony, she saw the soldiers below moving the furniture while a big truck stood in front of the iron gate.

—Rima, Rima, hurry.

—Nothing deserves my attention, said Rima as she glanced at the street.

—But the neighbors are moving, said Lina.

—Did we say hello to them? Did they say hello to us? said Rima.

Lina watched her from the corner of her eyes as Rima carried the coffee tray back to the kitchen. "And the key," thought Lina. "Will they give us back the key?"

The neighbors had been always there, but at the same time,

they hadn't been there. No one greeted them. No one invited them. They constituted a city within a city. Neither Lina's mother nor Bahiya tried to penetrate the icy wall which stood between the two worlds. But the neighbors didn't try either. The only messenger who crossed the threshold was the soldier, Saber. He used to come once in a while, his hand, as usual, on the pistol which dangled from his back pocket. He used to leave a pile of paper money in her mother's hands. She never counted it. And, without saying a word, he would leave, disappearing in the hallway like a specter.

During the long months Lina didn't hear anyone commenting on the neighbors' broken toilet, or door handles, or the floating water in the sinks. No one mentioned the possibility of going to the authorities, because the neighbors were the authorities, and no one was above them. Although Lina felt that her mother suffered from a strange feeling of persecution, she never heard her complain. All in all, Bahiya sometimes used to repeat a word that she heard from her brother: "The barbarians, the barbarians" every time her eyes fell on the captain's children throwing stones at one another on the sidewalk.

As the sun began to set, the street grew lively. Abu Amin poured a bucket of cold water on the sidewalk, and then spread his watermelons on a striped rug, hung his lamp on a branch of a tree as usual, and began to sing with a hoarse voice. The ice-cream vendor moved from behind his cart, and called to the boys who were scattered up and down the street playing ball, or shooting marbles. The butter vendor put his sleeves up and cut half a kilo of goat cheese for the fat neighbor, chattering with her endlessly.

Where did the sound of the violin die? Lina thought as she looked at the silent record player. Outside, cars blew their horns for the boys to disperse, and the big ball hit the fat woman on her head as she crossed the street.

At the entrance of the building there were new faces. And, in the midst of the confusion, Lina saw the captain give the apartment key to a man she had never seen before.

* * *

108

Lina stood excitedly on tiptoe behind the slightly opened door. She heard her mother say to Aunt Samiya with a voice full of worry:

—She grew up before her time.

—Who would remain young these days? said her aunt, puffing out cigarette smoke.

—But she is still a child, insisted her mother.

—A child who reads adult books? asked her sister Afaf mockingly.

Lina held her breath. She leaned against the wall. Her blood was frozen in her veins.

—Where did you find the book? asked Aunt Samiya.

—On her desk, said Bahiya.

She remembered suddenly that she had forgotten to hide one of Marx's books in the library.

—You are responsible, said Afaf to her mother.

—What do you mean?

—You let her fall under Rima's influence. Haven't we told you a thousand times it is enough to have one dirty Communist in the house? Afaf's voice grew louder. Lina thought that the passers-by in the street had stopped and were listening.

—God keep the evil away from us, repeated Aunt Samiya.

—Which evil? said her mother angrily.

—Don't you see that your daughter has been reading Marx, Max, Fax. . . I don't know his name, muttered her aunt.

—She will cause you trouble, said Afaf, laughing maliciously.

—Yes. She will cause us trouble, repeated Bahiya.

Lina heard her mother get up from the sofa. She was afraid the women would discover her hide-out.

—Oh God. Why does she want to grow before her time? said her mother, her voice choked with tears.

* * *

No one said a word to Lina at supper. The family was celebrating the return of her brother from the front line. She watched her brother-in-law, Hisham, smoke nonstop and stare at the sky.

—Ah, the tobacco! said his wife as she coughed.

—Is it from Latakia? asked Aunt Samiya.

—Latakia? Hisham gave a short, contemptuous laugh. Of course not, he said, it is American.

The servant was going and coming to the balcony carrying plates of fried eggplant, omelet, and salad, while Bahiya was busy setting the table and folding the white napkins into elaborate shapes.

—How much weight he has lost, said her sister Su'ad, pointing her finger to her brother who was sitting at the head of the table.

—From eating cockroaches in the army's soup, commented her aunt.

—Ssshh. Her brother put his forefinger on his lips warning of danger.

The smell of grilled chicken came from the kitchen. The cats were mewing on the neighbors' roofs. Lina amused herself by looking at her face in the silver knife and thought that the supper would begin in politics and end in politics. Suddenly, she felt tired and wished she could excuse herself by pretending that she had a headache or a stomachache or anything else. But she was afraid of the consequences. She expected her sister Afaf to comment on the book that had been on her desk, or to start a fight with Rima.

Everyone was waiting for the kitchen door to open and the maid to appear, carrying the grilled chicken legs in a big silver dish: Aunt Samiya sat at the extreme right of the table, far away from the hanging lamp which was swinging in the warm breeze, Lina's two married sisters sat nearby with their coiffured hair, bright jewels and endless whispers. Ahmad, her brother-in-law, was amusing himself by twisting his thick moustache as he sat comfortably on an easy chair. Rima bent her head to the left and began to tap her long fingers on the empty Chinese dish. Was she uncomfortable? Lina wondered, not wishing to look at her sister's chalky face.

The door creaked. Heads craned. Her brother-in-law Hisham put up his white sleeves.

—We won't need knives, he laughed. His belly shook.

Lina saw her brother look at her with half sleepy eyes, then turn to the servant and ask:

—Do you have a breast?

—Breast? Ha, don't you like legs? commented Ahmad, then laughed loudly.

Aunt Samiya frowned, then coughed a little. From the kitchen door her mother came, carrying a plate of watermelon and a small basket of white grapes.

—The chicken will get cold. Don't wait for me, she said, then turned towards the servant and asked:

—Did you get the Coca Cola?

Ahmad laughed loudly as he soaked a piece of chicken in the garlic and lemon sauce.

—Won't we drink something else? He pretended to be innocent. But when he saw Aunt Samiya shift about on her chair and mumble to herself "Forgive us, O Lord, forgive us, O Lord," he put the whole chicken leg in his mouth and began to chew, even on the bones.

Bahiya poured the cola slowly in the glasses. The servant walked around with a bottle of sweetened lemonade. Lina put her glass up in the air, smiled at Fatima and said:

—A little bit please. Then, after it had been poured, Lina pushed the glass to her mouth. The heat had already chapped her lips.

Her brother smacked his lips happily while cutting the chicken breast with knife and fork. After he chewed a little, he turned to Rima and asked:

—When will you start working in Aleppo?

—At the end of September, if nothing happens.

—What do you expect to happen? interrupted Su'ad.

Her brother's mouth was still full of chicken when he muttered with a low voice:

—A lot, a lot.

Bahiya reached for the chicken dish, lifted the heavy metal cover, then pierced her fork into a fat chicken leg.

—Is there any complaint at the border? whispered Hisham.

—Oh please, protested Aunt Samiya, who looked around in fear.

—No one will hear us. Su'ad held her shoulder gently, trying to calm her down.

—Since graduation day at the university the leaflets have been distributed to the officers encouraging them to revolt, said her brother quickly.

When Lina looked at her sister's face, she saw Rima smile for the first time while chewing a piece of fried eggplant slowly.

—And who will revolt this time? asked Hisham, rather worried. He wiped his mouth with his napkin and belched.

—Not the leftists? asked Ahmad. The words got stuck in his throat.

—Probably, said her brother briefly, putting his fork and knife in a plate full of bones.

Lina moved nervously on the chair. But when her eyes met Afaf's, she put her head down and pretended to be eating.

Su'ad put a number of tomatoes sprinkled with vinegar and oil on her plate, then raised her head slowly and said:

—Does that mean that 'The Big Brother' has lost control?

Lina remembered that her family had agreed to call the colonel "The Big Brother" to keep absolute secrecy. The image of the fat, short man shaking hands with the graduates came to her. His chest was decorated with scores of medals.

Bahiya stood up, clapped her hands for the maid to come, then helped her in changing the plates. Hisham took out his pipe.

—But you didn't eat enough, protested her mother.

—No. Thanks to God, I've had enough, said Hisham.

The smell of watermelon came out of the plates. The mouths began to move again. Then Su'ad asked her husband if he would like some goat cheese. He didn't answer because his mouth was full. He only shook his head positively.

—I asked my partner yesterday what will you do if the leftists take over? said Hisham as he puffed his pipe. 'Nothing,' said the man. 'He who marries my mother becomes my uncle.' Hisham laughed loudly, and then began to cough endlessly.

The maid hurried, brought him a glass of water. His wife ran towards him and began to hit him lightly on the back. Lina thought that some passers-by had stopped under the balcony and raised their heads.

—The man is wise, said Aunt Samiya. Everything is predetermined.

Lina saw her other brother-in-law shake his head and stuff his mouth with a big piece of melon.

Rima put her fork aside, then raised her head quietly. She had decided finally to speak.

—Were your evenings boring at the front? she asked her brother.

There was a long silence. The mouths stopped crunching the melon pieces.

—We played cards every night, said her brother contemptuously, and put his head down.

—Did you think you would do otherwise? asked Rima in a hoarse voice.

—Perhaps. But to see our enemies coming closer and closer to us every day and beginning to plough the No Man's Land, their automatic weapons directed to our heads, then to sleep soundly is something hard to swallow. Khalid's voice was trembling.

—The army's main concern is to occupy more houses and import Mercedes, said Bahiya.

Lina saw her mother put her forefinger on her lips and heard her whisper:

—Ssshh.

Aunt Samiya shifted about her chair nervously, then beating her chest she said:

—Why do we bring harm on ourselves?

Hisham put his pipe on the table, turned to Lina's brother and said confidently:

—If the Palestinians don't want to fight for their own country why should we fight for them?

The heads were frozen in one direction. Lina saw her mother get up, carrying the empty watermelon plate.

—The Palestinians today and us tomorrow, said her brother coarsely.

—And who said that, man? Ahmad laughed.

—The small land of Palestine is not enough for the Jews of the world, said her brother. Then he wiped his mouth and pushed his plate away from the edge of the table.

—Why do the Jews of the world migrate to our poor country? mumbled Afaf, putting on lipstick with one hand and holding the mirror with the other.

The men paid no attention to her.

—You spoiled our supper, said Aunt Samiya. God preserve our homes and forbid our dispersion. Then she pushed her chair back and belched softly.

—Amen, repeated Bahiya stupidly, then followed her mother to the kitchen.

Lina gazed at the lamp hanging from the ceiling. She felt as if the years were running backward. From the window pane of her classroom she had seen the specters of thin girls wearing rags, and when the pupils turned around, a question burned in their eyes, the Arabic teacher said:

—Do you see the Palestinian refugees?

She remembered that a child with a red nose and blue eyes asked curiously:

—Why are they poor?

—Because they lost everything, their country, their homes, and perhaps their fathers, answered the teacher, then she wrote on the blackboard: 'Palestine.' When she turned towards them they were trying to spell the word with difficulty. Before the bell rang, she pointed to the word again and whispered: "Engrave it on your hearts, children."

The kitchen door flung open, and the maid came in with a tray of coffee.

—I won't sleep tonight, said Aunt Samiya, raising her hand in protest. The maid stood confused, looking at the guests' faces.

—Is it too sweet? asked Su'ad, moving her elbows lazily on the table.

—No, mumbled the maid.

—O.K. then give me a cup.

—Don't you know that I don't like bitter coffee? Afaf stretched her head after she put the lipstick and the mirror back into her bag.

—I will make some more coffee, said the maid, then, leaving the small coffee cups on the table, the vapor rising in the air, she turned on her heels and left.

Before the servant disappeared behind the kitchen door, Hisham yelled:

—Don't boil the coffee too much next time. Leave some foam on it.

* * *

The summer passed by with its stifling breath. The watermelons began to disappear slowly from Abu Amin's carriage, and white grapes appeared instead. As the sun rose, the old man would hurry to the local fountain, fill his bucket with water, and return to his place on the sidewalk, where he would wash the grapes with affection and spend hours arranging them and decorating them like an artist drawing a picture. When the street became full of life, Abu Amin would stand, the buttons of his unwashed white shirt open, and he'd cry loudly:

—Oh sweet grapes. Who would buy some?

Lina used to wake up as he cried, and when she hurried to the window to open it she would hear the eternal dialogue:

—How much is the kilo?

—70 *qursh*.

—No, 50.

—50? The salesman would laugh.

—How much then?

—60. This is the last word by the life of my son Amin.

The haggling over the price would stop when the buyer heard the last word. Abu Amin would not lie when he swore by the life of his son. The old scale would clatter. One stone would replace another, then the grape vendor would wrap the grapes in a torn newspaper, his face beaming with joy. Lina would hear the money clinking in his hand.

The room was lit with sunlight when a moist wind blew in from the sidewalk, carrying with it the gossip of passers-by and the laughter of salesmen. As soon as Lina gazed through the shining glass of the square window and saw the flower vendor sprinkle sleepy bouquets of violets, she was overcome by a great desire to go to the countryside. She remembered that Aunt 'Aisha wrote from the summer resort "Why doesn't Lina visit us?" and Bahiya had commented then that "Lina liked to move from sofa to sofa and from book to book." She wanted to laugh out loud. She noticed her fat neighbor yawn lazily on the opposite balcony, pulling her hair pins as her eyes watched the street with curiosity.

—When will you have your breakfast? asked Bahiya as she opened the door and put her head half way into the room. The tea will get cold.

—What time is it? Lina asked, half asleep. Bahiya played with the golden chain around her neck nervously. Lina saw her squint, look at the small round watch which hung on a chain almost to her navel.

—After eight, she said and slammed the door angrily.

From the hallway came her mother's voice:

—Cover the cup of tea till she wakes up.

—Do you think she'll wake up? Bahiya's voice grew louder like a siren.

Lina rushed to the bathroom, carrying her towel and hair brush. In her haste she stumbled over the bucket of water and detergent the maid had put in the hallway. The water poured on the tiles. Fearful of Bahiya, she threw her towel on the floor and dried it carefully.

The windows of the house were all open, and the noise of the passing cars didn't die out for a moment. Lina shut the bathroom door behind her and breathed deeply. Will she put the wet towel on the edge of the tub or in the wash basket? And what will Bahiya say? How tired she felt! She didn't want to start a battle early in the morning. As she brushed her teeth, she thought of her eldest sister. Poor Bahiya, a woman with no occupation! She would enter one room and leave another carrying the duster. She would put this brass vase on the edge of the window, then would change her mind and take it to the table. She would switch the radio on, leaving it for a while, blasting everyone around, then she would put the volume down, forgetting that she actually had it on. One day Aunt Samiya was frozen in her place on the sofa. Her face was pale. She whispered, quite frightened:

—There is no power save in God. Is the Devil speaking with us here in this room?

Since that time, the family discovered that the radio had been on for many days. Now, whenever someone passed by, he would extend his fingers unconsciously to put the radio off.

There was a loud knock at the bathroom door.

—Yes? said Lina, upset.

—Still washing? asked Bahiya nervously.

—Yes.

—Shall we wait for you till noon? said Bahiya. When should Fatima clean the bathroom?

Lina dried her face quickly. In the hallway she saw her mother pointing at her silently to hurry to the dining room. She choked back her laughter, then said:

—I'll go today to see cousin 'Aisha in the summer resort.

—O.K., replied her mother. That'll be good for you before school starts.

The tea was cold when Lina lifted the wet saucer off the cup and put it underneath. Then she began to crunch the toasted bread. Her eyes were gazing at the olive bowl full of oil. When she moved her head a little, her picture quivered on the clear surface of the liquid. Suddenly, she thought of the small pool in one of the Zabadani's orchards and the naked peasant boys throwing water at each other.

She ate the fried eggs without any appetite, then cut half an apricot with her knife, pierced it with the fork, and swallowed it in one gulp.

—Did you prepare your bag? asked her mother, as she dried the Chinese plates and put them in the cupboard.

Lina took out a folded paper from her pocket indifferently and murmured while putting the pencil between her teeth:

—Will I need a sweater?

—If you sit the whole day on this chair you will not find a place on the bus, scolded her mother.

—But it's not nine o'clock yet, protested Lina.

—Really? Bahiya put her head inside the half opened door.

Instinctively, Lina found herself jumping from the chair, leaving crumbles of bread and white cheese on her plate, going backward on her toes and imitating Bahiya.

—Oh, the wicked. I'll break your neck,

Lina heard the ticking of the golden chain and her sister running after her, howling like a ghoul. She laughed, then she started hiccupping:

—Aaaa. . .

But before Bahiya was able to bend Lina's arm, Fatima came between them saying in a quiet voice:

—Aren't you ashamed of yourself?

When Lina slipped away to her room, and turned the key in the lock, she thought she heard Bahiya's hand give a terrible blow to Fatima's face.

*   *   *

The sidewalk was water-logged when Lina left home, carrying a light bag in her arm. She heard the gutters of the nearby houses moan as she walked slowly, carefully choosing her steps, and she saw the maids pouring buckets of water from behind the rails of hanging balconies.

She put her head down and hurried, stumbling over remnants of garbage. Her heart was full of bitterness. Bahiya's frowning face and Fatima's wet eyes came back to her. Then her sister's words got mixed up in her mind till they changed into a sharp screech. What made her into a scapegoat? Why did Bahiya pour all her bitterness on her? all her failure in life? Lina tried to dismiss from her mind those discordant echoes: her mother's muttering, her sister's cries, and the maid's whimper. But the echoes insisted and formed what was like a chorus playing constantly.

There were steps behind her all of a sudden. When she looked around she recognized the face of the boy who had been following her for more than half a year, standing under her balcony in the rain, in the wind, in the heat of August, raising his head like a Romeo waiting for a sign from Juliet, taking her to school at 8 o'clock in the morning, then coming back to see her in the afternoon. Although he never attempted to talk to her, she was sure he was yearning for even a slight sign from her.

His innocent face brought Werther's figure in Goethe's novel to her mind. Against her will, Lina found herself remembering with wild joy the memories of Werther's life, which was like a garden in which poisonous weeds grew and suddenly overflowed with the muddy water of the river and vanished.

She breathed easily, moving the bag from one hand to the other. Her home was far away now. A vague feeling came upon her when she started to descend the hill towards the river. The boy's face merged in her mind with that of the legendary "Crazy Lover," then she thought his breath was quickening and his arms became the eight legs of the octopus.

She picked up her feet and began to run. Cold sweat was trickling down her temples. As she turned behind, the boy's face had already disappeared into the crowd.

*   *   *

The driver took her bag and pointed for her to go on the bus. There were only five peasant women wearing bright costumes and some boys who were running from the front of the bus to the back, making a terrible noise. Lina sat by the window in the first row. She let the morning newspaper lie on her lap indifferently. A man in the square beat on his drum routinely, and a red rumped ape was dancing. People were watching. But the scene didn't make her feel better. She was bitter, and the reasons for her embitterment were both near and remote. She felt the years were stretching endlessly, and she was a prisoner of a world she hadn't chosen. A feeling of restlessness returned to her. She was afraid her vision would be blurred, her vague emotions would choke her. When the bus began to move towards the wide Beirut Avenue, she put her head against the window and wished she could sleep.

Through her half closed eye-lashes, the ghost of Werther came to her with his wet black clothes and big worn-out hat. When she stretched her trembling fingers to touch his weary eyes, she saw him jump into a wooden hearse and lie in it. The six men wearing black suits and gothic hats appeared. They pushed the hearse in front of them followed by red cheeked ladies. And in a certain grave the hearse was left to fall slowly. Lina heard the sound of a rope grating a bit. Then the wood snapped, and the funeral guests threw red roses in the hole while the rain dripped from their hats. Through the crumbling graves came a fat man. His face was wrinkled. He was carrying a spade in his hand. As the earth began to fly about, a monotonous voice came from the hearse, then it was muffled slowly. Lina saw herself sink down at the grave torn into pieces, frightened and shattered.

How much time had passed? She didn't know. She woke at the sound of a crying child while the bus was crossing a street lined with apple trees on both sides. The sun shone through the window, burning her face. Her sense of life's din outside and the fields bathed in the bright light made her sit straight and push away all the gloomy thoughts which had invaded her since morning.

How hungry she was! She thought, hoping there would be stuffed green peppers with meat and rice, onion, tomatoes and mushrooms at her aunt's house. As she gazed at the laden fruit trees in the remote orchards, she imagined her cousin 'Aisha standing there with a tray of baked apples decorated with cream and syrup.

The villagers' shops were half closed. The owners were lying lazily on the sidewalks under the warm rays of the sun. Flies flew around the olive baskets that were perched in front of the entrances without covers, or the wooden apple boxes crammed on top of one another.

She hurried along in the desolate street, moving her bag from one hand to the other. Peasants' wagons pulled by strong mules broke the silence once in a while; their old wooden wheels squeaked wearily on the paved road. How the grapes looked shiny and ripe under the sun and the peasants with their rosy cheeks and withered hands laughed around their earthenwares.

As she began to ascend the hill towards the house of cousin 'Aisha, a voice of a peasant singing came to her ears from a distance and, through the swaying foliage, she saw barefooted children run in the gardens and play hide and seek around flower beds behind a fence of mud houses.

The city was far away with its noise, smoke, and cigarette butts lying on the sidewalks, its tin cans floating on the river, the sweat of its inhabitants hurrying in the narrow lanes, its tanks rumbling past the sunken streets, the faces of its soldiers withered from the blazing sun. Lina saw a horde of storks fly suddenly toward the sky, soaring all at once. She followed them with her eyes and then began to run as if she were hanging from their long legs. She swung right and left as a hot autumn wind came to her face, but instead of soaring she felt like she was falling slowly and that the earth was opening up to swallow her into its dark labyrinth.

At the top of the hill she gasped in fear as a summer guest appeared on the edge of the fence, slowly promenading and issuing a dull sound with his walking stick. When she turned curiously to look at his face, his black hat cast a gloomy shadow over his eyes.

There was no grilled meat with onion and mushroom, nor were there stuffed green peppers with pomegranate sauce when she arrived at cousin 'Aisha's house. Everybody was having a siesta. The servant opened the door for her with half sleepy eyes.

—You, at last, she said, then took Lina's bag and asked her to come in.

The yard fountain was bubbling endlessly and the apple trees were laden with fruit.

* * *

Lina felt weary that evening as she bit into a piece of toast spread with butter and powdered with sugar. She felt Rasha's hand press on her elbow and saw Khadduj, Rana, and Omar surround her. Their eyes were full of smiles.

—At last you came, didn't you?

—One wonders though how you've left your books behind!

—But I want to see you.

—Oh, really?

—Yes, truly.

—Why do you talk to her like that?

How did the night mingle with the day? How did she forget the city? her friend Samira's image? the echoes of those heated political discussions? She didn't know. She just wanted to run in the fields, to listen to Rasha's trivial chattering, to fill her lungs with the air of the country.

—You're still reading Marx? Are you?

—Who?

—The philosopher.

—Why don't you admit?

—Mama said that.

—Well.

—But you are afraid.

—Afraid of you?

Rasha splashed water over her. Then the battle started. The three teenagers pushed her towards the fountain. Omar pulled at her dress, Rasha at her arms, while the servant watched and laughed out loud. Lina shivered as the slimy water touched her skin; she laughed shortly, trying to free herself from the hands of the two girls.

—Are you afraid?

—We'll drown you in the fountain.

—Come on.

—You won't do that.

—O.K. You'll see.

Omar let her dress loose and ran towards the wall, trying to catch a small lizard. As his sisters saw what he was doing they began to jump up and down.

—The lizard. The lizard. Put it in her back.

Khadduj ran to calm the children. But the boy was faster than her. All hands clasped, feet kicked. Then everybody fell on the grass; the frightened lizard slipped away from the fingers and disappeared in the garden.

—Aren't you all tired?

—Who?

—You. All of you? Who else?

Kisses were exchanged, then voices grew louder with singing. And as the servant disappeared in the room to make the beds and spread the white clean sheets, the feet jostled one another on the bathroom floor, and the smell of soap grew stronger.

—Good night, said Khadduj.

—Good night, all of them said.

* * *

—I don't know, cried Lina, avoiding Rasha's persistent questions and quick steps.

—Is it possible that you haven't fallen in love?

—Why would you care to know?

—Aren't we friends?

—Do I have to expose myself in front of my friends?

—Why not?

—I don't know.

Lina stressed her last sentence in a soft voice, then began to run toward the hill leading to the vineyard.

"Why does she care to know?" murmured Lina to herself. "Why does anyone care to know?" "Isn't it marvellous to be without friends? to ascend the hill without anyone following you, or asking you endless questions, or feeling other bodies shoving you and competing even for your own steps?"

—But certainly, you're not going to remain an old maid like Bahiya?

Rasha's words rang in her ears. She imagined her friend's little feet transfigure into a hundred feet stamping violently on the pebbles, scrambling to reach the top of the hill.

At the edge of a broken fence, Rasha stopped her. She was gasping.

—Do you know what I read last winter? asked Rasha, then laughed loudly. I 've never told this to a living soul. It was January, or February. I don't remember. I saw by chance an unabridged copy of the *One Thousand and One Nights.*

Lina turned quietly to her friend. It pained her that only a couple of minutes ago she had thought of pushing Rasha out of her world.

—I was alone in my room. The wood was crackling in the stove. When my mother put her head in the door, I told her instantly: "I don't want to be disturbed." "Really?" said my mother, astonished. "I have an exam," I said, quickly trying to hide the book under a heap of papers. As she disappeared in the hallway, I ran to the door, locked it quietly, then sat flipping through the old mouldy book. But honest to God, had anyone caught me that day I would have been done for.

—What is this serious thing you've read? laughed Lina and leaned against the fence.

—Well. After I'd read the tale of the Hashash with the upper class ladies, I don't know if you have read it, and I laughed at the man while he roamed around the black stone in Mecca and cried: "O Lord I ask you to cause friction between my beloved and her husband, so I could make love to her." I was bored a bit, but suddenly something caught my eyes. It was a tale entitled " The Disease of Lust in Women and Its Remedy." All my senses were alerted, and I began to devour the pages. The heroine of the tale is the daughter of a sultan. But she is very different from the other heroines I know of.

Rasha uttered a devilish laughter and began to rip the grass nervously and tear it to pieces.

—What do you mean? The tale began to interest Lina.

—You know what I mean. Rasha's childish voice rang excitedly.

—Is this the secret? asked Lina, feeling disappointed.

—No. Of course not, murmured Rasha apologetically, lifting

her head as if gathering the remnant of her courage.

—Well. I'll tell you the story from A to Z. When my mother disappeared in the hallway, I locked the door, and I sat next to the fire reading the tale of the Sultan's daughter who fell in love with a black slave. He deflowered her, and she was crazy about doing it to the extent that she couldn't go one hour without it. When the girl shared her secret with one of the servants, she was told that nothing like the monkey could make love to a woman, so she got herself a monkey and made love to him day and night till her father found out and wanted to kill her. The tale told of how the girl disguised herself in a Mamluk costume and fled to Egypt. There she stayed in the desert. Everyday she used to buy meat from a young butcher, then she would go home to cook for herself and the monkey. After they ate, she would bring the wine and they would drink it. Then, she would take off her clothes and the monkey would make love to her about ten times till she swooned. As I reached this part of the story, my heart was beating violently. I let the book slip from my lap, hurried to the door, made sure nobody was there. Then I found myself lying on the bed, taking off my panties, putting a pillow between my hot legs, and moving madly. Rasha was suddenly silent. She hid her face between her hands, and she began to sob.

Lina couldn't say a word. The story had stunned her. In front of her stood the figure of Rasha with her full breasts and long legs, all reflected in the images of other girls she had often seen loitering in front of doorways, their eyes full of loneliness. Through their coquettish gestures and hoarse voices she found herself groping like a bat in the darkness for her own soul.

—Do you despise me? asked Rasha after a while. Her throat was swollen, her eyes red.

—No, said Lina briefly.

—But you are a liar, a liar, said Rasha and hit the muddy fence with her fist, then ran quickly towards the foot of the hill.

Lina attempted to follow her and called imploringly:

—Rasha, Rasha.

But the girl didn't turn back to look. Her figure grew smaller and smaller till nothing was visible except her long black hair billowing in the wind.

Why didn't she say something to her? Why didn't she console her? She regretted it and wished she could learn how to open her heart to other people. Suddenly, she felt as if a hand was severing her head from her body. Then she saw, as in a dream, her head floating on the water decked with thorns. As she gazed into her own dark eyes, she issued a soft sigh. Was her face the face of a priest with its pallor, wrinkles, coldness, and rigidity? She wanted to flee from her silence, from the grapes lying lazily in the vineyards like eyes of glass, from the mountain picnic that had become a frightening nightmare. But as she began to run in the dusty paths, leaving behind the sodden drenched fields, the face of Helen who launched a thousand ships and the burnt Troy towers came back to her, then Faust's words: "Make me immortal with a kiss, O beautiful woman" rang in her ears.

On the shoulder of the road that led to the valley, Lina stopped in front of a small white house, trying in vain to drown the obscene images that burst around her from nowhere and made her blood boil. How much she wanted to sin, but she was afraid of something unknown, of those winding vaults which pulled her to the womb of the earth.

She closed her eyes, lest she see the scrawls which she often read on the dirty walls of toilets in her school. She closed her ears, lest she hear the immoral laughter which awakened demonic desires in her. Suddenly, she felt her throat swell, her face flare. As she looked around, the fields were deserted and from the muddy earth came the smell of dung.

She stood silently in the middle of the road. The image of the violet-eyed, brown haired boy traversed her memory, but when she waved her hand faintly to clear the coming fog from the valley, she felt like he was standing next to her after a year of estrangement, his face shining with wild joy. She wanted to bury her face in his chest, to feel his strong arms, but a peasant woman dressed in black appeared from nowhere, crying into the hills after her lost goat.

Lina hurried away. Her heart was beating with disappointment. The sun started to set.

—Good evening, the woman said to her.

—Good evening, murmured Lina unintelligibly.

A herd of sheep passed by. She heard the tinkling of bells on the necks of the bony cattle, and through her wet eyelashes she saw herself soaring in the heights, like the legendary bird her grandfathers had called the phoenix. How many years had passed? Five hundred? Six hundred? She couldn't remember. But she felt her wings were burning slowly and the fire was scorching her young face. When the wind blew and scattered the remains of her ashes into the universe, she was resurrected anew, and she wished nothing but to fly.

*   *   *

Lina leaned her head against the entrance door one cold autumn morning. Her eyes were full of tears. She watched the car that took her sister Rima roll on the gravel and then smoothly drive onto the asphalt road, passing scores of closed shops. Her mother was standing on the sidewalk, waving with both hands.

—Write to me.

The words of her sister rang in her ears. Then there was complete silence. At the top of the stairs stood Bahiya; her hair was tousled; her eyes reddened from weeping.

No. She won't waste her life among old women, Lina thought. A feeling of abandonment invaded her suddenly. She didn't believe that her sister could leave her alone. But when she slammed the gate and began to ascend the stairs, she was afraid she would never get out of her cell.

Morning will come; evening will follow. The maid will go on scrubbing the floor once with a sponge, another time with a piece of cloth. Bahiya will tell her: "There is no water in the bucket," and the maid will answer protesting: "There is water." Bahiya will pour more detergent in the bucket and will smile when she sees the powder float on the surface of the water and begin to bubble.

The maid will lift her rough hands, look with expressionless eyes at Bahiya's finger pointing to the tiles. When mother passes by and cries desperately: "Cleaning, day and night?" Bahiya pushes her contemptuously and says: "And who will clean the house? Sit on the sofa and give us your silence." Lina will see her mother shuffle her feet on the floor as if walking to her grave, then she'll hear her murmur to herself from behind the open door: "What have I done to you, oh Lord? What have I done?"

There was a sudden bitterness in Lina's heart against Rima. She wanted to run barefoot in the street to stop the car that took her to Aleppo, to the other world. Lina didn't wish to think that she would sit one day on the sofa like her mother, blaming God. Her mouth was full of laughter. She will read Plato's *Republic*. She will underline the just city described by Marx. As soon as she gathers her thoughts, she will not let chaos rule her life. But the commanding voice of Bahiya yelling: "Scrub the floor" still rang in her ears and the maid with her clipped hair and hunched back still bent, sweeping the floor endlessly as if under the curse of a wicked witch.

Everything around her is hostile, revolting and ugly, she thought as she slipped under the warm sheets. She wished to sleep and to forget the world. But these fragmented visions, these remnants. . . What should she do with them? Nothing is logical. Nothing. Her sister has left her alone now. In her despair she buried her head under the pillow as if fearing to confront the world anew.

*   *   *

The idiot's voice woke her. As she got up lazily and pulled back the heavy curtain, the glare of the sun poured into the room. From behind the dusty window panes she saw people gathering in a circle around the idiot and clapping. Her eyes fell on the old fortuneteller coming towards the square, pulling her patched red dress and howling at her seven dogs. As she opened the window, children ran to the woman screaming in nasty voices: "Hello,

hello mother of seven dogs." The woman chased them away with her kerchief, which was like a broomstick.

The people made a place for the woman. Her dogs sniffed the tail of her dress, their tails erect and swaying merrily.

—O fool, shouted the butter vendor as he tightened the belt of his baggy trousers, what did you dream of last night?

The people's heads swayed like cornstalks in the fields. Then they cried at once:

—Oh fool, oh fool.

Lina looked at the street. In the glare of the sun she could distinguish with her weary eyes the neighborhood fool limping in the midst of the circle, opening his mouth wide and gazing at the hostile faces like a wounded bird. The shoeshine boy approached him, loosened the rope that tied his arms to the back, then returned to his place. The fool began to jump in the air, and everybody clapped. Even children stopped paying attention to the fortuneteller's dogs. They lined up behind the adults, trying with their small heads to look through the circle.

—In the country of Waq Waq, said the cross-eyed fool winking and laughing loudly. The mountain's inhabitant will travel, cross the rivers and the valleys. He will have his hands on his head. In his pocket there will be a crooked knife. A waterskin will dangle from his neck. His shoes will float on the sea, but he will walk barefooted.

—Won't his feet bleed? asked one housewife ironically as she carried her basket laden with vegetables, prepared to leave. The fool ignored her. He was dancing in the circle like a dervish who had lost his soul in his love for God.

—The mountain's dweller, did you say? asked a short man putting his hands on his bulging belly, perplexed.

—The vision comes from God, said the fortuneteller, as she nudged the man.

—What do you know about God? asked a narrow-eyed woman.

The fortuneteller trembled with anger. As she turned halfway, ordering her dogs to be quiet, her blue tattoo looked like it was expanding under the glare of the sun and devouring her right cheek. Suddenly, a man with twisted moustache stepped forward and addressed the fortuneteller:

—Quiet. Let's hear the fool's dream.

The cross-eyed fool didn't see what was happening around him. His fearful look was lost. In its place was a more confident one, perhaps a bit dreamy.

—The killer will be killed. This is the law, said the fool.

—Who is the killer? who is the killed? asked the fortuneteller, gasping and beating her bosom with her fist.

—Don't listen to him. He's a poor man. A policeman stepped forward and yelled ironically as he played with his thick stick.

Lina listened carefully. Her heart was throbbing without an apparent reason. Then, she saw the children run to the fool as he carried a bird in a cage and sang in a dreadful voice: "My bird. My bird." Someone threw something at his back; then laughter grew, as the fool began to run around the circle madly trying to get out of the trap that others had set for him. But as he stepped forward, the crowd pressed together and vied in rubbing his ears or slapping his face or spitting on him.

Lina pressed the window with her hand. Her throat swelled. She didn't know what she could do. Many people passed under her window and close enough to the circle, but they never showed any interest in what was happening. Even the policeman did not differ from the others. He seemed amused by the beating of the fool.

The muscles of Lina's face became contorted as she saw the officer with the puppet face pass the crowd slowly without looking right or left. For the first time she saw his tightly buttoned suit. His expressionless face made her think of Rasha wearing a white dress covering the knees and standing in the wind at the hill leading to the vineyard, and she heard her say: "You are weak. You'll die before us all. I am strong, because I don't pity other people or burden myself with their worries."

The ring began to break down. Lina saw the bird's cage fly from one hand to the other, and the fool stretch his arms in the air like a beginning ballet dancer trying to retrieve it. The man with the twisted moustache opened the cage's door and laughed loudly. Through the narrow crack the bird escaped to the roof of the opposite white house, then disappeared in the air. It was as if a magic hand had changed the fool into a wild beast. As soon as he saw his bird and lonely companion fly away, he attacked the crowd, howling like a wounded animal. The people then began to move away. Their laughter echoed in the street.

On the sidewalk, Lina saw Abu Amin shuffle his feet, then kneel next to the fool, hug him, and sob.

*   *   *

It was 3 o'clock in the morning. The rain was still pouring on Abu Amin's carriage, which was covered with a heavy sheet of plastic, and the cold wind of February caused the window shutters someone had forgotten to close to moan endlessly. On the dressmaker's threshold, the fool slept covering his head with a thick canvas while Abu Amin stood in the dark square staring defiantly at the green light which came from the minaret of the neighboring mosque.

He looked around carefully. Then, on tiptoe, he walked toward the sidewalk, removed the plastic sheet from his bed, and took out a half broken umbrella. He touched it joyously, then opened it. As some of its wires appeared and the loops broke, he closed it again. He stretched his arm under the plastic sheet and got an old hat with no edges. He stepped forward twice, exchanged the umbrella with the hat, the hat with the umbrella, then looked around him. His head was dripping with water. There was thunder. He opened the umbrella and stood in the middle of the square. Suddenly, he felt as if the graves were opening beneath his feet. He began to run madly; the umbrella went up and down, the rain beating it violently like a devil striking the twelfth hour on judgment day.

The wind blew his hat from his hand. Then the air filled the umbrella till its ribs bent outwardly. When he tried to close it, there was a frightening squeak. A shower of water scattered across his eyes. He issued a vulgar curse, but at that moment the voice of the muezzin was lost in the thunder and fire.

Bom, bom, bom.

He pointed to the light behind the minaret. Then he wiped his forehead with his wet shirt. His eyes were wide.

—Cities buried under debris, he said in a hoarse voice. Children are hunted like rats and Your lemons fall from the sky and burn the wheat, the sickles, and the people. Why do You want more than that? And why do You pretend You are a just king?

He raised a threatening fist in the dark. But a mixture of thunder and bullets stifled his cry. Whispers through the lanes leading to the mosque grew louder:

—Oh Lord, hide our sins.

He threw the broken umbrella, pulled the hems of his baggy trousers to his knees and began to wade into the water. There was lightning then, and the graves opened up. His son Amin ascended on the back of a horse from a razed grave with no tombstone. His face was shining like the moon. As the grieving vendor ran to touch his dead son's hand, he heard a voice coming out of the bowel of hell: "Do not despair, Abu Amin. Your son has come back as the king of Syria."

* * *

Laughter filled the air as Lina began to ascend the hill on her way to school one cold morning. Flags fluttered on balconies, and military music blared from loudspeakers erected in the streets. People crowded around the newspaper-stand to read the bold headlines printed in red: "Fall Of The Military Dictatorship," "The Druz Mountain Put An End To The Dictator," "Alliance Of Progressive Forces Opens A New Chapter In Our History," while others loitered on the sidewalks listening to the broadcaster's voice, their hands in their winter coat pockets and their shoulders raised from the cold.

The dairy shop was empty when Lina stuck her face against the window to see the time. Her breath fogged up the glass. She could distinguish no one but the old man as he stood in front of the coal-filled brazier, warming his wrinkled hands. It was a couple of minutes to eight. Lina began to quicken her pace. She was surprised, though, for she didn't pass many students on her way. As she reviewed the day's time-table in her mind, the world suddenly blackened before her eyes. Eight o'clock mathematics. Nine and ten o'clock Arabic Language. Eleven o'clock religion. She saw herself yawn as she imagined herself sitting at her uncomfortable desk for two hours for the Arabic language class, listening to the teacher's monotonous voice as she explained Jarir's poem satirizing his contemporary Al-Farazdaq, trying to convince the class that the world had not known a satirist like the eighth century poet, writing up on the board long and boring columns of similes. She saw her classmates' heads bow obediently as they began to write down important points: the occasion of the poem, imagery, meter, rhyme, and style. But there was something that bothered her. She didn't know why she had to memorize that Al-Farazdaq had short legs, or a hunched back, or an ugly face. There was nothing in this satire to make her laugh. Often, she preferred to turn her head toward the open window and follow the housewives with her tired eyes as they pinned up the washing on the roofs, or polished the window panes with threadbare rags. She secretly envied them sometimes. They had nothing to think about. And on warm winter days she often saw them sitting on their balconies coring zucchinis and stuffing them with a mixture of meat, tomato, and rice, or peeling potatoes and soaking them in water, or changing babies' diapers on faded mats. It disturbed her that whenever she bent over the desk trying to dismiss those female specters, the smell of wet, damp nappies filled her nose, and images of mouldy cellars assailed her across desolate gardens.

At the school gate stood the principal with the green spectacles laughing loudly as she shook hands with a number of teachers. From the bottom of the hill Lina saw a few girls descending toward her, brawling with their swollen satchels and their boots caked with mud. Then a car rushed past her, a red-headed girl stretching out of it. "No school today Lina. No school!" shouted the girl waving her hand. Before turning on her heel she saw Amal running toward her, holding her skirt shyly, her long black hair flying in the breeze.

They walked through the side streets to avoid the crowd. The pale sun had already dried the wet pavements. Cigarette butts, torn papers from some pupils' exercise books lay strewn along dirty gutters. As they passed the dry-cleaners, a very strong odor of chemicals filled the air. They saw boys not more than ten years old hang the clean clothing on lines stacked one after the other, their eyes heavy with sleep. As they crossed the road they came across a park with trees laden with rain. Lina breathed the fresh air and said:

—Aren't you happy?

Amal didn't answer. Her head was down. Her shoes rapped monotonously as she paced down the sidewalk to the gate. She stopped a moment before turning, then raised her eyes and stared aimlessly at the pruned trees.

—He was expected to fall, she said as if talking to herself.

—The Colonel? Lina asked as they were about to enter the deserted garden.

Amal nodded and bit her lower lip.

—And will they kill him? Lina asked.

—I doubt it. Amal was silent for a moment, then said sarcastically, but don't worry, he won't become a beggar.

—Who's worried? protested Lina, and she watched her friend's pale face become a small pool of colors in the sunlight. Then silence prevailed.

What was irritating Amal? She wished to know. Lina walked slowly toward a pond full of floating moss, kicking pebbles to hide her agitation. Through her half-closed lashes, she saw drops of rain dripping from the trees' leafless branches and falling onto her cold face. She stopped a moment, as if something had just crossed her mind. She searched in her coat pocket, then pulled out a pack of dried apricots and offered some to her friend. But Amal shook her head and smiled gently.

—Are you still going to the secret Communist meetings? Lina

asked, munching slowly but noisily on an apricot.

—No, Amal replied gravely. She clung onto the metal railing around the pond, as if afraid to speak.

—Fine then. What's the matter? Lina gulped down the spittle in her throat and felt her hands freezing.

—We can't agree on certain things. Amal murmured gently. She closed her eyes in a spasm of sudden despair.

—What things? What do you mean? Lina asked, astonished.

—Don't forget, I am Palestinian, Amal stressed every letter.

—Is there a contradiction between your being a Palestinian and a Communist? asked Lina.

—Maybe not, but there are positions I do not understand. It's something Raja told me. Do you remember her? She has short blonde hair and she wears thick prescription glasses. You met her a few times at the meetings, Amal said.

Lina nodded, trying to recall Raja's pie-shaped face. Then she found herself saying, leaning close to her friend:

—What did she tell you?

Breathing with difficulty, Amal slipped her hand into her pocket, then pulled out a white handkerchief and twisted it around her fingers.

—It was during the summer, Amal said, just at the end of summer when I met Raja after her return from an international conference held in Moscow. She travelled secretly via Lebanon. I ran up to her and embraced her warmly. I wanted her to tell me everything about the conference, about the proceeding and her general impressions. But she stood before me like a statue. Her face was sullen. Her eyes were narrow. 'If you think I'm going to tell you everything that happened to me then you're mistaken,' she told me in a horrid voice. I was very surprised at her dry tone. Wasn't the conference exciting? Wasn't Moscow beautiful? 'No. Not at all.' Then did you fall in love with one of the comrades. . . She didn't let me finish the sentence. 'Actually, I met some Israeli comrades,' she said almost mockingly. Her comment hit me like a thunderbolt. I felt like such an idiot. All these years and it never crossed my mind that there were Communists in Israel. I saw her spit suddenly, as if she were trying to loosen a knot in her tongue. Did she meet them in Moscow? 'In Moscow? Of course in Moscow, where else? Mars?' she said furiously. Then she turned to me and glared into my eyes. 'The head of their delegation shook hands with me, then asked me if I were Syrian. I said: No, Palestinian. 'Palestinian, eh,' he nodded and I saw a pale smile across his face. 'Well, well, I am Israeli.' I withdrew my hand quickly and froze on the spot. I didn't know what to say. We were both attending a peace conference, myself and the man standing next to me.' Amal paused. What could I have told her, Lina? She is a Palestinian like me. Maybe you don't understand what I mean.

Lina put her head down. She couldn't find the right words. Her friend's voice seemed to be trembling. She found herself saying foolishly:

—But they are there. How can we deny their existence?

—Who? Amal turned to her, sparks flying from her eyes

—The Israelis, Lina said in a soft voice.

—And I? And my people? We don't exist?

The question struck Lina's face like a burning flame. She hastened to say:

—I didn't mean that.

Silence prevailed. Moscow was one of the first capitals to recognize the establishment of the Jewish State on Palestinian soil, Lina thought mournfully. How could Raja not have realized that? Why the shock? As she walked slowly around the edge of the pond with her hands hidden in her pockets, gazing aimlessly at the stagnant water, the ghost of the Israeli delegate came to her across the wet paths. Was he born in Poland? Or was he from great Russia? She imagined him standing in front of her with his long overcoat and black hat. She heard him prattle with other comrades about the rights of man.

A rotten stench rose up from the pond, then it started to rain. Through the mist, Lina distinguished her friend's face on the other side, and read the resistance of the vanquished in her eyes.

* * *

136

The street was empty as they began to run, the collar of their coats turned up, their heads buried between their shoulders. A car passed them quickly, and the drizzle mixed with mud splashed around them. Before the car disappeared, the driver opened the window, put his head out and shouted mockingly:

—Huhu. . . .!

—The pig, murmured Amal.

Under the awning of the bean vendor, they halted for a while. They were trembling. Behind the glass, the customers' faces were blurred. Lina saw the vendor with the flabby muscles scoop the beans from a big pot, and pour them in earthenware bowls while the vapor blinded his eyes. They didn't say a word. How could she break the silence to convince her friend that she too felt like the castaway Palestinian? Words crowded in her throat then stuck again, like gum sticking to trees. As she tried to open her mouth, she could only whimper like a child. From the wet lanes, a fragrant wind full of childhood memories blew on her face. A caravan of refugees passed in front of her half closed eyes and the echo of a broken song came back to her:

Am I Your true son, oh Lord,

Or am I a foundling?

She tried in vain to remember the words. Had she heard them from a priest who lived in Haifa? The images were mixed in her mind. But the image of the man with the long black gown began to come to her across the bare trees that lined both sides of the street. Was he in a church? On the top of a mountain? Did she see him with her own eyes or had she read about him? No, she couldn't remember. His stern face returned to her, and she heard him chant in a hoarse voice as if he were a bloody God:

I will fill the hearts of the inhabitants of the land with
fear
I will destroy them all for your sake
But I will not do it all at once
lest the land becomes desolate
and the beasts of the field multiply against thee

Little by little I will drive them from before thee
until your spring be increased and you inherit the earth
And after I set thy bounds from the Red Sea to the Sea of Palestine
and from the desert to the river
I will deliver the inhabitants of the land into your hand
and you will drive them out before you.

She trembled a bit and imagined the man's head to be cut off his body. Then it began to roll down on the wet sidewalk. But his mouth was still opening and closing. The wind carried unintelligible murmurs. The wrinkled faces of the refugees, faces without bodies, crowded the trees, and she heard discordant voices like the eagles' sometimes, or the wailing of women at other times. But in spite of the variation in sharpness, all voices repeated:
Am I Your true son, oh Lord
Or am I a foundling?
Lina turned her head suddenly and stared into the eyes of her friend who was standing next to her. The rain had almost stopped.
—Shall we go? she said, rubbing her cold hands.
As Amal nodded, the door of the bean shop flung open and a man with a flattened head appeared on the threshold. From inside came the smell of pounded garlic.
They walked slowly across the wet street, reading the advertisements for movies stuck on walls, staring at the window shops filled with merchandise. The sun began to appear. In moments, life buzzed again in the city. Children came out of their sardine-like apartments and began to play football in the midst of the streets. Cars blew their horns in protest; drivers put their heads out the windows and cursed right and left.
As a young boy selling the daily newspapers passed by, Amal called him, then gave him a quarter. Lina stood in the sun, gazing at the pensive face of her friend. "What is left for her?" she thought. There was nothing to hold onto anymore, and she relaxed her tense fist. All meanings, all values had to be built up from scratch in the loneliness of her individual mind. A sudden

feeling came upon her, and she wished she could run barefoot. How lost she was at a cross road, but free at the same time from all the chains that imprisoned her in the past.

When a youth with thick black moustache passed by her, leaving a leaflet entitled: 'Workers of the world unite,' in her hand, she crumpled it violently and threw it in the gutter.

* * *

The train whistled. Feet shuffled in close succession down the corridor which divided the carriages, and the laughter of the children grew louder. When Lina stretched her head out the open window, a moist wind touched her face. Her eyes barely distinguished the conductor, whose head resembled a hazelnut, closing the doors and then jumping onto the steps of one of the carriages. The station platform was immersed in darkness when the old train began to move. The heads of the school children stretched out the windows and their joyful shouts echoed in the air. Above the squeaking of the doors, the clamoring of the engines, and the cries of the children, the singing of the night crickets could be heard rising up from the sleeping fields. Then Damascus began to disappear slowly behind the trees, and nothing appeared on the horizon except for part of the slope of Mount Qasyun decked with lights. It seemed to her that the ghost of Abraham was slowly climbing the mountain on his way to the cave where he was born. Then, she saw him stare at the stars. Was the story true? she inwardly asked herself. But she knew there was another cave which the common people called the Cave of Blood because its rock was still red from the blood of Abel, the son of Adam who was killed by his brother Cain. Where had she read that? She tried in vain to remember. Then she felt she had to laugh. The voice of her Aunt Samiya returned to her across the years: "Qasyun is holy, my daughter. Abraham prayed upon it, and Moses and Christ, even Job and Lot (may God bless them all and grant them peace.)" She could not understand her aunt's desire to make every river, every mountain and every plain sacred. The mere

139

idea of Abraham ascending the mountain did not make her love its big shadow towering over the city any more or less, nor its brown dusty peak, nor the stone houses clinging to its barren surface.

The train was swamped with primary and secondary school students. Each class occupied a number of specially-designated carriages; the teachers began to move around periodically from one place to another to keep order and guard against the possibility of any mixing of the sexes. Some girls, however, outwitted their teachers: whenever a teacher appeared behind the glass door, illustrated magazines would be pulled out, circles would form to sing, or literary discussions would begin. As soon as the teacher disappeared into the corridor, the laughter would rise, heads would pop out of the windows, and kisses would be sent through the air to the boys in the other carriages.

The conductor appeared and disappeared, opening doors and closing others. His silver whistle hung from the pocket of his blue faded jacket; a set of keys rattled in his hands. The girls would follow him from time to time, joking with him and stealing his blue cap with its frayed edges.

Then the dark grey air began to retreat towards the horizon. In moments the sun rose like a golden disk. Hands reached out for the baskets and bags. Cheese sandwiches were taken out, cups of tea were poured and can openers exchanged. Then some of the boys from the other carriages called out. Heads peeped out and fresh date pastry, slices of fried brain with eggs, and love letters passed from hand to hand.

—You're anti-social, said a sharp-toned voice.

When Lina raised her head it was Nuha, one of her classmates standing in front of her, carrying a basket of apples and pointing for her to take one. Before she was given a chance to answer, Wafiqa opened the door of the carriage. She was short in stature and had a head that touched her shoulders. Faces turned towards her and then Nuha said:

—Let's have a poem.

—Yes, yes, a poem, the others called out, and they began to clap their hands and bang on the floor of the train with their high-heeled shoes. Wafiqa didn't move. Instead, she closed her black eyes and put her hands on her stomach as if she was getting ready to pray. The girls suppressed their laughter and pointed towards Wafiqa, who stood motionless. Then Nuha moved a few steps closer and said in a mocking sort of plea:

—When will the bird sing?

The girls jumped off their seats and hit their thighs as if they were in hysteria and began to ceaselessly repeat: "A poem!. . . A poem!."

—Okay, said Wafiqa, slowly opening her eyes.

How Lina felt like lamenting for her. How she wanted to run to her and to shroud her from their teasing laughter. They joked about her short neck, and about her breasts clinging to her navel. They were not interested in her reading poetry or prose. But she remained immobile, and found herself nervously chewing her fingernails.

—In the solitude of the night I cry for. . ., the hoarse voice filled the carriage.

—You cry? Who do you cry for? The muttering rose and the gestures increased.

—Let her finish it, said Nuha.

—Oh my Helper, oh Helper of the poor.

—Allah! Allah!

Then without excuse or warning, some of them began to leave the carriage, or stand at the windows to shout at the boys, while the girl with the short neck stood reciting a poem about her love for God to empty seats.

The train quickly glided through the fields. The smell of the grass rose up from the wet earth. Mount Hermon appeared with its white "hat" forever against the line of the horizon. When Lina closed her eyes, the image of scores of anemones blossoming on the Golan Heights came back to her, and her nostrils were filled with the fragrance of the wild flowers bathing beneath the rays of the sun. The village of Al-Himmah glimmered in the dark corridor of her memory like an oriental bride laden with gold and silver. Then she imagined herself taking her clothes off on the bank of the Yarmuk River, her face wet with grapefruit blossom and her breasts covered with lilac-colored grass.

The seven mineral springs. There are Al-Maqla and Al-Rih. She began to count on her fingers. "Oh, what were the names of the remainder?" In the house of her cousin 'Aisha, with its small garden, there was a bathroom with a pool to which you descended down two steps, or maybe three. She couldn't remember. But the water from each of the three taps was from a different spring. One day her cousin had pointed to the tap with the red spot and had said to her: "Be careful, it will fry your skin." How weak she had felt the first time she plunged into the pool, and the smell was like that of rotten eggs enveloping all her senses.

There was a clamor of feet going back and forth. Darkness reigned as the train passed into the tunnel. Lina, in spite of the screaming of the students in the neighboring carriages, heard the noise of frantic kissing and she thought she felt an unknown hand groping for the backsides of the laughing girls. When the sun flooded the carriage again she saw a boy with dishevelled hair escape out the door, while Umaya, with her fat cheeks, sat next to the window, bashfully straightening her skirt.

How naive she was. Lina wanted to laugh, but she was choked intermittently with rage for several minutes; then was overcome by a feeling of desolation. From the sides of the hills, she was reminded of the image of her naked body, and the words of the boy, who stood summer and winter under the balcony of her house, rang in her ears. Her face burned suddenly with shame, and she found herself getting up from her place and running from carriage to carriage, searching for the face of a friend.

Around the doors of the train, boys jostled with distressed faces, carrying trays of evil smelling biscuits and bars of melting chocolate. They were shouting, "One for one franc!" Some of the pupils left a small piece of money in the pockets of the sellers without buying anything, while others ran searching for a shop which sold cold drinks. On the steps of the train, Lina saw the History and Arabic teachers beckoning the girls to come back and get in order. Then the railway platform was immersed in shouting, and the boys ran out to explore, carrying bags with camping equipment upon their backs. Some of the adolescents whistled, hanging about lazily with their hands in the pockets of their tight trousers in front of the girls.

*   *   *

—Lina, aren't you going to swim? one girl raised her head from under the water and shouted loudly.

Lina was standing at the entrance of the bath. The hot steam blurred her vision; the smell of rotten eggs filled her nostrils. She found herself putting her left hand on her cheek, opening her mouth widely and yelling:

—No!

The echo returned her voice mingled with the splashing of water in the pool and the laughter of the naked girls. She wished that Amal would hurry up in drying herself, so they could go to the fields. Sweat was pouring profusely from her forehead, and she felt her shirt sticking to her skin. When her eyes caught the girls' scattered shoes in the corridor, their bags and baskets, their underwear and socks full of holes, she was nauseated, and found herself opening the door and carefully putting her head out. But the cries of the girls in the pool forced her to close the door again. Through the lonely ray of sun coming from the bath window, she saw her friend Amal standing naked in the corner, her bosom polished like a mirror, her hair thick like night. The image of 'Unayza, the beloved of Imru'l Qays getting out of the brook in the heart of the desert came back to her: her complexion like the first egg of the ostrich, neither white nor yellow; her face shining like a lighthouse in the dark. Then she thought that she saw Imru'l Qays standing there after he hid the clothes of his beloved and her bathing companions, and when she looked around she heard him laugh like an idiot.

How foolish she was in her literary visions. It hurt her that she had never known pleasure in the company of other people, nor the lightheartedness of young girls in her age. Her childhood was dead, probably lost. She couldn't experience joy, or immerse herself in frivolous activities, or laugh with full lungs.

That shell! How much she wanted to destroy it, or let the waves play with it from within and without. Her life was always regulated, in spite of the rebellion that stirred in its inner hallways. She didn't care a bit if the waves pushed her fiercely and drowned her altogether. She wanted to loosen up, to laugh if someone splashed her with water, to tell a dirty joke, to forget everything she had learned about morality and immorality, even to mock Wafiqa, the girl with the short neck, to dabble with good and evil. But no matter how much she tried, how much she did, she remained priestlike in her heart: serious, dull, and with a moral philosophy.

*   *   *

Life was buzzing outside when the two girls headed towards the bank of the Yarmuk river. They passed by the white country houses. Boy scouts were pitching tents and working like a hive of bees: some fixing the tent pegs, others spreading the sleeping bags, some gathering hard sticks, others lighting a fire. No one paid attention to them. The two girls walked parallel to the rail track without exchanging a word.

The village was full of joy. And from the trees laden with grape-fruits, the voice of a singer came to them. The smell of grilled meat mixed with the scented herbs filled the air.

—If paradise be on earth, al-Himmah is its site, no doubt. If it be in heaven, then al-Himmah is its earthly counterpart, Lina found herself saying. Her eyes were burning from the flame of the red anemones on the fences.

—Paradise? And since when do you believe in it? asked Amal mockingly.

—I don't know, said Lina, but the yellow chamomile makes me dizzy, just like dancing makes a dervish forget himself.

—And are you going to be one of those beautiful women who look like hidden pearls in the oyster shells in order to excite the hearts of the pious men? asked Amal, who laughed so loud that Lina thought the singer in the nearby field had stopped singing, and that the red anemones had started to burn.

—No, said Lina bitterly, but the image of the garden with its flowing rivers charms me. Don't you see what I mean?

—No, said Amal coolly. The content cannot be separated from the form, and Mohammad's paradise with his men lying on rugs, wine glasses in one hand and the hips of beautiful women in another, cannot fascinate me.

—I didn't think of that, said Lina, half apologetic.

—Of course because the colors had charmed you. This is the difference between you and me. Don't you see? You are not a Marxist.

Silence prevailed. Lina suddenly felt like suffocating. She was bitter in her heart against the girl standing next to her. It seemed to her that the grapefruits were beginning to fall in the fields, and that the insects were eating parts of the fruits and making them look like gouged eyes. When she wanted to conjure the image of the chamomile to her mind, her eyes caught the cow dung on the desolate path, and the buzz of flies rubbing their wings on the stinking dark excrement rang in her ears. Then she turned to Amal and said:

—The question is political. Don't you see? Mohammad had addressed the unsophisticated Bedouins, telling them things they would like to hear.

But Amal didn't let her finish her sentence; she interrupted her by saying:

—Are you justifying Mohammad's behavior?

—Why not? The most important thing for the ancient Arabs was drinking. How could he have made them understand what paradise was? said Lina.

—Okay! Amal laughed curtly. But why do we have to buy his ideas today?

Lina did not reply. The image of paradise as depicted by the poet Al-Ma'arri came back to her. She heard the heathen poets mutter, joke, and quarrel without cease. She began to laugh. But when she looked around, her friend had disappeared. Through the long weeds the shriek of a bird, as if in its final agony, came to her ears, then silence fell. In the stagnant river, the apparition of a sailing boat appeared, then vanished. Suddenly, Lina started to run like crazy, the gnats dancing in front of her and veiling her sight. From a distance she saw her friend standing like a palm on the disused railway line, pelting the road that led to Haifa with handfuls of grass. At that moment Lina felt a fragrant wind like wine begin to blow from the sea, and the ghost of a train without passengers was crossing the fields.

* * *

The history teacher stood near the window, reclined against the white wall, her back to the light, her hands with long nails covered with bright red polish. As she spoke, her body, along with the golden chain that decorated her neck, swayed back and forth.

Lina sat at the front desk as usual. The supervisor made them sit in certain places from the beginning of the year, the short girls in front, the tall girls in the back. But the teachers sometimes used to change the plan that the supervisor had drawn carefully and asked a student to sit elsewhere, particularly if they discovered quite early that two girls were talking non-stop to each other, or could possibly start a commotion in the classroom, or they were copying from each other during the monthly tests. Lina thought that the girls who usually sat in the front seats were the brilliant ones, not only because they could listen to everything the teacher said, but because they were always the youngest in the class. They never flunked, nor were they preoccupied with the problems of love and engagement. Lina didn't want to accept this generalization altogether. There were other factors involved which made the girls brilliant. The opportunities available to a girl from a bourgeois family were nil, or almost nil for a girl belonging to the working or the peasant class. The face of a peasant girl full of surprise as the political science teacher brought in the recording machine one day came back to her. The girl who had recently come from Horan snuck in during the break to the classroom and touched the machine with horror, then fled as the tape began to roll and the voice of one of the political leaders, as if it were inhuman, roared, for she was not able to control the speed.

Lina's eyes followed again the deft movement of the history teacher's fingers, or the waning sunlight fading away from the roofs of some brick houses. The teacher's monotonous voice rang in her ears as she summed up sometimes gravely, other times mockingly, the history of the Crusades and how Pope Urban the Second one autumn day in the year 1095, in a field outside the city of Clermont, depicted to his audience the supposed oppression under which the oriental churches lived and encouraged the Knights of Christianity to invade the Holy Lands. The people threw their hats in the air and shouted in Latin: *"Deus Lo Volt."* They tore their garments into the shape of crosses, which they attached to their shoulders in imitation of Christ. The pope's appeal spread like fire in the south of France, in Lorrain, in Champagne, and into Normandy, and Flanders.

The voice of the teacher grew louder or became softer, but the tale always remained interesting and easy to understand. Unconsciously, Lina found herself draw on the open notebook in front of her pictures of heavily armed knights, their body armour was of mail, their heads were hidden under helmets with small holes around the nose and the eyes, and in their left hands they carried round shields. Her eyes moved madly from one crusader to the other as if trying to conjure in her mind one image of the frightening face she often saw in history books.

As the teacher moved towards the blackboard, the sunlight, which had been blocked by her posture, now poured into the room. Lina heard the swish of the teacher's long dress and her fingers pressing the chalk, then the sound of a nail scraping the board followed by sharp murmurs.

—Did they all come for religious purposes? asked the teacher, without expecting anyone to answer.

—Of course not. The reasons are numerous; they could be social, or economic. . .

Lina saw her scribble unintelligibly on the blackboard, speaking excitedly of the First Crusade, of the paupers who thought their journey would lead them to Salvation Path, to the New Jerusalem, coming down from heaven as if it were a bride adorned for her bridegroom, to its twelve gates, its light which resembled crystal jasper.

Lina bit her lips, put her hand on the open notebook as she realized that the teacher had spotted the drawing of the crusading knights; her cheeks began to blush. But the teacher smiled faintly and continued to speak, disregarding Lina:

—Had the pilgrims who were armed with lances and swords found the New Jerusalem? Had they obtained the reward as promised by their religious men? Had they cleansed themselves from sin by killing the Arabs, the owners of the land?

—The fierce summer heat was waiting for them, said Nuha giggling and cracking the knuckles of her right hand.

—And the sand storms, added Samira.

The class laughed loudly. Lina took advantage of the break and yawned. The image of the crusaders one stifling day in July came back to her. They were marching across the Galilean hill country on their way to Tiberias and camping in a waterless region. Their lips cracked from thirst; their eyes smarted from the smoke coming from the fire that the Moslems had lit. In her joy, the magic word "Hittin" rang in her ear, and she remembered putting the magnifier on the map of Palestine one time to see the small town west of the sea of Galilee and to recall in her memory the ghost of Saladin surrounding 18,000 of the knights of Europe, defeating them and capturing their king Guy. She wished she could remember the exact date but she couldn't recall numbers, not even the number of her house, or the telephone. She hid her laughter and tried to convince herself that the battle of Hittin had taken place undoubtedly at the end of the 12th century. Eight hundred years had passed. What a joke! She gasped as she looked at the friendly face of the teacher, and she heard Maryam with the childish voice whisper:

—I believe that history repeats itself.

—What do you mean? asked the teacher. Her eyes glowed with strange joy.

—The knights of Europe, muttered Maryam, they come to us once with crosses on their chests and once with the stars of David.

There was silence for a while. The girls' heads were down.

Then the teacher moved towards Maryam. She knew that the little girl was born and had grown up in the city of Haifa. She said to her, in a warm voice:

—Do you believe that?

The girls' heads turned to Maryam who was sitting in the fourth row. They noticed her pale face and tearful eyes. Some whispered; others laughed. Wafiqa put her finger in the air. But the teacher didn't look at her. She stood up and began to croak like a frog: "Please, teacher, please."

The teacher held her history book, flipping its pages in embarrassment, then she gazed at Maryam's face and said:

—Why do you interpret history as a personal event? A tale like all other tales?

Maryam did not answer. Her hidden emotions exploded without a warning. Through the fading light of the sun, Lina saw the dark skinned girl rush outside, hiding her face with her hands. Suddenly, she felt that the frightful net of "History" was stretching across the continents and oceans to swallow her. The bell rang. Books flew in the air; laughter mingled with the clinking of golden bracelets. And in the long dark corridor, the city of Jerusalem appeared to her with its twelve gates like a bride awaiting her bridegroom. In front of the shining ramparts, tall men with broad shoulders stood; each one of them held a golden ring and a key made out of brass. When she asked silently about the eternal groom, elbows jostled, necks craned, and noise grew louder. Suddenly, she felt she was suffocating, so she started to run. Her heart was throbbing. Cold sweat trickled down her back. Then, she thought that the ghosts of strange looking women wrapped in black were following her wherever she went. She wanted to cry, but something pulled her to the womb of the earth and tangled her hands and legs.

Through the holes of that net in which she found herself captive without a crime or a choice, she heard the clinking of the suitors' swords in front of the bloody city's ramparts.

* * *

149

The playground was crowded with girls. Noise drowned the tiled roof of the school. On a table close to the door Zahra, the girl with the thick spectacles and the visible Adam's apple, stood holding a long roll of paper bearing irregular scribbles, showing it to everyone who passed by, quickly answering all questions and offering her pen to the questioners, insisting they should put down their names and addresses.

As Lina walked across the crowd, the voice of Nuha came to her from behind:

—Have you signed?

—Signed what? asked Lina.

Nuha's face burned with excitement. She pulled Lina blandly like a child and said to her pointing to the worn out paper:

—To eradicate illiteracy.

—Who supervises the program? asked Lina.

—What is the difference? Nuha's voice was angry. Her upper lip curled up to reveal her incisors.

—Because I want to know, said Lina quietly.

—Okay, the Ba'th Party, answered Nuha.

At that moment, Zahra came towards them and gave Lina the pen, saying:

—You don't have to be a member of the party. Her Adam's apple jogged up and down. She was trying to smile.

A small ring of listeners closed round in a minute. Questions were asked; answers were mixed up. Suddenly, the rosy-face of a girl thrust between the shoulder blades of Zahra and Nuha glancing from one to the other catching the flying phrases in her flat sugar beet-like ears. As Lina turned around to call Amal who was standing at the door, a short, thin girl rushed to the ring and said in a sharp thin voice:

—But the Arab Nationalists do the same thing.

All heads turned towards the hunch-backed girl with the black hair. Her eyes were tiny, like rats' eyes, and on her face was a smirk. Nuha jerked her shoulders and without looking at the thin girl, said:

—We don't deal with the Arab Nationalists.

—This is strange, said Lina. The scene amused her.

Zahra gripped the thin arm of the girl, and without paying attention to Lina's remark, said breathlessly:

—You belong to the Bourgeoisie!

The girl struggled to free herself from Zahra's fist, but in vain. A thin foam hung on her lips. She continued to say:

—Of course, we teach the illiterate how to read and write 'not Communism'.

A thin voice came from the ring:

—Ha, ha, ha!

The girl standing next to Lina whispered in her ear:

—But their aims are the same. Aren't they? Unity, freedom, and socialism.

Lina laughed, but didn't know what to say. Some girls began to withdraw quietly from the ring, and she heard one say wearily:

—Ah, let them fight from morning to dusk. The matter doesn't interest me in the least!

Zahra relaxed her grip on the bony girl and let her run like an arrow outside of the ring. Then, watching the girl run away, she began to speak with energy and confidence this time. She mentioned the problem of illiteracy, especially in the villages, the difficulties the volunteers encounter in attracting a greater number of women, the peasants who believe that reading and writing are unnecessary luxuries.

A dark girl raised her hand in the air and bleated like a sheep:

—Cheers to the party.

No one paid attention to her. Meanwhile, Wafiqa, the short necked girl, stepped forward, enunciating her letters clearly:

—Had you taught the Quran, the peasants would not have thought that learning was a luxury.

Laughter grew loud. Lina saw the lame girl nodding her head approvingly, and she heard her mumble to herself:

—This is true; this is true.

—All we need are the Moslem Brothers! Nuha said, smacking her lips. Is this what you want us to do?

—God preserve us from the infidels, said Wafiqa. She stressed each letter till her golden tooth showed.

Lina blushed. She couldn't listen to this bickering anymore and didn't understand why the girls did not attempt to convince one another instead of mocking and wounding. As she turned on her heels to go, she heard Zahra say in a soft but querulous voice:

—When shall we separate religion from politics like they do in the civilized countries?

—We won't let you do that except over our dead bodies, yelled Wafiqa jumping in the air. Her eyes were full of flames.

Lina withdrew quietly. She was feeling sick. She imagined a ship without a captain sailing aimlessly; her passengers spoke different languages and each one of them wanted to steer her. In the midst of the issuing confusion, the winds blew and the ship drifted toward an iceberg. As the dark fell, a visitor with a spongy face arrived. His cloak was black and fluttering. Before they fell on the ground, they cursed each other, they spat in each other's eyes, then they turned their faces to the stranger and they lay down on the ship's floor like rotten corpses.

At the top of the staircase, before she could push her way through the throng of students, Lina turned in the direction of a voice who said to her:

—You are an independent thinker. But by withdrawing into yourself, you belong with those who don't care.

Lina recognized the face of Samira. She waved to her without saying a word and began to descend the stairs quickly, as if running away from an inferno.

No, she won't let anyone buy her soul, she thought. The sweat dripped from her forehead. The image of priests in the Middle Ages came back to her. Their long robes fluttered as they roamed from village to village, showing people the salvation documents and promising them paradise. In the midst of her confused thoughts, the girls around her took different shapes of dusty-footed priests carrying parched papers and ran after her to tame her by force.

She hated violence in all its forms. But the mental violence surpassed everything in her view. She could not get used to living with it or to accepting it. She was confronting it daily in her home, in her school, in society at large. All she wanted was to grow alone, independent from anything that could exert pressure on her mind or deform it. But the figures who always ran behind her, always trying to tame her by any means, were disguised in different clothing and behind different masks. Where should she start and where should she end? Her mother sometimes, Bahiya always, her brother, her brothers-in-law. She put her head down as if the world were falling upon her. And she remembered the words of the principal when she had given the girls their final marks at the end of the year:

—Life is full of chains. We have to accept them, she told them, nodding her head with certainty.

—Chains? Lina had repeated, then found herself biting at a small pencil. Anger choked her. She swore secretly not to surrender. As she watched the girls step forward like lambs, their heads down, their cheeks pale, she thought the principal's face had changed into scores of familiar faces around her. She realized then what the word "chains" meant, and she began to laugh. She always had to say "YES"; she had to accept everything her mother said, or Bahiya, or the religion teacher, or the party girls in the school. She had to obey. She was not supposed to think or argue. And if she was allowed to think, then she had to take the decision of the majority as her own. The group was over the individual, the family over everybody, and the men were the ones who form the consciousness and values of the nation.

At the bottom of the staircase, Lina passed by the principal who seemed to be trying to escape from the religion teacher who was conversing with her earnestly. The principal's body was bending, her left foot to the back, her right foot in the act of moving while she gathered the edges of her long skirt about her for the ascent of the dusty stairs. Lina heard her say nervously:

—Alright, Mr. Karkutly. Whatever you see suitable. Undoubtedly.

As Lina began to cross the corridor, a voice called her:

—Where are you going?

Before she turned, Amal, who had been running from the opposite room, stood in front of her, panting.

—I want to walk, whispered Lina.

—And the sport class? Amal tilted her head. Her long black hair scattered across her face.

—I have no desire to attend it, said Lina. She began to walk quickly towards the door.

—Wait for me, called Amal, then she rushed to the classroom to look for her bag.

The doddering porter was sweeping the corridor as they passed by. He didn't notice them. Then they saw him stand for a moment, leaning against the stick of his broom, wiping the sweat from his forehead with a dirty handkerchief and staring out one of the open windows.

They crossed the road without saying a word to each other. As they neared the curve, Lina could hear the thud of the ice-cream pestle at the big wooden barrel go up and down and the smell of the peeled green pistachios mixed with sugar and walnuts filled the air.

—Shall we go to the old city? asked Amal as they passed by the shop of the wine seller. The bald-headed Greek was dusting the wine bottles in the window with an old feather dust bin.

—Okay, said Lina.

The crowded bus was about to move as the two girls pushed the door and lightly jumped inside. There were no empty seats as usual. The conductor with the thick black moustache came towards them, pushing people with his elbows, yelling in a husky voice:

—Please! Please!

Lina put two piasters in his open hand and said: "Students" as she pointed to herself and to Amal, who was standing next to her. The conductor ripped two tickets quickly, then said to Amal:

—Show me your I.D., beautiful!

The two girls exchanged looks as the man took the I.D. and examined the picture and the name carefully. The bus stopped suddenly. Many people got off, many got on. The conductor hurried away, glancing lustily at Amal, searching in his pockets for half piasters to pay to the irate passengers who claimed that he forgot or wanted to forget to give them change. In the meantime, a fat and veiled woman stood at the steps of the back door carrying a baby. Behind her rushed a group of school boys hitting one another with their worn-out leather bags. There were two men who wanted to get off the bus. One looked at her and said kindly:

—Ascending is from the front door, sister.

The woman did not pay attention. She pushed the man with her elbows, trying to keep the baby close to her breast. The boys ran behind her, stepping on everybody's feet and cursing each other in a vulgar language. The conductor yelled at them. Then Lina saw the two men jump to the street, their faces flushed with anger as the bus continued its journey towards the old city.

Her gloom returned to her. Restlessness began to eat her anew. No, she did not know peace in her soul. The noise of the boys annoyed her; their silly voices made her feel more than ever that she was different from others. She regretted having said yes to Amal to go to the old town. She dreamt of gardens that did not exist, more beautiful than the ones in the new suburbs. She was desperate to erase the horrible vision about the world around her, that squalor which spread like cancer, that chaos which enveloped everything. The image of Damascus with its long narrow lanes, its crowded shops with copper trays and jugs, curved swords, manuscripts written with gold water, embroidered tablecloths, and brocade appeared in front of her like a veiled bride, and as she stretched her hand to touch the silver bracelets, the vision became blurred, then disappeared.

Although the bus passed in front of a jovial array of lit up shops and young girls wearing light clothes, their arms hidden up to their elbows in baskets full of taffeta, velvet, and silk, the gloom did not leave her for a minute. Through the withered branches of the trees she saw Port Said Street with its modern travel bureaus, ice-cream kiosks, photographers, the theater which showed silly Egyptian movies, its cafes crowded with men smoking narghile and playing backgammon. The smell of the stagnant river, glorified by the poets throughout the ages, filled her nostrils. As she looked from behind the dusty glass window at the people flowing towards the Hijaz station, she thought that the city had escaped death. As her eyes fell on the antique clock of the station, she realized it was not working. A vague dissatisfaction grew within her and consumed her as soon as the bus stopped by the Ministry of Justice and people began to push each other. On the sidewalk, men in worn-out clothing sat at tables and filled out various applications for the illiterate customers, while some peasants slept on the ministry's steps and the sun burned their wrinkled faces.

*   *   *

The same huddled shops, the same hungry faces, the same drawn out accents, the same ugly odor, Lina thought as she walked next to her friend across covered lanes which hardly saw the light. At the corner, an old man with a bucket of olive oil in his hand was about to cross the street. He glared at them and then looked away, muttering in an angry voice:

—Good gracious.

The two girls hurried without looking back. Then Amal put her hand on her mouth to stifle a fleeting laugh.

—Did he see the devil in us? asked Lina perplexed.

Amal let her hand drop and laughed indulgently. Then she said:

—Women without veils. What do you expect?

The passers-by turned around. A fat woman with breasts dangling to her naval heard Amal's words. She stopped in the middle of the lane and beat her chest with her hand, muttering beneath her thick veil:

—God save us from the new generation. Then, she slipped away, gathering the edges of her long black coat quickly, as if fearing to be smitten by the plague.

—Is this the one you want to make a Marxist out of? whispered Lina mockingly as the black ghost began to disappear.

—Undoubtedly, said Amal confidently. You are a defeatist.

—Thank you for your kind label, answered Lina. But when are we going to witness the miracle? Soon?

—What a strange person you are! Could the revolution happen in a year's time? Or in two years? Amal gnashed her teeth angrily.

—And did the revolution take place? asked Lina.

—Of course. Look. Am I like my mother? Are you like your mother? she asked, then halted for a second as if trying to catch her breath.

—No. You are right. But the majority are not like us, Lina said, moving her school bag from one hand to the other.

—It is our duty to change them, said Amal. She stressed the word "duty."

—Change them? Lina repeated the words sadly. Then a tide of anger surged within her. How many years would she need? Change them? Ha. How could she make Amal see her frightening visions? Oh, that naive optimism, that fantastic resolution, without a clear plan, or a studied program, without wise leadership.

The remnants of torn advertisements on the walls hit her eyes. And in the midst of her doubt she began to read the words in a loud voice: "Vote for the Moslem Brothers," "The Syrian National Party needs. . ." Then, she was silent. The last word was torn and above it there was a picture of one of the candidates of the People's Party.

—Why are you so pessimistic? accused Amal. Don't you believe that the revolution needs time?

—Time, time. That's what you all say. But I will grow old. I'll be walking like a beast before I see anything change. Lina's eyes were full of anger as she pushed away her friend's sticky hand.

—Perhaps your children will see the difference, Amal smiled slyly.

—And who will guarantee that to me? You? asked Lina.

—No, said Amal. History alone will guarantee all that.

—History? Lina did not finish her sentence because a young teenager took advantage of the crowd and pinched her thigh. Another put his hand on Amal's breast. As the two girls turned, stunned, the teenagers melted away into the crowd of vendors and buyers at the end of the Hamidiya bazaar.

How much the idea of imprisonment had worn her out. She

was not able to wander in her own city on her own, neither in the crowded, nor in the deserted lanes. There was something threatening at all times. She couldn't defend herself against the fingers that wanted to violate her body by force. She was burning within, not because the boy had pinched her against her will, but because everything around her, in her home, in her school, in her city, followed the same pattern, the same style.

Lina saw Amal fix the collar of her blouse. Her face was contracted, her hands were the color of saffron.

—Did the boy hurt you? asked Lina. She had seen his hand press into Amal's breast.

—Of course he hurt me, replied Amal, but he is the victim of repression.

The problem of sex as Amal saw it was very difficult to solve, and she read about it in books. But she couldn't, honest to God, tell how it would be best solved. After all, she had other problems to think about. But she was sure the whole matter ought to be put in a larger perspective.

—Are you going to pay with your own life and person the debts the grandfathers had left behind? asked Lina.

—Undoubtedly, answered Amal. For the sake of a just society.

—And do you believe that the ordinary people would discard the idea that woman was the punishment and pleasure, an idea that had taken root at the beginning of mankind? insisted Lina again.

—Things usually change, Amal stressed her words.

—Why didn't they change all these years? Don't you see that all social forces were against change? Don't you believe that whenever one put up a ladder to ascend, the crowd gathered and brought him down by force? Lina continued to press.

—Nonsense, mocked Amal. A man's country comes first and we have no place for individualists, be they poets or mystics.

Lina felt the insult bitter in her mouth. How could she explain to Amal simply that their country was nothing but a cat eating its own children? How could she make her see the same dark bottom of the precipice that she herself saw? How was it possible for one to dream of a clear sky, full of stars, before one faced the real horror?

As they crossed Jupiter Temple, school boys were buying and selling old books in front of small bookstores on both sides of the street, while unshaven men dozed in the courtyard of the Omayyad mosque under the sun. Lina and Amal turned right and continued to walk in the midst of dark lanes with low roofs and adjacent shops. They saw the silk merchants measuring the colorful material with long rulers, cutting meters of velvet for the peasant women who stood under fading lamps, carrying their babies. And at the beads bazaar, they saw women busy trying on cheap necklaces. They heard the continuous sound of hammers and the bazaar of clogs with its shimmering colors loomed like a spot of light in the heart of a dark tunnel.

What was she seeking in her long search? Lina thought as she wandered with her friend from lane to lane and from bazaar to bazaar, as if something eluded her.

At the end of the gold market, she stopped and watched breathlessly through a half-opened door as an old goldsmith gently hammered the edges of a pure silver necklace. His face was lit by lamplight. She held her breath a moment in order not to disturb the man's creativity. She stared in admiration at the rubies which studded the glittering silver triangles. Wasn't the man like God in his posture? she thought, watching his long fingers play with the necklace. As she pushed her way clear to the store, she saw the goldsmith bend over an old table and use his thin pincer to fix the trembling beads of sapphires. Lo and behold, through his fingers the city of Damascus with its eight gates stood in front of Lina like a silver box. The eastern door flung open, and from the corner appeared a white minaret studded with emeralds and sapphires. Who was it that was supposed to descend at the end of the world? She wasn't sure, but the red stone was refined and pure, refined and pure as the breast of a girl in her twenties.

A wagon pulled by two horses, loaded with oil barrels passed by the jeweller's shop. The shouts of the driver and the rattling of the old steel interrupted Lina's radiant vision. Then the goldsmith raised his head. His gaze met her wet eyes and, without saying a thing, he bent again down to the silver necklace, polishing it and chiselling its edges. The sound of his file drew her back across the years, low and faint like the rustle of leaves, like the whisper of ponds, like the bells of a dream. As she turned around to leave, his face shimmered in her mind, and his necklace turned the narrow lane into a tunnel of silver. She saw her friend waiting for her at the sidewalk, closing her ears with her fingers, waiting for the heavy carriage to pass.

* * *

The smell of the dawn filled the room as Lina opened her weary eyes. Ah, the early summer! The light hit her face, but she lay still. A faint melody sang in her ears. A hidden spirit, pure as dew and swift as wind, filled her soul. She began her journey from the world of sleep to the world of wakefulness slowly, like a flower opening up as the light pours in.

Who had sat next to her on the bed and talked to her during the night? she asked herself, still in ecstasy over her enchanting vision. Didn't she see his face, which was fatigued by travel? Didn't she hear his voice coming across the desert?

The ideas poured upon her from every corner, vague like mist, confused like a dream. Then, she saw herself repeating nonsensical poems, a mixture of lines written by famous lovers. As she raised her hand a bit to remove the veil of sleep from her eyes and to hear her own voice, not the voice of others, deformed but enchanted pictures followed her and fluttered around her like storks, some without necks, others without legs. The boy with the lilac eyes and the brown hair appeared to her, flying on the back of a cloud. How had she lost him in the crowd of the city? How had she forgotten the smell of his clean shirt? She stared at his face as if staring into a clear mirror, but he laughed at her and fled like the wind. In her despair she hid her head under the pillow to keep from gazing at the empty void.

Where did the poems that rang in her ears at dawn disappear

to? And why did her tongue stumble through broken rhythms, stutter, and then stop? She began over and over, repeating the first line. The noise of a twittering bird at the window sill came to her, and light drenched the room.

Suddenly, she raised herself up, and leaning on her elbow, looked for a pen and a paper. But she did not find anything on the table except Ibn Hazm's book *The Dove's Necklace*, with its fancy moorish cover, and the silver letter opener that she had bought one cold day from a boy as she crossed the white bridge on her way to school. Her arms stretched lazily toward the drawer. She slowly pulled it open, groping with her hand for its contents. The stapler was there. She heard the tiny staples fall from the box in the midst of ballpoint pens. Finally, she got hold of her diary and on the first page a grey Parker was fastened to it.

She fixed the pillow stuffed with combed wool behind her back, putting the notebook on her bent knees, then she began to write stanzas of the song as she had heard it during the hour hanging between dream and wakefulness. She took care to write neatly on the unlined page. And as she was drawing the letter "M," humming the faint tune to herself, she saw the boy with the brown hair approaching her, begging her not to stop singing. Then, she found herself standing in the midst of a field laden with apple blossom trees on the shoulder of the town, singing in a hushful voice to a noisy group of students, singing to him alone about a man who refuses to die, about a soul transfigured into a golden bird that awakens the drowsy sleepers, about a harbor with no old people, about a goldsmith who defies time. As she stopped singing, the noisy voices of the students filled her ears, and she smelled the grilled meat. From the edge of the field she saw his eyes open wide like a Chinese fan and she felt as if she were standing face to face with his naked soul, scrutinizing its deepest secrets and watching its most private thoughts. Then his eyes followed her, at times lowered, at other times withdrawn, like a chameleon's stare at the shifting sun.

How had she trusted him all these years? How did she love him silently like a nun? He came towards her through the mist, laughing as she met him one night in that flying wheel, the upper buttons of his shirt were open and his hair billowed in the wind. As their seat stopped at the highest point and it seemed like their heads were touching the reclining mountain over the shoulder of the city, she felt his fingers play with hers and she heard him say in a worshipper's voice: "You are beautiful," but she pulled her hand away. There was something frightening in his voice, and she saw his eyes become two black spots, then blaze like a conflagration. She felt he wanted her soul, so she resisted him. No, he did not want to meet her as a human would meet a human; both are there, both are separate, yet both are together. He wished to draw all of her into him, to make her weak so she would depend on him. And she thought if she let him have his way, he would crouch on her, clutch her as if intending to pull her heart from its place. As she saw his face, which had no reserve, no restraint shining under a sinister moon, she gasped like a wounded animal and jumped from the rocking chair even before the wheel stopped and the man with the colorful hood could help her descend.

No, it was not love. When one falls in love, one does not feel she is in a cell and that her lover is her jailer. She wished to be free and she did not find any contradiction between freedom and love. But he was registering all her moves, and looks, and was jealous even of the breeze that touched her face.

She doubted he was listening to her song about the goldsmith enameling the gold, about the man who, like the phoenix, appeared through his ashes, young and fresh to live a new cycle. He did not care about what she said, what she thought, or what she felt. She was his beautiful woman, his doll, and, like a child who filled the world with his cries, he fought everyone around him to keep her for himself. And she saw him look around lest someone notice her. He wished to veil her from top to bottom.

Despair overcame her, then her abrupt anger routed the lingering vision in her soul. Where could she go? There was no place and on whatever spot she chose to stand, she stood alone. Endless bars sprang in front of her and behind her. Bitterness began to surge in Lina's soul, and she felt that she should smash something. No, she would not give in. She tightened her lips in a terrible resolution, as if the image of the holy city with its golden bird who sings for eternity had appeared to her eyes in a dark moment, so she turned her face towards the light, leaving the vision humming in her ears.

But his jealous eyes haunted her again. Distorted reflections of his image poured on her like small moons, the boy who followed her on the stairs with a bunch of daisies in his hand begging her for a kiss, the boy who told the neighborhood boys that she was his beloved and stood under her balcony in the sun, in the rain, in the wind as if he were a statue, the boy who threatened to strangle her and strangle himself if he saw her on the arm of another man and wrote her broken poems, the boy who sent her a bad translation of *Othello* and once in a while gave her old yellow books.

She told herself for the thousandth time that she did not love him. She wanted a friend, not a master or a slave. But he wasn't unique in his strong desire to possess, or in his wild passion to self-abasement. She saw in him the image of the oriental male, the eternal gloom, the mad hallucination, the excessive sensualism. She said to herself for the thousandth time that her love did not mean selflessness, but emphasizing and maintaining the self; not the loss of her humanity, but its restoration.

She threw her diary aside. The sun filled the room, and life began to buzz in the street. Why was she weary? She slipped under the sheets and wished she could see again the image of that holy city which eluded her.

*   *   *

26 July 1956

We gathered around the radio. In a loud voice Jamal Abdel Naser was proclaiming the nationalization of the Suez Canal. There was no sound in the deserted streets. A soft hiss fell from a window, and quickly evaporated. Even the birds were sleeping, as were the frogs and the babies. No other sound competed with his voice. As I turned my head towards my mother, I saw her cry silently. My brother paced the room, back and forth, his hands glued to his back.

—We will build the High Dam, said the president to his listeners. The value of the Dam is greater than the land it would irrigate and the electric power it will help to generate. It will be the symbol of a nation, and an incentive to the nations of Africa.

Amal, who was visiting us that evening, jumped from her seat and cried as she shook my hands in an excited manner:

—I can't believe that! I can't.

Laughing voices burst forth from the empty streets, drenched later by the tapping of tambours and the dancing steps on the asphalt. The radio poured out songs of the Egyptian peasants mixed with the hysterical cries of the spectators. We couldn't distinguish the source of the noise. Damascus and Cairo, long emaciated by yearning, were now transformed with a magician's stick into one city.

Who could have thought that the poor fisherman, who stood for days under the burning sun, flinging his net in and out of the water, yearning for a basket full of fish, would catch a copper long-necked bottle that had been thrown to the bottom of the sea hundreds of years earlier?

30 July 1956

The city was still enchanted as I walked with Amal towards the river at sunset. We had nothing in mind except the nationalization of the canal. Amal laughed nervously as she spoke:

—Do you believe that they will leave us in peace?

—Who? I asked alarmed.

—The shares' owners, she said contemptuously.

29 October 1956

The Israelis crossed Sinai at night, lowering parachutists over the Mitla passage, 25 miles east of the Suez. They moved on quickly.

We gathered in the school playground in the morning and demanded to be trained for arms and to have a prompt first aid course. As the principal stood in front of us with her light blue dress, folding the morning newspaper, gazing absently at our angry faces, we assumed she would laugh at our naivety and force us to return to our classes. But we saw her take a couple steps, tapping the floor with the heels of her shoes, leaving something in the hand of the tiny-headed supervisor with the monkey-like eyes. And in a quiet, toneless voice, still staring vaguely at our faces she said to us:

—You are right. There is no reason for studying now.

Cries dashed back and forth, mingled with the shuffling of young girls' feet.

31 October 1956

—Perhaps we have to fight from house to house, said the history teacher, as the radio announced the news of the British and French forces attacking the land of Egypt.

Quietly she stood, then walked to the window: a vision of sorrow under the pale autumn light.

2 November 1956

A frightening night. In my dream I went from home to home in deserted Port Said. An ominous silence presided over the city. Dirty dishes on tables had not been cleared by the fleeing owners. As I examined some portraits that had been flung on the floor near a window, I heard a hail of bullets coming from the direction of the sea, then I saw a herd of locusts cover the face of the sky.

5 November 1956

—Bolganin. Bolganin. The voices drenched the city lanes. Children ran carrying colorful rockets in their hands. As the radio announcer asked the shoeshine boy in the martyr square whether he believed that the Soviet Union would shoot its destructive weapons on London and Paris, the boy shouted in a loud voice:

—Long live our friends the Russians. Long live Bolganin.

6 November 1956

In the windows of the crumbling houses in the old city, they stood day and night, waiting for the aggressors. Even the children waited. Their hands were laden with bombs and machine-guns.

From their hiding places they riddled isolated patrols with bullets. Some British described them as people with no moral scruples and claimed that the soldiers have gotten used to walking backwards in the streets of Port Said.

Isn't it ridiculous to talk about morality, especially when they were the first to violate all moral codes by occupying the land of Egypt?

22 December 1956

At night, a soldier climbed (just before the evacuation of the British troops from Port Said) the flagpole that was behind De Lesseps's statue and nailed an enormous union jack to it. As he slid down the pole, he left a thick smear of grease. His action reminded me of the irrational behavior and stupidity of man. National chauvinism does not help anyone.

25 December 1956

De Lesseps's statue tumbled into the canal carrying in its right hand the French flag. Who would have ever thought that he who dug the canal would sink in it?

I said to Amal as we walked along the river bank toward the university that understanding between nations is quite impossible. I saw her look at my face astonished, then I heard her mumble something to herself. She could not understand the meaning of the word "impossible."

1 January 1957

I saw Abu Amin dance in the square like a dervish. Darkness had enveloped the city, and I could not sleep. As I pressed my face on the windowpane, I thought I saw him point to a ghost somewhere in the air. The wind was blowing outside and snow flakes were dripping from the roofs' edges. I did not see the idiot sleeping on the threshold of the tailor's shop.

As I went to bed that night, I dreamt of birds with green legs, and of sapphire beaks hiding in the wide space. I was surprised. I listened to various sounds. As I was looking around, the sky opened and a little boy with blond hair and rosy cheeks appeared, and I heard him say: "I am the lost Messiah."

When I got up, frightened, the birds had already disappeared,

but the balconies of distant palaces were still falling like stars from
the gates of the sky.

*　*　*

The girls stood in the school playground in little groups and
began to gossip endlessly. One said:

—Did you know that Wafiqa will be getting married?

—Oh, no. Who will marry her?

—Every worm-eaten corn has its cross-eyed farmer, remarked
the same girl mockingly.

—Is it the religion teacher? asked Samira.

—No, said the girl.

—Well, who then? The heads closed in curiously.

—I know, said Wafa', then laughed like a devil. A professor at
the university. Isn't it?

The girl nodded approvingly.

—What does he teach? asked Zahra.

—Arabic, said the girl in a low voice.

—Couldn't he find someone else?

—Love is blind.

—Where did he see her?

—Most probably he didn't, said Samira.

—Didn't see her? all said at once.

—Of course not, said the girl.

—But the engagement will not take place, whispered Umayya.

—Did you say it will not take place? all asked.

—No, she said, looking around as if someone were listening.

Lina bent her head forward. The girls' eyes were opening and
closing. And she heard Umayya say in a low voice:

—We wrote him a letter. She and I. She pointed to a big girl
with huge breasts standing next to her.

There was silence for a while, then the girls exploded into
laughter. Lina was shocked. How could they have done that?
Through the laughing masks, the sorrowful face of Wafiqa came
back to her, and she heard her voice broken with rheum, mixing

with the sound of the train wheels. She saw the notebooks of the girls fly around her while the dust of chalk fell on her hair like snow flakes.

How naive she was, she thought passing through the long dark corridor and in her nostrils felt the ugly smell of mould. The classroom doors were closed and silence reigned in the deserted halls. And from the walls, oozing with humidity, the colorful pictures of her schoolmates looked down on her, then the face of an innocent girl pointing to a big map on which was written: "My Country is from the Ocean to the Gulf" arrested her for a while. Who painted that? she asked herself and stared with difficulty through the gloom. Her eyes were tired and she could not see anything. How could one build a country before one builds the human being?

At the landing of the stairs, the deformed ghost of Wafiqa, neither an engagement ring on her finger nor a crown on her head, stood in front of her, and from behind the crumbling walls the laughter of girls came to her mixed with the sobbing of the gutters. She hurried along; shame burned her cheeks.

Why hadn't she said something? And why had she slipped away from the ring? The mist enveloped her mind as she walked home and the road looked desolate under the drizzle of rain. Was it possible to remain silent? she asked herself for the thousandth time as she crossed the wooden bridge, listening fearfully to the sound of her steps on its shaky boards. And from the open kitchen windows the smell of crushed garlic came to her. She saw the housewives standing behind oil pans. The mist began to disappear from her eyes. The person who witnessed a crime was no better than the criminal. Fear invaded her but no one passed by. Where could the others have gone? She began to run across the wet lanes as if she were searching for a face that eluded her in the dark.

One more year and she will go to the university, she said to herself. Through the drizzle of rain loitering on window panes she saw hundreds of boys walking through the long hallways, gossiping merrily, smoking and laughing. Everything will be different, Lina thought as she glanced quickly at the clouds. She too will lean against the wall, gathering the edges of her skirt shyly, talking about her concept of the divine city, not as a city of heavenly existence but rather as a conceivable earthly state. Perhaps the others will listen to her and they will strive together to create the new human being she often dreamt of in her dull evenings.

She passed by a row of closed shops, and she did not hear a sound. The wind was chilly. As she looked askance towards the frozen drops of water on the sidewalk, she saw a bird fly and then land on the edge of a brick house. How was it that it still lived in the frost? she wondered, staring at its small grey bosom. Its beak was black, its wings short, and it seemed to her soft and fragile like cotton candy, but its dark plumage resisted the wind.

—Ah God, a faint cry escaped her mouth. Her cheeks were aflame, her limbs trembling. She strode on in the deserted lane as the clouds drifted silently in front of her.

Where was her childhood? Those chains that pulled her always to the womb of the earth? Those voices that warned her that she was fragile, fragile and soft like a breast of a dove?

She envisioned herself rising from the grave, casting away her shroud, listening to the singing of the eternal bird. And through the grey mist she saw the gate of the divine city shining on the shoulder of the street.

*   *   *

There was fried cauliflower for lunch, meat stuffed with almonds and pine seeds, thin potato chips sauteed with cheese sauce. She had never liked cauliflower. She remembered the servant telling her that cauliflower caused stinking smells. Hiding her laughter, Lina had sat at the table looking askance at Aunt Samiya, squeezing lemon on the tender white cauliflower and licking her fingers hungrily.

—Rima won't be coming then during the holiday? said Aunt Samiya after a while, narrowing her eyes as if squinting through the hole of a needle.

—No, said the mother gently.

169

—It's your fault, said the aunt. Her hands were trembling. This is the result of education!

An uneasy air hang about the room. Bahiya seized the sauceboat and put it in front of Aunt Samiya.

—Shall I pour you something over the meat? she asked in a low voice, avoiding her aunt's eyes.

—No, said Aunt Samiya sharply. The veins of her throat were tense.

—Ah. The girl has no future, sighed Bahiya, whether she has had an education or not.

Aunt Samiya knitted her brows as if angered by Bahiya's state-ment. After she chewed the meat in her mouth, she put her el-bows on the table, leaned close to Lina's mother, then said, al-most whispering:

—Did you hear what happened to the daughter of our neigh-bor, the merchant?

—No, replied her mother. Her face bent towards her plate of cauliflower.

Aunt Samiya wiped her mouth with the white serviette, then said in a weary voice:

—She hanged herself on her wedding night.

Bahiya stopped chewing her fried bread. Her mother's finger was stuck on a root of celery dipped in radish sauce with walnuts. Silence prevailed. Then the door opened and the servant ap-peared with a basket full of oranges from the Dead Sea. She put it on a red mahogany sideboard. And before leaving the room Bahiya said to her in a whimpering voice:

—Pour me a glass of water.

From the corner of her eye, Lina watched the servant hold the silver jug quietly. The water bubbled in the crystal glass with the long neck as she poured.

Her mother waited till the door was closed. She put the celery wearily on her plate and said:

—Ah well, she's gone to a better world.

Aunt Samiya sighed and bowed her head in assent.

— Was she a . . .? asked Bahiya. Her fingers were tapping the stem of the glass.

—I don't exactly know, said Aunt Samiya. Some say she was pregnant.

—And you, did you see her? asked her mother.

—She always stood behind the window in her colored cotton jumper. Her hair was loose on her shoulders.

—And her parents? said Bahiya.

—They let her do whatever she wished, replied Aunt Samiya, licking her cracked lips and yawning. The boys used to pass day and night under the window.

—And did they find him? asked her mother.

—Who? said Aunt Samiya. Her head leaned forward as if she were about to fall asleep.

—The guy who made her. . .

—Ah that, said Aunt Samiya. I don't know.

Bahiya stood up carrying the ceramic pot of potatoes wrapped in a white napkin and went from person to person. But Lina did not want to eat. Her mouth was dry and under her tongue she could taste a sharp bitterness. From the edge of her heavy eyelids she watched her mother exchange the plates of salad, olives, and cheese with Aunt Samiya, then she heard the noise of forks and knives mixed with Bahiya's low laughter.

* * *

During religion class, Lina sat with her arms folded, listening to the scraping of chalk on the blackboard. Professor Karkutly went to and fro around the desks, distributing the corrected exam papers, commenting on the girls' essays, being extra careful not to let his long cloak touch the edges of their wide skirts. He told them that their answers were scandalous, and the fact that they neglected to quote the Quran and the Tradition indicated the laziness that overcame them while getting ready for graduation. Then he took Zahra's paper, held it up in the air and said:

—Aren't you ashamed to give me a paper blotted with ink?

He only praised Wafiqa. According to him, she was the ideal

Moslem woman who knew her position in society, and accepted what God had decreed for her. The professor then was silent for a while, staring at the girls through his stern eyes. Zahra moved on her bench with difficulty, turned her head toward the window to hide her smile, while other girls buried their faces in the open books and scribbled funny drawings in the margins.

What was it that made him angry? Lina lifted her eyes slowly as silence filled the classroom. She saw his finger pointing at her and heard him say with disgust:

—Heretic.

Short whispers ran through the air. Heads craned curiously, following the professor who moved towards the window with loud steps; his back to the girls, and the worn-out heels of his shoes causing a creak on the floor. The eyes rested on his white turban.

Lina's eyes were full of sleep, and the rain was beating strongly against the crumbling roofs of the houses. The smell of mould oozed from the eaten-up walls of the classroom. She saw herself in a single file line of women with shaved heads, walking barefoot. The cries of children with no eyes sounded in the remote caves of her mind. Listening feebly to the distant echoes amid the silence of the room, she noticed Professor Karkutly turn around suddenly like a preacher on a pulpit, clasping his hands, speaking in a very low voice:

—Didn't Islam honor women? Didn't it venerate them? And who prohibited the burying of the newborn girl, but Islam?

His voice trembled, and his hands shook. He stepped then one step forward, looking right and left into the girls' eyes. He stretched his arm in the air, his face contracted.

—Might was right in pre-Islam till Islam came. The newborn girl was buried alive till Islam prohibited that. Is there anyone who doubts this?

The resonant voice reverberated in the room. The girls' heads bowed with piety; their questioning eyes withered.

Then he came toward Lina, clefting the air before him with his thick cane, wagging his wide grey cloak, flashing his rotten yellow teeth. And when he stood beside her, he pulled out her essay with fingers wrinkled from excessive washing for the ritual ablution.

—Perhaps, you didn't think much about what you've written, he said in a controlled voice.

Then he spread the essay out on the desk and pointed to something:

—Here, about God and justice, he said while his Adam apple was always in motion. He wasn't just when he created women. . . . Hum. . . Isn't this heresy?

And before he gave her a chance to reply he folded the essay, left it in front of her and said:

—You are a poet. But your talent is not dedicated to the will of God.

The classroom drowned in laughter. Whispers flew in the air, and one girl with crooked teeth said: "Let's read the essay," and the braces on her teeth flashed out. Wafiqa stretched her short neck and there was a large grin on her face. A dunce girl sitting next to the window clapped, then put her fat hands on her face, wagging her head right and left and laughing in a high-pitched voice.

But as Professor Karkutly banged the desk with his fist and said with contempt: "Imbeciles!" a hush fell on the classroom.

So she was serving the devil all these years! Lina bowed her head and stared stupidly into the void. And the word "religion" lay heavily upon her heart with its short elegant letters. So all that haunted her mind about justice and equality was heresy! Doubt began to pierce the fog of her mind, she pressed her face against the bench and closed her eyes. In the dull light, the figures of women from past centuries passed by, their shrouds were dusty, their eyes were half open. When she ran in the winding lanes of sleep, terrified like a child, the cry of the auctioneer in a Baghdad Bazaar came to her mind, mixed with the tinkling anklets and the merchants' laughter.

She lifted her head slowly, and with trembling hands she found herself arranging a long index, scribbling on the paper in front of her with unclear handwriting:

Islam and polygamy
Islam and the veil

Islam and the Paradise Huris
Islam and testimony
Islam and the relationship between husband and wife
Beating and deserting in bed
Life imprisonment of women who commit adultery
Islam and inheritance

And under the title of "Woman and Popular Literature" she wrote:

God's preference to the Male over the Female
The male is a subject while the female is an object
and the subject is much better than the object
Women are disloyal, stupid and irreligious

Under this subtitle she wrote quickly the lines of a poem that came back to her through her foggy mind:

Women even if they pretend chastity
Are wombs tossed around by hovering vultures
At night you have their secrets and talks
At dawn their legs and wrists are for another
It is like being in an inn: you stay overnight, then you leave
But you have no idea who will take your place.

Her face was full of anger. She pressed the pen on the paper. But a gentle kick from the girl on the bench behind warned her of the professor's stern gaze. She hid her papers quickly, and put her hands on her temples as if listening to a sermon.

* * *

The boys' laughter filled the air. Colored paper lanterns were trembling in the warm wind of May. From the window of the dressing room, Lina watched the guests coming up the steps which led to the roof, waiting for a while to gather their breath, then passing into the theater. Girls with white flowing dresses and tight gloves loitered at the entrance and ushered the visitors, raising their heads, stretching their arms in the air. Why was she afraid? She pressed her face against the glass, murmuring broken sentences to herself, trying to remember a short dialogue between herself and Othello. Suddenly, she felt that she had forgotten everything, and that her legs didn't support her weight anymore.

One of the girls was practising the piano, while the actors pushed one another on the stairs of the back-stage, snatching their clothes, fixing their beards, tying their belts. Under the pale glow of a lantern, the art teacher with the heavy thighs bent over the face of the girl who was playing the role of Brabantio, Desdemona's father, and was painting her forehead with wide grey lines, dabbling the brush in blue and black on the cheeks of the girl in order to make them wrinkled. As Lina glanced at the dressing table, crossing her hands behind her back, silently waiting for her turn, she saw the wigs heaped carelessly on top of scores of white and black beards. Pearl necklaces mixed with silky embroidered handkerchiefs and ruby rings poured out of the open drawers.

The pattering of girls' heels going and coming was heard, and from the dark corridors of the stage came the sounds of hammers, followed by footsteps pulling pieces of furniture, and stifled laughter. At that moment, the door was opened, and the angry face of the principal peered. Lina saw the lean girl hurrying to the corridor, putting her fingertip on her mouth, murmuring with fear: "Sssh" while the prompter buried her small head in the text of *Othello,* ready to start reading.

—When will you begin? the principal asked the art teacher and moved her eyes amidst the painted faces, then approached the man with the pinkish shirt and white embroidered pants. And as she saw his sword hanging down from his wide belt, she sighed in a loud voice, then said pleasantly:

—Am I in the presence of honorable Cassio?

She bent her head a bit, putting her right hand on her side as if suffering from rheumatism, squinting her green eyes, examining the girl's face which hid behind a big feather hat with curiosity, then she cried breathlessly:

—Ah Lord. Isn't she the young Samia?

The girl bowed shyly, raising her hat in the air, showing her grey wig, then the laughter of Roderigo, the idiot, came from the hallway, followed by the sound of Bianca's jewels and the dancers' castanets.

A correspondent for a local paper came running to the principal. Lina saw him scribbling something under the glow of the pale lantern, while his photographer stood in the middle of the room with sleepy eyes, watching Othello, who was standing in front of the mirror wearing his earrings, rubbing his face with a piece of burned cork, murmuring a tune to himself.

As Lina let the art teacher accentuate her eyes, she felt as if the girls' faces were stretching from all the windows till they almost touched her golden hair. She felt their warm breath on her painted cheeks. "The divine Desdemona," their murmurs filled the air. At that moment, music began to come from the orchestra pit, mixed with the chat of the audience and the laughter of the actors.

From her place behind the mirror, smeared with make-up, she saw the servants hurry in light steps holding the torches, waiting to hear Brabantio's cry in the midst of the night: "Strike on the tinder. Give me a taper." Iago hung about, rocking himself from his heels to the tops of his toes rhythmically, thrusting his left hand into the pocket of his tight pants, holding the text of the play in the other, repeating to himself in a whispering voice:

—Put money in thy purse, I say. It cannot be long that Desdemona should continue her love to the Moor.

As Lina was getting ready to stand up, pulling her long white dress from the waist, touching her rouge painted cheeks carefully, the Arabic teacher came towards her, panting, and told her in a low voice to walk straight on the stage and to speak clearly. Then Lina saw her rush into the corridor, waving her arms and dispersing the group of actors like a flock of seagulls. She pointed to Iago in a gesture to follow her.

Lina's heart began to beat. She knew that in a few moments the curtain would go up and that strange eyes would watch her gestures in the dark. And, perhaps, he would be sitting there among the audience, his face burning with jealousy, and in his arm a bouquet of flowers. She stepped towards the window. Her cheeks were aflame, her limbs were trembling. From the audience a muffled noise came to her, then sudden footsteps of the servants. As she put her forehead against the glass, his boyish face loomed, and through the faint light of the lamps she saw his eyes full of desire. What was it with him that awaited her except a turbulent life between light and darkness, between love and hate, between peace and violence? And how many years would she need before crossing that city which she built in her dreams to the land of the Barbarians? Perhaps years, perhaps months, perhaps days. But she was dead sure that the bridges, all the bridges she built around herself, would be destroyed by him, and that the sleeping beasts within her soul would inevitably be awakened.

The thought of the part she had to play humiliated her. She was nothing. A white puppet with blond hair desired even by the idiot. A white ewe run by a black ram. A land carack boarded by pirates. And the words of Othello rang in her ears: "Are not you a strumpet?" Then, she saw him throw some coins at her feet. In the perplexity of her thought, the world of man and animal got mixed together, and those erotic images came to her, one after the other. She heard Iago say to her father: "Will you have your daughter covered with a horse and your grandsons neigh to you?"

A few moments afterward, she found herself on the stage surrounded by scores of lanterns. From the hall came the whispers of the audience. Time passed, and she stopped seeing those innumerable faces in the dark, watching her. She laughed and cried, and in her fantasy she loved the black man and saw in him the image of that boy who followed her, on the stairs with a bunch of daisies in his hand. Then Emilia came. The stage was dimly lit. She gave her a nightgown, put the wedding sheets on the bed and left her alone.

Sweat trickled down her face as she lay on her back, staring into the void. When she heard his heavy footsteps and saw him standing behind the transparent curtain, her breath quickened.

—Don't kill me my lord, her trembling voice filled the space.

On the pillow on which he often kissed her, she felt his big hands close around her neck. And in that instant a voice full of fear yelled:

—Don't strangle her.

There was silence in the hall. And, through her wedding sheets and her shrouds, a noise came to her from behind the stage, and she heard Emilia's voice reverberate: "My lord, my lord." Tears began to fill her eyes, then feverish steps were heard on stage followed by brazen clashes of swords and the crash of bodies on the floor.

—Cold, cold my girl, said Othello, as if singing.

She could hear the girls sobbing from the first rows in the hall. Then, Othello's body fell upon her. As the curtain fell, the hall filled with applause.

* * *

III

WOMANHOOD

Bahiya moved between the cupboard, which was filled with Chinese plates, and the big wooden chest in the dining room, carrying the dust bin in her hand, listening to the radio whose volume she had raised in the kitchen. She stopped suddenly and asked Lina, who was drinking her third cup of coffee:

—Aren't you going to the university today?

Lina raised her head lazily and murmured, almost asleep:

—Do you really care?

—Yes, I do, said Bahiya in a sharp voice. She snapped the empty coffee cup, letting the dust bin fall on the floor. We clean and you make everything dirty.

Lina laughed and, from the corner of her eye, she saw Bahiya rush to the kitchen like a storm, empty the coffee dregs into the sink, then turn around, yelling loudly:

—Don't forget I can ask. . .

—Oh really? said Lina mockingly, I'll write you my timetable for next week if you like!

Her mother came running from the living room, and stood excitedly in front of the door.

—Aren't you ashamed of yourself to start fighting with her early in the morning? she said to Lina, then stepped forward to the kitchen, saying to Bahiya breathlessly:

—Turn down the radio. The noise deafens me.

Lina slipped away from the dining room, put her coat on in a hurry and didn't even take her books. As she descended the stairs, she saw the servant shake the lambskin from the window, speaking to someone behind her, then she heard Bahiya's voice which split the ear:

—Am I the maid's daughter to clean the house?

*   *   *

The lane was strewn with donkey dung. Peasants had tied their animals to the thin trunks of the trees and left them there till they could remove the boxes of fresh fruits and vegetables to the nearby shops. Lina walked carefully, choosing her steps amid heaps of wet dung and straw. As she began to cross the square towards the university, she saw the grocer follow the idiot, trying to beat him up. The idiot was cursing God in a vulgar language.

She began to run across the deserted lanes. The cold wind stung her face. She wanted to forget everything: Bahiya's yelling, her mother's murmurs, the idiot's cries, the smell of donkey dung. But the disturbing voices continued to follow her, and the images of squalor in her city persisted. A faint sickness overcame her. Suddenly, her head became heavy. She stopped running, and closed her eyes for a moment. From one of the open windows, the sound of a faint pipe came to her. Then it grew louder till she thought that the sleepy lambs on the foothills would begin to wake up and move in herds towards the city.

As she raised her head curiously, she felt the rays of the sun warm her face, and the whole world laughed with her. She continued to walk, more lightly as a child who had loosened her heavy clothing. In the midst of her happiness, she saw Ibn Hazm coming towards her across the streets of Cordova, insisting in a voice weakened through the ages that life's goal was to be free of anxiety. But when she grabbed his feet to ask him more questions, he slipped from between her hands like a shadow.

The convent stood in the alley that led to the river, a white-washed stone house with many rosebushes in its garden. As she stood stunned in front of the cypress walk, she told herself that Alhambra kings came in the evening to the garden, and when the mist disappeared from the brick roof of the convent, they hurried away behind the ramparts of the city. In her dream, the convent became Granada University, and she read words written on its metal gate with gold water: "The world stands on four pillars only, the wiseman's knowledge, the great man's justice, the prayer of the virtuous, and the daring of the courageous." As she tried to recall the ghosts of the Castilian students discussing philosophy and astronomy with their Moslem colleagues, a young nun looked from one of the windows, stared for a while at the horizon, then began to water a plant on the window sill.

Lina hurriedly put her hands in her pockets, listening to the songs of the wandering vendors coming from dark shops on the edge of the street. As she began to descend the hill, the wind penetrated her coat and the water of the river looked bleary, like glass. The two minarets of the Sultan Salim's mosque and scores of domes hanging over open yards loomed from behind the tall poplar trees. As she crossed Beirut Street towards the victory bridge, she imagined that the deserted cells of the monastery were suddenly filled with dervishes; she could swear that she heard their dancing footsteps on the edge of the pool.

She laughed loudly. But as she saw a tourist with fair goatee, wearing shorts and a white shirt, standing in the wind in front of the national museum, she hurried away, buttoning her coat carefully, swinging her bag to and fro. She thought that the guide would lead him from room to room, unveiling the seven masks of statues left by her grandfathers before the dawn of history. Suddenly, the word Palmyra rang in her ears, then began to ebb slowly. And from the dead letters, a city rose in the midst of the desert, and she saw Queen Zenobia dragged in golden chains behind the chariot of the Roman victor. But her thoughts were dispersed by the military barracks to her right, with its high windows and dark-colored brick. As she tried desperately to dismiss the gloomy images of the past, the students' faces in the outer garden of the university came upon her.

Nine o'clock. There was a plenty of time for the philosophy lecture. She crossed the entrance of the law school, took a left, then walked down the dark corridor which led to the office of the Arabic professors. When she knocked at the door, a hoarse voice answered after a moment saying:

—Come in.

Lina turned the door handle carefully, opened the door, and halted in the grey light that came through the cobwebbed window.

Her professor was sitting behind his desk, sipping tea and flipping through student papers. He raised his head slowly, then gave a friendly smile and said:

—Come in. Come in.

Lina closed the door quietly, and approached the desk.

—I came to pick up my paper, she said in a quiet voice.

—Ah, of course, he said.

And she saw him stand, and walk towards a shelf full of manuscripts. He pulled out a pile, dusted it with his hand, then began to flip through the papers quickly. He halted a second, raised his head and looked at her vaguely:

—Your name is Lina. Isn't it?

—Yes, she said and stepped forward.

—And you wrote about the blind poet of Ma'arra? he asked.

Lina nodded her head, swallowing with difficulty. Her heart started pounding violently. She saw him pull out her paper, then take a white handkerchief out of his pocket, wipe his bald head quietly, and without looking at her eyes, she heard him say solemnly:

—Perhaps, it would be better to talk about the subject.

There was a knock at the door. The face of an old servant popped in.

—Does the professor wish a hot cup of tea? asked the peasant voice. The water is bubbling on the fire, and he has to go to the interior ministry for something.

—No, no, thanks, the professor's voice filled the room. Then, the door was closed quietly, and silence prevailed.

What did he want from her? She couldn't guess. She saw him go towards the stove turning his back to her. As he crouched carrying a piece of wood in his hand, the faint sunlight fell on his oval skull.

—Do you like al Ma'arri? His trembling voice came to her

through the crackling of the wood. I mean, do you sympathize with him?

—Yes, said Lina.

She saw him rise slowly, rubbing his hands, a dry expression on his face.

—Do you really believe that procreation is a sin and annihilation is the only hope for humanity? he said, then walked to the window. His voice was trembling excitedly.

Saddened by his angry tone, she was silent. Through the silence, the noise of footsteps in the corridor came to her mind with the echoes of distant laughter.

—I did not mean to discourage you, he stuttered after a while, stroking his chin gently, but you are young, and al-Ma'arri is nihilistic; he doesn't believe in anything.

He left the window and came towards her in slow steps, then he smiled and said:

—Is it possible for the rose to believe that death is our ultimate goal?

Lina looked at his kind face and tried to keep her voice from shaking:

—But man is like a broken glass, isn't he? Is there someone who can put his pieces together? she asked.

She saw him bow his head and walk to the stove; then she heard him say in a voice full of desolation:

—Then you don't believe in God.

—No, said Lina, there is nothing that makes me believe in Him.

He turned towards her slowly, and she saw his restless soul watching her through dark eyes, then he burst out:

—But we need Him. Don't you see? He walked to the window quickly; his limbs trembling and a scornful smile on his face.

—No, no. You can't possibly take away from us this only hope, he said in a faint voice.

—Then, you admit that He is our opium, I mean this God, said Lina in a kind voice. But he did not answer. She saw him open the window, silently raising his head towards the sky. At that moment the bell rang and the laughter of students filled the damp corridors.

He came to her with quiet steps, put his hand on her shoulder, and then said:

—You know something? I am older than you are. And I am not as religious as you might think. But I believe that doubt leads us to destruction. The goal of life is happiness, and if we deprive ourselves of the last illusion we have, we are undoubtedly lost. Do you understand what I mean? You are young and beautiful. Sweat began to drip from his face; his lips trembled.

—What will you do when you reach my age?

His weary voice fell on her parched heart like a hammer. She did not know what to say. The door opened, and the grammar professor came in.

—Good morning, he said briskly.

Lina took her paper and rushed outside.

She had to live in a perpetual dream, to believe everything, to make the illusions facts. She could not understand why she had to go on studying. From the scores of closed doors, the comic specters of the department came to her: the chairman holding special sessions for girls, because he did not approve of both sexes being under the same roof; the portly geography professor who read his lecture from a book he wrote or translated many years ago; the library clerk who ascended ladders, disappeared for at least an hour among the books, then yelled from the small window upstairs: "The book is loaned;" the grammar professor who wasted weeks discussing a word and how the ninth century grammarians had different opinions about its function in a sentence. They all came to her in their tall, or short, bodies, their innocent or roguish eyes, in their oval or flat heads, holding hands and laughing in faint voices. As she stared at their dusty faces and strange clothes, she decided that God had forgotten them asleep in one of His caves for three hundred years, then, suddenly, He woke them up.

* * *

In the auditorium overlooking the university hospital, Lina sat among hundreds of students. As the philosophy professor with

184

his light hair and short stature came in and ascended the platform lightly, throwing his heavy briefcase on the long wooden lectern, gazing at the faces which looked from the balconies, the cigarettes were extinguished, and the room grew quieter. Before he took out his lecture notes, he went to the blackboard and wrote in big clear letters: "Plato's *Republic*."

Notebooks were taken out of the briefcases, sharpened pencils squealed on the desks. A student in a yellow sweater, sitting in front of Lina whispered:

—Did you see? The professor changed his tie for the sake of Plato.

His neighbor struck his heavy boots on the floor, laughing rudely. From the back seats, confused voices grew louder, followed by impolite laughter.

The professor wiped the chalk from his fingers, then he tested the loudspeaker. As he put his papers on the lectern, the echo repeated the faint sound of something cracking in the auditorium. After drinking a glass of water, he began to recite his lecture. He enumerated at first the characters of the Dialogue, pronouncing them in French. Lina heard the student sitting behind her imitate the professor with difficulty because the letter "p" does not correspond to anything in Arabic; then someone said in a dry voice:

—Shut up.

The professor explained Cephalus' definition of justice, (Cephalus was a businessman), and agreed with Socrates that wealth did not make one necessarily honest, or truthful. The student with the elegant suit and glossy hair whispered, quite disturbed:

—Is he a communist?

—Ask him, said a blue eyed girl, then she hid her face in her notebook, giggling stupidly.

The professor was silent for a while, then he said solemnly:

—Of course, there is Polemarch, (he meant Polemarchus), who sees that justice is giving every one his due, helping one's friends and injuring one's enemies.

The peasant student bent towards her and said naively:

—This is logical.

Lina glanced up quickly at him. His shaven face was impassive.

The professor refuted the new definition and proceeded to show that justice cannot involve injuring a human being, for its very nature involves goodness and virtue. Suddenly, a veiled girl rose in the balcony, stretched her arm over the rail, and waved her hand to attract the professor's attention. She began to shout in a hysterical voice:

—But the Quran said: "An eye for an eye, and a tooth for a tooth."

All heads turned towards her at once. A ripple of laughter passed around. When the echoes died down, the professor wiped his mouth and said dryly:

—We are not talking about the Quran.

Some students clapped; others whistled in protest, but the professor knocked at the wood with his fingers, then proceeded with his lecture.

—Whereas Thrasymach (he meant Thrasymachus), the sophist (and he stumbled pronouncing the word), for him, justice is political and involves the struggle between the strong and the weak. He sees that injustice is strength, and justice weakness.

The students' ears opened. Eyes were glued on the short man standing behind the lectern. The girl sitting to Lina's right said in a faint voice:

—Isn't this Thrasy. . .(and forgot his name), ah never mind. Isn't he right after all?

The peasant student laughed hoarsely and wrote in very clear handwriting on a piece of paper:

—Thrasymach.

The girl shook her hand in his face, dismissing him from her sight.

The professor bent over an old Arabic translation of Plato's *Republic,* quoted some passages, then was silent for a moment as if he had lost his train of thought. She had heard some say that he was a radical leftist, that he had studied in Paris during the Second World War, and that he didn't mix with anyone. She often saw him at the library poring over old manuscripts. When she greeted him he did not recognize her. She looked at the clock hanging on the wall. Ah, the dull day! And from the narrow windows she saw the medical students with their white shirts hurry to the hospital. The wind howled outside.

—But I think that the divine city can't be found on Earth, said Plato. "Perhaps," answered Socrates, "there is a pattern of it laid up in heaven for him who wishes to contemplate it. But it makes no difference whether it exists now or ever will come into being. Man can order his life by its laws." The professor's voice trembled. His eyes were glued on one of the windows.

The student with the oblong skull took out his creased handkerchief and whispered to the girl sitting to Lina's right:

—Give him the handkerchief. Doesn't he have the face of a besotted man?

The girl bleated in a weak voice. The rims of her eyes seemed red from excitement. Then the bell rang. Before the feet shuffled outside, the peasant student asked in a loud voice:

—Do we have to read all six books of the *Republic?*

*   *   *

The student union was loud with noise when Lina carried her cup of coffee, looking for an empty seat. The tobacco smoke blurred her eyes. She halted in indecision at the doorway for a few moments. And, through the faint light of the lamp, she saw heads raise and observe her curiously. She glanced right and left, frowning slightly, and when her sight cleared, she noticed Amal chattering in a ring of students, leaning her elbow on the table.

—Hello, said Lina, tapping her friend on the back. A guy with golden spectacles rose and offered her his chair. Before she could protest, he bent and said:

—I have a lecture. Then he hurried to the door, carrying a heavy briefcase with him.

Lina did not recognize anyone except the girl with the white fur from the French Department and the Algerian guy who sometimes attended her pre-Islamic poetry course. After she put the cup of coffee on the table, she took off her coat and said to Amal:

—Where have you been hiding these days?

—In the lab, laughed Amal.

—Experimenting on the corpses of the poor, said a guy with a red moustache, craning his head from the edge of the table.

—What do you mean? asked Lina surprised.

Amal nodded her head approvingly. Her smiling eyes were fixed on the guy's plump hands.

—And do you believe we dissect the corpses of the rich? the student with a checked suit said, turning his head nervously to one side, his cheek twitching.

—What's the fuss for? A corpse is a corpse. Plus she has to experiment on something, said the girl with the dark skin.

The hands clapped and the laughter grew. Then the Algerian student got out his pocket-book and noted something in it. He showed what he had written in French to the girl with the white fur and said:

—*C'est vrai?*

—*Oui, oui,* the girl giggled, glancing at the notebook. Her eyes were painted a light green shade. At that moment the terrace door opened and the figure of a woman wrapped in black stood in a faint shaft of the sun.

—Is that Wafiqa? Lina looked up quickly.

—In the flesh and blood, whispered Amal. Did you hear that she belonged to the Moslem Brotherhood and that she was organizing religious seminars regularly in her house?

—Really? said Lina, astonished. But the glasses that hid the eyes, the black veil and the long wide coat? What does all that mean?

The guy with the red moustache laughed, showing his yellow teeth colored by nicotine, then he said in a barely audible voice:

—But these religious seminars can't possibly last, can they? A few days and Naser comes to Damascus.

The girl with the dark skin stretched her neck with a puzzled expression on her face, then whispered:

—Can't they go underground, though? Lack of democracy won't serve anyone.

—Well, sure, said the guy in the checked suit. But there is no place for reactionaries in a socialist country.

—And who said the country will be socialist? asked Amal mockingly without looking at the guy's eyes.

—This is what the Communists say, he said contemptuously. Then he rose.

—Now, what's the quarrel for? intervened the girl with the white fur, leaning her body languidly.

The guy grinned and said hastily:

—Ah nothing. All I want to say is that the new state, Syria and Egypt, will be exactly as we want it to be. There is no reason for pessimism.

—Why don't we eat something? said the girl with the white fur. Hunger always makes us quarrelsome, doesn't it?

—Be my guests, said the Algerian guy. He rose quickly and went to the counter.

The sound of laughter followed by enthusiastic clapping and feverish footsteps came from the garden. The young man in the checked suit rushed to the balcony door. Others rose to their feet, talking and gesticulating from narrow windows towards the road leading to the medical school. And in the midst of this hustle, a sharp voice of a student reciting a poem came to Lina.

—Are they Naserites? asked the union's boy several times as he put the empty cups of coffee in the tray and wiped off the table with a dirty rag. No one would answer him.

Then Lina saw the girl with the fur coat open her leather handbag, her hand rummaging in its contents. She picked out a folded paper and snapped the catch, sighing loudly.

—Did you read the leaflet? asked the guy with the red moustache, pointing his fat finger at the crumpled paper.

—About the unity between Egypt and Syria? said the girl with the white fur. The fire work undoubtedly will be very interesting, won't it?

The quiet sound of her voice and her noticeable lisp were very pleasing to the guy sitting at the edge of the table. He laughed in a hoarse voice and said, almost whispering:

—It seems that Mademoiselle does not see Naser's image on the sky as the poor do.

—Ssshh, said the girl and shifted about in her seat with apparent anxiety. But as she saw the Algerian guy back with a tray heavy with cheese sandwiches and orange juice, she changed her tone quickly and whispered: *"Ah, très gentil, très gentil."*

From the balcony door youthful faces, bearded faces, dark faces, excited faces, serene faces, appeared, but all were looking for the lost Mahdi, the stolen dream.

They ate silently as a hoarse voice repeated outside: "Unity, freedom, and socialism." Remnants of sausages and half-smoked cigarettes were thrown on the deserted tables. No one wanted to say a word. The Algerian student seemed as if he were listening attentively to the speech of someone being interrupted by applause. Then the pallid face of a short guy appeared in the corridor. With their weary eyes, they followed the little fellow as he went to the counter, bought himself a glass of juice and strolled to the corner, indifferent to the noise around him. Wiping her nose with the back of her hand, the girl with the dark skin bent down over her plate, whispering in a weak voice:

— Isn't he the Communist representative in the student union?

The guy with the red moustache bit his lips. Amal's restless eyes became still and cold like ice. After the guy poured the orange juice down his gullet, he stopped a minute to adjust the high turtleneck sweater and put a cigarette in his mouth. Then he dragged his right foot slowly, looking contemptuously at the crowds of heads behind the windows.

Before they sensed any danger, they saw the little fellow throw a coin in the juke box and the voice of a singer blared. He then walked slowly back to the table, spat the cigarette butt out of his mouth, and turned his shoe on it.

—Shut off the juke box, yelled a voice from outside.

Angry hands motioned from the windows. But the little fellow ignored the noise about him. He sipped some more orange juice, then took a coin, tossed it up then let it fall on the table. A big guy rushed from the balcony and grabbed him by the neck. Then others came. One shouted: "The dirty Communist." As the little fellow attempted to run away, they pulled his legs and he fell on the ground. He tried to roll over on his stomach and cover his face with his arms, but as he got to his side, he was kicked in the groin. He screamed, and as he tried to raise himself on one knee, someone took a short step forward and kicked him in the face. He fell on his side, his arms folded across his stomach; the blood gurgled in his mouth as he tried to scream.

Lina was stunned for a moment, then she rushed towards them shouting: "Leave him alone, leave him alone!" They had already formed a circle around him and were kicking him in the temple. She saw his eyes roll back, his head lolled for a moment then thumped to the ground. They told her to go to hell and banged their fists on the tables. One of them asked her if she truly wanted to see the dirty Communists rule the new state. Another assured her that some day she'd understand. They laughed and sprawled on the chairs, nudging one another, watching the man's face bathe in blood.

Heads popped up from windows and students gathered in doorways and from around the counter, asking what had happened. One speaker interrupted his speech in the garden, then someone yelled: "The cops!" and the crowd began to run outside the student union. Some jumped from windows; others tried to climb over the outside fence of the garden. Amal came towards Lina, dragged her by the hand, and they ran toward the Law School. The ambulance sirens screeched outside while stones were thrown in the air. Cold sweat trickled down her back. Before she could lean against one of the walls, she saw a sign which said "The Moslem Brothers oppose Naser's regime" swoop through the air and thud against someone's head. Arms were raised. The mob flowed forward then backward, infuriated faces pressed together and, from one of the windows of the Law School, a loud speaker screeched and told the students to break it up, warning of the consequences of the army's interference in the university's affair.

A few meters away, a fat student grunted suddenly as if he had been struck in the stomach with a club. She saw him sit down and gaze into the empty space. From behind a window someone said: "Let the Israelis sleep quietly, for we will kill each other before the turn of the century."

In the dark corridor Lina and Amal stopped for a while, breathing heavily. As they continued to walk past the empty classrooms, the noise began to recede. They passed the room of one of the janitors. Through the slightly opened door they saw the old man praying quietly; his face was full of love, and his hands raised to the sky.

*   *   *

He stopped her on the steps of the library, putting one foot before the other. When she turned behind, almost frightened, she saw the sweat trickle down his face, his hands tremble.

—Lina, I want to speak to you, he said in a low voice.

Without answering him she ascended the flight of steps lightly, then stopped at the top landing, putting her bag at the stone edge, gazing at his unshaven face with difficulty.

What did he want from her? And why had he insisted on following her day and night? In the university and outside it? Othello's words, before the Moor strangled Desdemona, came to her deformed, confused, and gloomy. How could she make him understand that love was fleeting, like a sound? Short like the lightning? And that she wasn't his beautiful doll?

He stood next to her in a shaft of grey light, then she saw him take his starched handkerchief, wipe his forehead and gaze at her vaguely. Before she smiled at him stupidly, she heard him ask her in a voice full of anger:

—Was it wise to go out with other guys to the student union, when everybody knew you're mine?

—And how did they guess that if you yourself did not spread the rumor? she asked mockingly.

—Rumor? How dare you say that? he said, and put his hand on her shoulder threateningly.

Lina took her bag and turned quickly toward the library door, but he stood in her way. She tried to escape, shouting in his face that even if she were his since birth, there would be someone who would try to steal this right from him.

—What does the Bible have to do with this? And why don't you answer my question? he said in a low voice.

—Answer? What do I have to answer? she said, her hands tight on her bag. Do you understand that I am born free? And that I can change my mind about you?

—But if one loves a bitch. . . . he couldn't finish his sentence because a number of divinity students with their black suits and long beards came down from the library.

She saw him descend a few steps to let them pass, raising his troubled eyes towards her. Before she could slip away, she saw him wave his hand threateningly at the foot of the stairs.

What did she want? She stood in front of the authors' catalogue. Her heart was full of bitterness; her feet unstable, as if she were standing on the back of a whale in the midst of the sea. She took out one of the drawers, opened it with difficulty, then flipped through the cards, gazing absently.

The letter "J." What was she looking for? The names rolled down. Al-Jahez, Jabla bin al-Ayham, Jarir, Jamil. Her fingers were frozen on the last card. And through the small printed letters the image of the Arabic professor standing in the dark auditorium came to her. She heard him say loudly: "Jamil's love for Buthayna represents nothing but the triumph of the soul over the body, chastity over sin, innocence over corruption."

Ah what a nonsense! How they stuffed her mind with trash! How they invented theories, and found excuses! And the swearing that led to love? What a joke! The desert lovers came to her with their wide white robes and embroidered black sashes. In the grey light she recognized their weary faces and hoarse voices, and she thought that only a sick civilization like hers could create people like them, the man as a worshipper, the woman as worshipped. She found herself mimicking her professor, hiding her mouth with her hand:

— Who gave Europe the cult of the dame?

Ah, then, it was worth it that the French troubadours wrote their lyrics; that Dante created his beloved Beatrice; that Don Quixote roamed the world looking for Dona Dulcinea; that Werther cried in his yearning to see Charlotte!

A wicked smile came upon her as she flipped through the cards. She told herself that all lovers were sick, and that they did not strangle their beloveds like Othello, only because they did not have a chance. She put the drawer back, closed it, and fetched another. In the middle of the hall, the library director was speaking with a student in a querulous voice. As he spoke, he raised his thick brows slightly and bit at his lips between phrases.

— Deek al-Jin, she gasped as she flipped the card between her fingers. The library director turned toward her for a moment, then she saw him take the student by the arm and go quickly to the daily newspapers office. Had she looked for him, she wouldn't have found him. She laughed bitterly. The damned Deek al-Jin! Had Shakespeare ever heard of him? Or perhaps read something about him in the Arabic tales that traveled via Italy to North Europe in the 16th century? A cold wind came to her face as the library door opened. The janitor appeared carrying parcels of new books. Before he arrived in front of the closed offices, he halted for a moment, then turned, raising his eyes towards a student dallying outside the reading room.

—Could you open the door for me, please? asked the janitor in a weak voice.

Lina's eyes were fixed again on the card of Deek al-Jin. His love for Ward, the Christian girl, his marriage to her, his long absence from his city Hums, the rumor, a cousin of his had spread, that Ward had a love affair with a young boy, the return of the poet and his killing the woman whom he had loved like nothing in his life.

How could Shakespeare have heard the story? She yawned and closed the drawer quietly. Didn't she read somewhere that *Othello* was taken from a Moroccan story collected by Giraldi Cinthio in his book *Hecatommithi* in the 16th century? She wanted to laugh loudly. The Moor of Venice, the poet of Hums. Ah, no difference! Both couldn't possibly belong to another race!

She walked excitedly to the subject catalogue, her limbs shaking with anger, her eyes full of tears. The peasant student passed by her, putting his hands in the pockets of his jeans, squinting as if searching for someone. Then he stopped beside her under the faint light and said jokingly:

—Working hard, eh?

Lina raised her head slowly without saying a word, letting the cards roll on the metal stick.

—Did you see the philosophy professor? he asked, bending down towards her.

Lina shook her head.

—I don't know if he will approve of my topic, he said after an instant.

They walked slowly toward the library door. Darkness had fallen on the city. The houses' lights glimmered from a distance on the foot of the mountain.

—Aren't you going to write on the Divine City of Al-Farabi? asked Lina.

—No, said the peasant student excitedly, then he looked vacantly at some hurrying figures in the dark. Do you know that my mother dreamt of it? He halted, his limbs shaking.

—Dreamt of what? the Divine City? asked Lina, glancing at his troubled eyes in the shadow of a faint lamp.

—Yes, said the peasant student.

They walked on towards the train station. There was something burning in the air. They passed the university hospital, and from behind a hedge of poplar trees, babies were crying in rooms bathed with light.

—It was the sacred night, he said in a frail voice, like a boy.

Lina saw him halt for an instant in the shadow, collecting his breath.

—I was milking the cow at dawn when I saw my mother running towards me, frightened. Her hair was loose; the buttons of her shirt open. Was she alright? I asked raising my head, wiping the sweat of my forehead with the back of my hand. She murmured something, then fell over a heap of hay, breathing with difficulty. I thought she dreamt of a fox stealing a hen, or the landlord asking for the crops, or the aged cow dying. I was not alarmed. She always dreamt, and we always laughed at her dreams at night. But there was something in her tone which forced me to carry the milk pail, leaving the cow to run to the open field, wagging her tail in the warm summer wind.

"Do you believe that our landlord has altogether disappeared?" she said in a childish voice. I saw her play with the hay with her rough hands. Undoubtedly, she was sick, I said. "I was in the field cutting watermelons, and the sun burned my face," she said and screwed up her eyes a bit. "Your father was at home busy with the landlord, checking the account. I had to work alone, to fill the carriage on the edge of the dusty road with watermelons before sunset. The landlord assured me he wanted to go early to the city. Ah, the weather was very hot. And that bending! It seemed eternal. Every time, I stood up, I felt an electric shock go through the bottom of my back."

"Where were my brothers?" I asked her. The dream began to interest me. "Why didn't they help out in cutting the melons, or at least in transporting them to the carriage?" I saw her smile fade, and I heard her say in a feeble voice: "I didn't have children in the dream. I was all alone, and the nearby fields surrounded me like the walls of a prison. I didn't hear a sound. Even the wind was silent. I did not see a tree, only watermelons that blocked the horizon. I was rushing like a shadow between the field and the carriage, carrying the watermelons against my breasts, and the sweat washed my face. Even the horse was tired of the heat. It did not eat the hay I left, and I often heard its tongue crack from thirst."

Her words called up a feeling of desolation in me, and I imagined that all the dead had risen from their graves searching for water in the deserted villages. "My fingers are full of blisters," she said and stretched her hands towards me as if wanting to prove to me that it was the truth. "I sat on the dusty road, leaning against the carriage wheels, wiping my face with the sleeves of my cotton dress, fixing my head piece which began to slip, because I was bending and standing all the time in the melon field. I only wanted to sleep then. But before closing my eyes, I looked in the direction of the thin horse. It too had fallen to the ground and was not able to get rid of the flies stuck to its eyes. Then I thought that a cold breeze had come from the east, and that the burning sun had begun to set. Suddenly, I felt a kick in my groin, and when I woke up frightened, I saw the landlord standing over me. He shouted loudly: 'You cursed woman. Did you sleep the whole day?' To my surprise there was not a single melon in the cart. I thought he would lash me with his whip, but he didn't do it. He pushed me to the carriage, then began to whip the horse's back madly. I didn't see anyone in the village. All houses were quiet. I didn't hear dogs barking. The carriage went on for hours crossing the land. Then, I could not recognize the street anymore. Everything seemed strange. At first, I thought he would take me to the city as a maid to his wife and children. But the roads were not paved, and I could not see one house in the silent fields. I thought I heard the neighing of a horse in the distance and reckoned that your father, perhaps, had followed us. Similar carriages to ours appeared slowly on the horizon, and after that there was absolute darkness."

I heard her sob, and I saw her hide her face in a pile of hay. "But, it is a dream. Isn't it?" I said, trying to quiet her, and I took her rough hand between mine. As she raised her eyes towards me, there was a shadow of a smile on her face.

"He threw me from the carriage," she said, squeezing her eyes as if trying to remember the rest of the dream. "I thought my skull would break open on the stones, but the earth was sandy. Then I heard him say as he beat the horse with his whip: 'The desert, that's what they deserve, the dirty peasants.' His figure melted away in the darkness. I couldn't even pray for him not to leave me alone. There was something like a big cucumber in my throat which prevented me even from crying. It did not take long though before other carriages came, one after the other, leaving behind men, children, and women."

197

"Was it the desert?" I asked her in a subdued voice, but my question trailed off into laughter. She did not seem to be angry with me. The dream had already possessed the whole of her. "We did not have a cover," she said as if talking to herself. "It was dark and how the children wept! When the dawn came I found your father sleeping next to a cousin of his. There were other peasants from other villages. All dressed differently. The sun shone and the noise grew loud. No one knew where we were, or how we could return to our villages. Then our neighbor who lived at the top of the hill said that to stay in the desert without food or drink would force us to kill each other. The village idiot began to compose a song about the peasants who found themselves suddenly without masters and did not know what to do with an unwanted freedom."

"A society of peasants, eh?" I said and began to crack my fingers. Her dream was getting very interesting. "We fought amongst one another at the beginning. Each one of us wanted to play the role of the master," she said, moving violently on the hay. "But one day, there was water under the sand." I could not listen to her anymore. I reminded myself that Plato chose the philosophers as rulers for his ideal city, and that Al-Farabi did the same, but my mother, who was and is illiterate, chose the peasants to build a new civilization.

The last words of the peasant's story sank into Lina's memory, and a vague picture of villages shining in the desert stood in front of her eyes. In her secret heart, she saw the humiliated people of the earth rise from the graveyards, throwing the dust from the collars of their worn-out coats, rushing like hurricanes towards the tightly closed gates of the world.

—Did the class differences disappear in your mother's city? she asked, embarrassed.

—Undoubtedly, said the peasant student simply. There was neither a master nor a slave, neither an owner nor an owned.

His tone touched her pleasantly. She wished that she, too, was convinced that private property could disappear.

—And the woman . . . did your mother dream of her too? she asked after a moment of silence.

She heard him laugh in a hoarse voice.

—You can't imagine that my mother has seen the foundation of the ideal city in a short dream! he cried and cracked his fingers nervously. But from the bits and pieces she told me, I was able to draw the characteristics of that city. No, I don't believe that women occupy a lower place than men. Indeed what surprises me is that the soldier who played his role in Plato's *Republic* was not to be found in her city.

—Did you ask her about the soldier in particular? said Lina.

—No, but I asked her about war, he answered gaily. There was no war, she assured me, because there was no property.

Rain began to drizzle as Lina took the bus from the Hijaz station. Through the window, mist-blurred, she saw the figure of the peasant student hurry on his way to the old city with his long black coat. The images of those armed men, grim, lean, and carrying revolvers in their pockets, glimmered in her mind. They all came to her under the drizzle of rain from their hideout in the history books, from Sean O'Casey's plays, from Diego Rivera's and David Siqueiros' paintings, from Franz Fanon's articles. She heard their raw voices, their hoarse laughter fill the air.

* * *

In the exhibit hall, men wearing white starched shirts and black short jackets stood sipping wine and talking in low voices. Two waiters were busy offering drinks and appetizers to the guests. A man in a light green suit hurried toward a group of women, some of whom were bare armed, others wore colorful blouses. They stood under a painting of a broad-foreheaded man with fuzzy hair who was screaming. The group swayed and reeled, turning upon itself like dancers in a haze of tobacco smoke.

Lina stood for a moment under the light of the hallway. It was seven o'clock. She felt embarrassed when she noticed some men gazing at her curiously. She cleared her throat, then stepped inside hesitantly. She saw the sociology professor standing under a picture of a naked woman in the midst of a little group of men. She heard one of them say in a low voice:

—Undoubtedly, a prostitute.

The sociology professor turned towards him, his eyes were red from drinking wine. He said naughtily:

—You are a hypocrite. If you despise her so much, why do you gaze at her?

—But she is inviting us. Look, said the man raising his head towards the woman who was lying on her back. Doesn't the portrait remind you of that famous painting of Goya? Her arms behind her head, her breasts standing up, her belly small.

—Yes, said the sociology professor with open scorn, but you are a married man. Aren't you?

—It doesn't matter, said a stout man, waving his index finger in the air.

Lina hurried; her face burned with excitement. She paused under the portrait of a woman holding a Spanish fan and covering her long hair with a black mantilla. Before she continued to walk, the man standing next to her said:

—But he paints like the impressionists.

—Do you believe so, my dear? said a thin voice, but you would love to be in her place, wouldn't you?

The man laughed loudly.

At the end of the hall, she met him face to face. He shook hands with her and said:

—Yellow is becoming to your complexion. He offered her a glass of orange and asked her if she were writing poetry these days, and wanted to know more about her plans for the future. She blushed, stared at his forehead, and spoke with difficulty

—How can an artist living in a bloody period of history paint the lanes of the old city bathed in light, or the olive vendors on the bank of a stagnant river playing cards, or Bourgeois women standing in front of mirrors, pouring French perfume on their bare bosoms? Is it possible that you do not see men being tortured in prisons, or hear shots in the distant barracks, or smell blood that stinks up the air? she asked him bitterly, once she had gathered herself.

—But the narrow lanes, he said almost jokingly, the olive vendors, and the Bourgeois women, are all there. Do you want me to stop painting women hatching children? Don't you know that these things always happen, whether there is a war, or not?

—No, no, of course, but I cannot understand your logic. Don't you see violence around you? And how can you ignore it? she said staring at the portrait of the woman with the untroubled face.

—He who paints violence gets lost in violence, he said. His voice trembled. Perhaps, had I lived abroad, I would have looked differently at things. Don't you realize that Picasso painted Guernica while living in France? No, I can't paint violence. All I can do is to scream. But I know quite well that I live in the forest, and that the echo will repeat my voice endlessly.

She saw him drag his feet with difficulty, take a glass of wine from a passing waiter, then gulp it at once.

—The artist's duty is not to portray vagueness vaguely, or disorder disorderly. On the contrary, he said, noticeably swallowing his saliva, then he was silent for a while. He took his white handkerchief, and wiped the sweat of his forehead.

—The artist, he murmured without looking at her eyes, cannot show chaos to others if he himself is lost in it.

—And Goya? How did he paint violence? she asked defiantly. He came towards her, his limbs trembling.

—You should not forget that Goya had to wait for six years before he painted the French soldiers shooting the Spanish suspects, he said, shaking his index finger nervously. Don't you know that Goya, during the war years, turned out a lovely series of intimate portraits?

—Does that mean I have to wait for a long time before I can see a painting showing this violence in which we both live? And is it possible that this violence in its different forms, that of the family against the individual, the state against the citizen, man against woman, the sane against the insane, the enemy against his enemy, would disappear one day? Lina asked him so forcefully that he did not answer. His eyes were full of horror, exactly like the peasant's eyes in Goya's painting, with the French soldier pointing a gun to his chest.

When she left the exhibition hall, darkness had fallen upon the city. From behind the trees which lined the sidewalk, the paintings of Goya came to her, one by one, and she saw a severed head hanging on a feeble branch. Then two tied hands walked towards her, coming from nowhere. But as she turned her face towards the city, frightened, she pictured corpses stripping off their clothes and blocking out the barren mountain.

*　*　*

March 25

I met the sociology professor in the bookstore close to the Officers' Club. He was wearing a grey sweater and had a bunch of papers in his hand. Asked me was it true I was leaving Damascus and why. Told him I wanted to keep my sanity. He laughed coarsely. Asked me whether I believed I could really do so in another country. Perhaps, I said hesitantly.

March 26

One cannot possibly grow in this city. Something in its air, in the cruelty of its people, in its withdrawal from the outside world, smothers the baby in the cradle.

May 4

He followed me to the bus stop opposite the Justice Ministry. Looked like an ewe fleeing from the butcher's knife. Said I have destroyed his life. A false claim. Said he would do everything to stop me from leaving the country. One word to the Secret Police, and I would be finished.

May 5

I put on the radio. The city was almost asleep. The voice of Um Kalthoom came to me, mixed with the cries of the hashish smokers:

>Ah, make the most of what we yet may spend,
>Before we too into the Dust descend;
>Dust into Dust, and under Dust to lie

Sans Wine, sans Song, sans Singer, and sans End!
Better for this heart to beat
And in the flames of love to burn
What a wasted day that passed
Without having loved.

I turned off the radio. Thought that sick love could only flourish in a sick civilization.

May 14

I assured Amal that no social revolution was likely to sweep this city. I wiped my fingers of the *Baba au Rum*. She frowned, then said I had a queer mind and I had read too much of the Bourgeois literature. Perhaps. I laughed and pushed the empty plate in front of me. But the socialist literature is not easily available. Not true, she said sipping the coffee rather loudly. Before the waiter cleaned the table, she looked in my face tenderly and assured me that I would go back to my faith in socialism one day. But the belief in socialism and achieving socialism are two different things, I said. There was no hope for me, she said jokingly.

May 29

I dreamt that my brother was waiting silently in one of the dark corridors of the Interior Ministry. There were also other strange figures whispering behind tall closed doors. An old man carrying a heavy tray full of coffee or tea cups passed by from time to time. Whenever a door was opened a pale shaft of light flew across the corridor, and the smell of cheap cigarettes filled the air.

Some time passed, and no one entered or left the employees' offices except the janitor. A bell would ring. The old man would get up from his chair at the end of the corridor, lift his head with difficulty, tighten his eyes, and he would read the number in the electric box which was hung on the wall, and then shuffle down the hall with his body bent forward and his hands dangling at his sides. Without looking at anybody's face he would open one door, put his head inside the room, then a man's hoarse voice would say: "Sweet coffee," or "Bitter coffee," or "Three cups of tea," then the old man would close the door, muttering something to himself, and he would pass by the people as if they were not there.

One time a man who was waiting in the corridor for long hours holding an application in his hand stopped him and asked him something, but the old man looked at him blankly, then uttered in a low voice: "Come back tomorrow."

Some people became restless. They paced the corridor back and forth. Their voices sometimes betrayed a deep anger. They cracked their fingers, read their applications for the twentieth time; they counted the change in their wallets, made sure that they had stamps and photos in their pockets. And whenever the old man passed by, they stopped him, reproached him, yelled at him. And when they got tired from pacing back and forth, from cracking their fingers, from reading their applications, they loitered behind doors, whispering and complaining.

Getting an exit visa was not a normal thing. A person's relations had to die abroad, or be lying on their death beds in hospitals. He had to supply the state with documents which proved his claim. Yet the state was not obliged to facilitate his business. The employees felt good when they complicated matters. They liked to impose their will on the citizens.

For these reasons, some people became restless. Had they known that after this long wait, which might last one to two months, after all this endurance of writing applications, finding reasons and justifications, buying stamps, and getting photos, had they known for sure that they would get the approval of the employee, and his signature, sooner or later, they would have then found all difficulties easy, and would have endured all troubles.

Not all people rushed the matters. On the contrary. The majority were patient, silent, with bent heads, played with rosaries and thanked God for his blessings. And when the office hours were over around 2 o'clock in the afternoon and the old man came to brush the people like flies, the group would smile contentedly and each person would mutter to the other person: "Tomorrow, if God wills."

Friendships were very often made amongst the patient group of people in front of the closed doors in the state's offices. It was normal to see the same faces daily and for a long time. During the first days hardly anyone said anything to anybody else. But soon the muscles of the faces relaxed, and the mouths moved. Even the old man began to loiter between those people as if he were expecting them also to order sweet or bitter coffee.

My brother's hair was white when someone called his name, and I saw him in my dream walking slowly, putting his right hand on his hip as if suffering from rheumatism. When he stopped in front of the employee in a room filled with smoke, he took a worn out application from the inside pocket of his jacket and put it on the desk without saying a word.

—Another application for Lebanon, huh? said the employee as he scratched his head, looking at my brother with scorn.

—No, said my brother wearily. I just want to inform you that I approve my sister's traveling to. . .

—Where is your father? asked the employee, astonished. We would like to have your father's approval.

—But he is dead, said my brother.

—In this case, the employee shook his head, no objection. Do you have a certificate to prove the death of your father?

—Yes, said my brother and started looking for the piece of paper in his pocket.

—And your sister. . . Isn't she married?

—No.

—And why would she like to travel alone? asked the employee nervously.

—She wants to pursue higher education, said my brother, trying to control himself.

—Higher education? And why would a girl pursue any education? Didn't you find her a husband? the employee asked coarsely.

—This is my approval, my brother pointed to the folded paper on the desk. I have no objection. His voice trembled.

—No objection? Hum? The employee opened the paper, then started reading in a disdainful voice:

To whom it may concern. I have no objection to my sister leaving the Syrian territories. Since I am her legal guardian in my capacity as a man, and because the law does not allow women to leave the country unless they get the approval of their fathers, or their brothers, in the case of the former's death, or their husbands in the case of their marriage, I guarantee that I will take all responsibilities and consequences of such an act.

—Beautiful. . . very beautiful, mocked the employee. He put his seal on the paper, and just before he dipped his pen in the inkwell to write the date, he rang the bell and waited till the door was opened and the head of the old man stretched out of the corridor.

—Sweet coffee, said the employee, then he yawned so widely that his golden teeth showed.

* * *

June 4

My mother told me that learning did not help me a bit. On its account, I rejected my family, society, religion, and country. Laughed insolently. Told her she should have arranged a marriage for me when I reached thirteen. Would God I had. And she sighed. Pushed the cup of coffee and stood up. Did she want me to hatch like her every nine months? Impudent, she said angrily. But when I turned my back, going towards the door, I heard her say almost imploringly: Don't forget you are a woman. And the woman hatches nothing but children.

June 15

I walked with the professor of modern literature to the train station. He was cross with me because I had described the story of the Cave People which occured in the *Quran* as a myth. And before we parted, he halted for a second, then asked me with a soft voice why I was angry at everything. Answered him I was tired of being an Arab, a Moslem, and a woman. Under the soft light of a lantern I saw his colorless eyes looking at me through thick glasses. Didn't he ever feel he was born in the wrong country? Asked him without any fear. But he did not answer.

June 18

I saw Petro's mother throw her garbage from the third floor

onto the street. The empty cans, the core of squash and tomatoes, the skin of apples and banana peels. It was quiet for a while. Then suddenly the balcony doors were flung open again, and piles of garbage were thrown on the dusty road. When I stuck my face onto the window I saw the rats of the neighborhood dance in the square, their fur sopping wet, their mouths stained with blood. What will we leave behind us when we are long dead? The Pharaohs' pyramids? The Crusaders' castles? The Moslems' mosques? or mountains of rusted tin cans, fields of broken Coca Cola bottles, and interesting chronicles about cholera and the plague?

Damascus. The garbage city. The rats' city. Without any trees. Without any gardens. Without any sparrows.

* * *

— *Il fait chaud,* said Janet to the Algerian student and took a small mirror out of her bag, wet the edge of a handkerchief with her saliva, then wiped the spots of green shade from her lids.

—*Et comment voyageras-tu après l'examen? En avion?*

—Yes, said the Algerian student, *je resterai a Paris deux ou trois mois.*

—*A Paris? Oh la la!* Janet jumped off the ground shaking her right hand nervously.

—*C'est magnifique, magnifique.*

Lina saw the short student with the broad shoulders gazing at Janet vaguely, then turning slowly to read the notice board. Janet dallied for a moment as if she had forgotten something, then she said like a spoiled child:

—*Je m'excuse. A bientot.*

Before she disappeared in the midst of the crowd, she turned a bit, waved her hand and said, almost whispering:

—*Bon voyage.*

The students began to fill the corridor. Their eyes were bloodshot, their nerves were raw. Some stood on the steps leading to the auditorium smoking cigarettes; others reviewed the brief notes in the margins of their books.

Through the open door, one could see the professor of Arabic

207

literature sitting near a pile of dictionaries. His bald head was shining, and before him on the desk lay some poetry books. He leaned back in his chair, inclining his head toward a student who was analyzing a love poem by the Andalusian poetess, Wallada. The grammar professor sat at his right, while at the other side of the desk the Quran lecturer amused himself by flipping through the pages of a thick book.

No, she wasn't afraid of the examination, said Lina to herself as she stood next to the Algerian student looking through jaded eyes at the passers-by. The janitor will appear after a while at the door, read her name in a weak voice, and she will follow him to the room silently, greet the professors, putting one foot in front of the other. The bald headed one will give her a poem about Seville, and she will sit in the corner for ten minutes, read the poem to herself first, analyze the poet's concept of the city, his relationship with it, his love and hatred, and when the professor of Arabic literature points to her with his finger she'll jump lightly, walk to the desk, then sit down, putting the book in front of her, and she'll begin to read. The Quran professor will move in his chair, letting his glasses fall over his lap. When she is finished reading the poem he will tell her that she knows the secrets of the language, and that her voice is good for singing. The other two men will nod their agreement. The grammar professor will ask her about the latest poems she's been writing, and she will answer him shyly with her head down. Nothing makes her chest heavy except that illusionary city with its silver subterranean vaults and tall gates that reach the sky.

The peasant student came towards her. She heard his feet striking flatly on the floor.

—Good morning, he stuttered.

—Good morning, said Lina. She saw him fan his face with the daily newspaper.

—The heat is unbearable, he complained, then he stuck his face against the examination door.

—Are they still on the letter 'J'? a student leaned forward and asked in a toneless voice.

—Yes, someone answered. He had red hair. There are two nice young ladies in the room, he said and laughed slyly.

Lina saw the stout student hide his face behind his book and walk to the window.

—They don't have to study. I mean the girls, whispered the red headed student and nudged another guy with his elbow.

Laughter grew loud. Some girls turned their heads as if they had not heard a word. A tall blonde girl appeared at the door. Heads turned; lips muttered something. Then someone flipped a coin in the air, and when it dropped, a foot stamped on it before it could be picked up. A thin voice said: "Heads." Some laughed insolently and shoved each other. Then, the lame student came panting and said that the oral history exam was delayed till next week. They formed a circle around him. One mimicked him. The red headed student said that the lame guy's testimony was not acceptable. Another tickled him in the stomach. Then they carried him on their shoulders as he fought to get down. One said: "Let's get drunk." Others pulled him, and he fell on the ground. When he tried to hit back, two fists hit him in the back, another in the kidney. They let him loose as the janitor appeared at the door of the examination hall, and said in a frail voice:

—Silence.

The peasant student laughed, quite embarrassed, and rubbed his hands. The veiled girl whispered:

—Let them go to hell.

Then they began to disperse. They walked away, adjusting their shirts and pants, smoothing their hair with the palms of their hands. Some stood in front of the windows pushing their genitals, patting them in place. Lina told the peasant student she was tired. The smell of coffee came from one of the janitor's rooms. The voice of the muezzin grew loud in the university garden. Before the students began to disperse for lunch, a hoarse voice said:

—Look here!

As they all looked behind, the lame student was standing at the top of the stairs, in his hand a revolver. They began to run in every direction. Lina saw the red headed student jump in front of her like a rabbit. The peasant student pulled her by the hand, and they rushed towards the hallway door. Then shots followed. At the end of the corridor, he dropped her hand, and she saw him fall with glassy eyes to the ground, the blood flowing from his neck.

* * *

They carried him on their shoulders. The June sun melted the asphalt. Even the roses on his coffin had withered in the heat. The mourners walked in narrow lanes, and a blind man sang something from the Quran. There was dust everywhere. The shops were half closed, and weary men dozed on their thresholds. They prayed for him in a simple mosque: its carpets were torn, its walls crumbling, its windows dusty. The echo repeated the thin voice of the muezzin. When they took him out, the air was hot; the flies singing. No one looked from the windows of the mud houses that lined the road, nor did the ice cream vendor cry as he usually did on hot summer days: "Alaska, Alaska;" his old cart was standing on the sidewalk, but he had vanished somewhere.

In a graveyard similar to those of the desert, they let him down in a narrow hole. He was lying on his back, his shroud as white as snow. They poured earth on him, and before they turned back to the dusty city, a woman's sob was heard:

—Ah Lord, where are you? And why do you kill the innocent?

* * *

Garbage was floating on the river as Lina and Amal crossed the Victory Bridge. Before they turned left on Beirut Street, they halted a little and smiled at the doddering sweeper who was carrying his long broom and pushing his grey cart with difficulty. Across the almost dry river came the voices of the workers from Damascus International Fair mixed with the noise of machines.

At the foot of the hill that led to the Guests Palace, they stopped for a while. Amal took her cigarette pack from her hand bag, lit a cigarette, then said in a toneless voice:

—You are determined to leave, aren't you?

—Yes, said Lina; it is difficult to be born at the wrong time in history, in the wrong place.

—But we can change this time, said Amal. Her voice began to tremble. All we need is faith.

—I am one person, said Lina. Alone, I can't change a thing. There ought to be others.

—But there are others. Don't you see me? asked Amal, scoldingly.

Lina halted, then said bluntly:

—No, I don't; maybe in my imagination, but not in flesh and blood. They are not born yet.

—But your dream is vague, said Amal in a faint voice, a vision of heavenly existence.

—Yet, from a historical perspective, it is clear that the vision of one century is often the reality of the next one, said Lina.

—Don't you see that the problem is purely economical? asked Amal. Your utopia could not be found unless the economic life is reorganized, and wealth is distributed.

—And this means that improving the environment will predominate, since with improved surrounding, man's mental and spiritual progress will follow as a matter of course. Do you believe that we would behave like humans if we were materially satisfied?

—You are idealistic, said Amal contemptuously.

— Because I insist on a primacy of man's mental and moral improvement? Don't you see I don't reject your materialistic theory altogether? All that I am trying to do is combine the two theories, the materialistic and the idealistic.

—This is impossible, said Amal. The two theories are contradictory, the materialistic insists that man is created and conditioned by his surroundings, and the idealistic asserts that man's mind is free.

—Both are correct, and I don't see the contradiction, said Lina.

At that moment, a squad of soldiers passed by them on its way to the Guests Palace. Uncouth faces, stained by the sun. As she strove to look at them with indifference, a faint feeling of shame rose in her heart. Through the glaring light, the image of the crowd rising and falling in the square like the dunes came to her, and a tall man stood on the balcony of that white palace. She saw him lift his hand toward the people and heard him say in a loud voice:

—Who amongst you will betray me?

They fell upon their knees beating their chests, shouting loudly:

Naser, Naser, Naser.

They turned towards the Star Square and went on for a while in silence. There were men playing backgammon in the garden of a house and smoking a waterpipe. From the half opened window, the smell of freshly ground coffee mixed with cardamom came to their nostrils.

—Aren't you afraid of loneliness? asked Amal, and threw the remnant of her cigarette butt in the gutter.

—I will take the risk, said Lina.

—Even if that means losing your family, your friends, your country? her voice trembled.

—Even though, said Lina, I am tired of those chains, whether they're called family, friends, or country. Since the death of the peasant student, I couldn't believe in anything anymore. But he came to me one night, leaving his shroud behind, and when I touched his neck, there was no wound. He told me again about his mother's dream of the peasants' city, and said that bitterness could not serve anyone.

—Do you believe that his city will become a reality if you leave? Amal halted a little.

The cruel words lashed Lina as if they were whips.

—Listen, she said to Amal, the ideal city will not become a reality if I were here or not. And if I stay I will end up either in prison or dead. Otherwise, I'll rot like the rest of you. I reject your false love that prevents me from seeing you as you are. I refuse to serve that which I don't believe in, whether it is my family, my friends, my country. I'll try the impossible to express myself the way I want, with the freedom I see fit. All that will not be available to me unless I go away from you.

They walked silently. Sorrow filled the air. The cries of a baby were heard. A woman appeared on the balcony putting up the wash. As they reached the end of the street, they stopped for a while.

—Goodbye, said Lina.

—Goodbye, said Amal.

In the shadow of the trees, Lina saw the pale face of her friend, her dejected eyes. Were they destined to leave as strangers?

The sun began to set on the foot of the mountain. From the city minarets, the voices of the muezzins grew louder, calling people for prayer. What was waiting for her in exile? She raised her head to the sky and gazed at those frail birds rising and falling. Suddenly, she wanted to run and run. Through the faint light she saw the deserted lane become a silver vault, then the image of the goldsmith in the gold bazaar came to her, and she heard his file across the years, frail and faint like the rustle of the trees, the murmur of the brooks, the bells of a dream.

Syrian History:
Chronology From World War II to 1961

(The First World War is won. The Arab Revolt against the Turks is successful. All the Arabic-speaking provinces of the Ottoman Empire in Asia are now free after four centuries of Turkish domination. In October 1918, Prince Faisal enters Damascus with his triumphant army. But Arab hopes of achieving a unified, independent state as a result of the victorious outcome of the war are soon to be squashed, despite assurances by Great Britain. Indeed, the consequences of the war prove to be disastrous for the Arabs. In April 1920, the Supreme Allied Council meeting in San Remo, Italy, partitions the Arab world into mandates, following the earlier Sykes-Picot agreement. Syria is to be broken up into three fractions: Palestine, Lebanon, and a reduced 'Syria.' Iraq is to remain undivided. Syria and Lebanon become a French mandate, and the French march from Beirut to Damascus on July 25, 1920).

JUNE 1940	France is defeated by the Germans. The posting of pro-Vichy General Dentz as High Commissioner in Syria and Lebanon brings the European conflict to the Middle East.
JUNE 1941	The Free French, British and Commonwealth forces invade Syria, oust the colonial Vichy administration and occupy Damascus.
1941-1946	Syria is jointly occupied by French and British forces.

MAY 1945	For the third time in twenty years, the French bomb Damascus, the oldest continuously inhabited city in the world.
APRIL 1946	French withdrawal from Syria. (Independence Day on April 17 continues to be a national holiday). Syria becomes a parliamentary democracy. Shukri Al-Quwatli is elected President. He belongs to the National Party which represents the interests of the Damascus notables.
MAY 1948	The defeat of Syrian Arab forces against the newly created state of Israel, product of the Balfour Declaration and the Sykes-Picot agreement. Palestinian refugees in Syria. Rising bitterness against the West. The beginning of political unrest and military intervention in government.
MARCH 1949	The advent of military dictatorships. Brigadier General Husni Al-Za'im overthrows the Quwatli elected government in a bloodless coup.
AUGUST 1949	Brigadier General Sami Al-Hinnawi overthrows Al-Za'im government. Both Al-Za'im and his prime minister are executed.
DECEMBER 1949	Col. Adib Al-Shishakli arrests Al-Hinnawi.
NOVEMBER 1951	Col. Al-Shishakli removes his associates by a third coup.
APRIL 1952	Al-Shishakli abolishes all political parties and creates his own party: The Arab Liberation Movement.
1953	Student strikes and unrest in the country. Al-Shishakli bombs the Druzes in south Syria and declares martial law.
FEBRUARY 1954	Al-Shishakli is overthrown by a military coup

led by Col. Faisal Al-Atasi and parliament is restored.

1954-1955	The Syrian Nationalist Party, devoted to the establishment of greater Syria, loses its influence in local politics, and in 1955 it is suppressed in the army. The majority of the officers now are Ba'thists: pan-Arabists and socialists.
	The Ba'th Party and the Syrian Communist party have an effective organization and definite programs. Both parties have aggressively recruited students, workers, officers and professionals to their ranks.
JULY 1955	The Egyptian Revolution and the abolition of the monarchy in Egypt. Agrarian reforms are implemented.
JULY 1956	Gamal Abd Al-Naser nationalizes the Suez Canal.
OCTOBER 1956	British-French-Israeli invasion of Port Said and Sinai. Mobilization of Syria; support for Egypt, and the growing pan-Arab unity movement in the Arab world. The Soviet Union becomes the new ally of Arab nationalists.
1958	Civil war in Lebanon as some Lebanese rally to Pan-Arab calls of Egyptian President Naser. U.S. Marines land in Beirut in accordance with the Eisenhower doctrine of resistance to 'international communism' at the request of Lebanese President Camille Chamoun.
1958-1961	Union with Egypt. In February 1958 Syria, under the leadership of the Ba'th party, gives up its sovereignty to become the "Northern Province" of the United Arab Republic (U.A.R.) of which Naser is unanimously cho-

sen president. Political parties are dissolved.

SEPTEMBER 1961   Military coup in Damascus. Syria secedes from the U.A.R.

FRANKLIN PIERCE COLLEGE LIBRARY

00101623

DATE DUE

GAYLORD			PRINTED IN U.S.A.